THE MURDER OF SHERLOCK HOLMES

David Fable

Copyright © 2014
All rights reserved.

ISBN: 0990852903
ISBN 13: 9780990852902
Library of Congress Control Number: 2014917684
Highflyer Press, Studio City, CA

To Kim for her love and infinite patience

1

WATSON

A clot of blackish blood oozed from the drill hole, ran down the side of his lifeless face, and onto the coroner's porcelain table. This was no hoax perpetrated by the greatest crime-solving mind of our age. This time he was truly dead. His hawklike features slackened into a pale-blue death mask. The drill hole showed like a dark bull's-eye in the center of a large indentation just below the line of his graying, brown hair. There on the table lay the greatest friend I have ever known—Sherlock Holmes.

"Subdural hemorrhage. That is surely what killed him, Dr. Watson," said the coroner as the last clotted blood drained from the hole in Holmes's skull. The coroner's assistant, a bespectacled, rail-thin lad of no more than twenty, was taking notes.

As a battlefield surgeon in the swelter of the Second Afghan War, I had witnessed the worst the world has to offer. I've seen rifle wounds large enough to put a fist into. I've seen bayonets broken off inside of men. I myself sustained a bullet to the leg, which I still carry around as an aching reminder of that hellish chapter of my youth. But all this was nothing compared to the sickness of heart and spirit I felt as I stood watching the chief coroner and his assistant conducting their business with the remains of Sherlock Holmes.

Suddenly, I felt nauseated by the smell of embalming fluid from the adjoining room where other bodies were in repose. I had to force my racing mind to focus on the dissection process in order to observe every detail and clue just as Holmes would have wanted. I couldn't help comparing my emotions to those I had felt twenty-one years earlier when I stood in a daze staring down at the churning waters of Reichenbach Falls. I could vividly remember how seeing Holmes's Alpine stick leaning on a rock at the edge of the waterfall turned me cold. How the sight of it led me to the inevitable conclusion that Moriarty had indeed fulfilled his murderous purpose. The experts' examination had seemed conclusive that Holmes and Moriarty had struggled and plunged over the falls locked in each other's arms. For three years I thought Holmes dead. And, yet, during that time there was still a nagging sense that somehow it could not be true. Intuition is a feeling that cannot easily be defined except to say that it is a belief held in the heart and mind based on emotion. Somewhere, deep inside, intuition told me that spring day in Switzerland might not have been the end of Holmes. It had seemed inconceivable to me that he would have knowingly backed himself into such a vulnerable situation. Additionally, there had been reports of Moriarty still lurking in the shadows of the criminal world and, of course, Holmes's body had never been discovered.

When, after that three-year period, Holmes reappeared, revealing that he had indeed survived his encounter with Moriarty, and that he had been laying low these many months traveling the Far East to avoid Moriarty's remaining assassins, my resentment at the ruse was overwhelmed by the sheer joy of having my intuition confirmed and my most valued friend back. I must confess that upon his return, I was a bit miffed by his explanation that any contact with me during those years would have possibly endangered him. Neither then, nor ever, had I betrayed a confidence regarding any matter or case until given the approval to do so by Holmes. No, my emotions on this day were far more intense than all the combined days of that three-year period during which Holmes was presumed dead, and nothing in my intuition prepared me for what I would learn about the murder of my best friend.

"Third, fourth and fifth rib appear to be broken. Lung puncture is likely," said the coroner as he leaned over to examine the collapsed right side of Holmes's chest. The coroner's name was Nolan. He was a short man with a handlebar moustache and sideburns that made him look more like a character from a burlesque show than a medical examiner. He had only had the chief coroner job for a few years, but had been in the department for twelve. I knew him to be a good man, accurate more times than not and always willing to cooperate with Holmes and myself when a case required it. He looked up at me as if to receive confirmation on his observations.

"Yes, punctured lung," I repeated.

News had already leaked out of the dreadful discovery of Holmes's body in a granary in Kent. It would appear in the papers the next day. The public would be clamoring for information and the journalists would give them plenty of misinformation and speculation, accomplishing their task of filling columns and selling papers.

The truth was that nothing was known about the circumstances of Holmes's death. Since his retirement to Sussex, I had seen him when I traveled out to his farm where he was forever minding his beehives. During those years, he rarely ventured to London or, for that matter, far from his comfortable enclave in the South Downs. He often remarked how soothing it felt to be surrounded by nature and out of the "gloom of London."

"From the looks of it, I'd say Mr. Holmes was hit with something flat like a shovel or the blunt side of an axe. Someone with great strength must have wielded it," Nolan continued to speculate.

I considered his words and tried to imagine Holmes being taken by surprise by some shovel-wielding assailant. Holmes had turned fifty-eight years in January, and though I grant you, none of us are as agile and skilled as we were in our peak years, to my mind he hadn't lost any of his acuity. It seemed unthinkable that he would allow himself to walk into such a trap or have such a confrontation. Holmes had enemies, many of them, mostly in jail. None would have the graceless audacity to think they could end the life of Sherlock Holmes with as crude a plan as that. No, unless it was a total fluke or chance encounter, Holmes would never be defeated by such a pedestrian plot. None of it made sense. Why a granary halfway to nowhere? A minimum of blood was found in that barn, but that could be owing to the fact that most of his injuries bled internally, or perhaps he was killed elsewhere and for some reason moved to the granary.

"One blow to the head and then one to the chest, that's what I think," said Nolan.

"Yes, I see," I responded, still lost in my own thoughts. "Quite possibly," I quickly added so as to not seem dismissive of Nolan's analysis.

Nolan could see I was distracted and apparently attributed that to the distress this event had inflicted upon me. He was not wrong, but also turning in my mind was the naked fact that I would have to be the one to solve this crime. How ironic a situation was this? The man most capable of solving this murder, the genius who had allowed me to join him in the greatest adventures of my life, was the victim.

"You don't need to be here for this next part, Dr. Watson," Nolan said sympathetically as he lifted a saw to commence the thoracic examination. "If I come up with any new information, you will be the first to know."

I nodded gratefully. The smell of formaldehyde was now beginning to choke me. As I have already stated, I am far from a squeamish man, but the circumstance of this visit buffeted me with waves of helplessness. I gave a last look at my esteemed friend. My vision became a surreal prism, blurring my sight. I raised the back of my hand to my eye and realized it was a tear that had altered my view. I withdrew from the dissection room.

• • •

A cold mist greeted me as I emerged from the morgue. Though barely half past noon, the afternoon sky had a dull, pewter cast befitting the circumstances of the day. I scanned the street for a cab. I knew the first person I wanted to question regarding the murder, but, before that, Mrs. Hudson had requested that I go directly to 221 Baker Street upon completion of my duties at the coroner and inform her of all I had learned.

Mrs. Hudson no longer lived at Baker Street. Having withdrawn to the country with Captain Hudson, they were now living in a home near Hampstead Heath. The Captain had retired a year ago from a successful career as a merchant sailor for the British India Steam Navigation Company. Early in his career, his route between England and Australia had earned him enough to purchase the Baker Street building as a home and source of income for the missus. He was frequently at sea for six months at a time, and I always thought it was a wonder that the marriage could survive such long bouts of separation. Lord knows I couldn't have been separated from my darling Mary for more than a few days.

At last a motorized hackney came bouncing down the street toward me. I must say I preferred the horse-drawn four-wheelers to the fume-ridden, internal combustion vehicles that had overnight taken control of the city. Ten years ago there was not a single motor-driven cab on the street, now there were 7,000 of them. It was said that they would reduce traffic in London since they are far shorter than the horse-drawn cabs, but as we all know that didn't happen, and, along with an imprudently high 20 mph speed limit, the streets had become a crowded and perilous place for pedestrians. On another occasion I might have waited for a horse-drawn cab, but as I was in a hurry, I did not have the luxury of choosing my conveyance. I climbed into the back of the hackney and directed the driver to take me to Baker Street.

• • •

Still feeling numb, I knocked on the door of 221A Baker Street. Mrs. Hudson opened it, her eyes red with grief. Despite her distress, Mrs. Hudson's courtesy was unflagging. "Would you like some tea, Dr. Watson?" she offered instinctively as she showed me in.

"Thank you, no, Mrs. Hudson," I responded and entered the sitting room.

Suddenly, the poor woman broke down in tears. She collapsed into an armchair, hands over her face, sobbing without restraint. If there was one person on this planet who had as much affection for Holmes as I, it was Mrs. Hudson. When it came to her world-famous lodger, she was the model of forbearance. She jealously guarded his privacy, tolerated his intolerable habits of testing firearms and noxious chemicals in his apartment and never questioned even his most outrageous behavior, for, though not a complicated woman, she recognized genius.

Mrs. Hudson was a few years younger than I. Her hair was usually brown owing to her frequent visits to the hairdresser, one of the few luxuries she afforded herself. As she propped herself up and wiped away the tears, I could see the gray peeking out around her temples. She was wearing low-heeled, lace-up shoes with rubber soles, which told me she had made the four-mile walk from the heath this morning, undoubtedly trying to calm herself after receiving the telephone call from me at 6:30 a.m. conveying the tragic news.

"I am struggling to organize my thoughts, Mrs. Hudson, but I will tell you all I know," I said grimly.

She managed to compose herself and sat up attentively. Before I could start there was a stout knock on the door, and Mrs. Hudson's son, Christopher, poked his head into the room. Christopher was twenty-one years of age and the image of his father. Though not quite as tall as the Captain, Christopher was still over six foot with the same sandy hair and gray-blue eyes. He had an intensity and forwardness that his father did not possess. He was just graduated from Oxford, having mastered several forms of science. He had been accepted to medical school though had decided to delay his entry to explore other fields of endeavor. Christopher had grown up underfoot, constantly rattling up the stairs to Baker Street B to watch Holmes conduct some experiments or analyze some evidence. I remember one occasion when Holmes was performing some ballistic test, and Christopher picked up the gun and stared down the barrel. The both of us nearly jumped out of our skins to grab the weapon away from the five-year-old. Thereafter, Holmes was always careful to exclude Christopher from the more dangerous investigatory practices. But when patience allowed (and Holmes would not have been considered one of the more patient individuals I have ever known, and was by no means a lover of children—in fact, I must say Christopher was the only child toward whom I ever witnessed him show any true affection) Holmes would explain to Christopher the particulars of whatever experiment he was conducting as the boy sat wide-eyed and cross-legged on Holmes's Persian carpet.

Since his return from Oxford, Christopher had taken up residence in Holmes's old flat. All of Holmes's research tools—such as his soil specimens from all parts of the city, cigar and cigarette ash collection, his kit for creating and detecting various poisons and his ballistic analysis machine—had been put in cellar storage. Without these things, 221B Baker Street lacked the cluttered character of Holmes's presence, but the remaining leather furniture, wood paneling and massive bookcases still hearkened back to that time when we shared some of the most extraordinary experiences.

"Excuse me. Mother, may I please hear what Dr. Watson has to say?" requested Christopher. He was unerringly respectful of his mother, and Mrs. Hudson was boundlessly fond of her only child.

"Yes, yes, of course, Christopher. You should hear everything. We all felt the same way about Mr. Holmes," said Mrs. Hudson. And then the tears came again, and it was hard to restrain my own sorrow when I saw the poor woman in such a wretched state. Christopher sat down on the sofa next to his mother and put a comforting arm around her.

"Yes. I should like to get this out as quickly as possible before I, too, succumb to my emotions," I said, commiserating. Mrs. Hudson continued to weep as Christopher fixed his keen stare on me.

I related to them what I had learned at the coroner's office and the circumstances surrounding the discovery of Holmes's body in the granary in Kent. When I finished, Mrs. Hudson could not restrain a loud sob. Christopher had listened to every word as if memorizing it for later recitation.

"And what does Scotland Yard think?" asked Christopher sternly. "Have they any suspects?"

"They are investigating as we speak. I know nothing more of what that might have yielded." I took a breath. The recounting of the facts tore at the open wound in my heart. For a few moments, the room was absolutely silent. "Are you all right, Mrs. Hudson?" I asked gently.

Mrs. Hudson had a vacant look in her eyes, as if in a trance. "Mrs. Hudson?" I repeated.

Her eyes refocused. "I'm afraid I won't be all right for quite awhile, Doctor. Certainly not until this murderer is found," she said forcefully. The fierceness in her voice reminded me of the tenacity with which she used to guard Holmes's doorstep.

"He will be caught," reassured Christopher as he fetched her a glass of water from a white ceramic pitcher with a hummingbird hand-painted on it. It had been a gift from Holmes when he returned from his travels to the Far East. Christopher handed his mother the glass of water, "And he will be hanged," he continued coldly, and then fixed his serious eyes on me. "May I examine the body, Dr. Watson?"

I was momentarily surprised by the request until I remembered the young man had taken his preparation for medical school and so obviously felt confident that he might have something to contribute. It seemed to me that there was little harm in allowing him to visit the morgue. There is nothing more desultory at times like these than having nowhere to direct one's energy. If visiting Holmes in the morgue would make the lad feel more useful, so be it.

"I believe I can arrange it, Christopher. Tomorrow morning, perhaps?"

"I'd prefer to do it today," he fired back.

We were all in a bit of a state, so I tried not to take exception to his rather demanding attitude. "I won't be available until later in the afternoon. There's someone I want to question first. I can meet you at the morgue at four. Will that do?" I said patiently.

"Forgive me if I sound strident, Doctor. I would like to see if I can help with any observations before there's further contamination," he said with consummate self-confidence. Apparently, in addition to the sciences, he had been tutored in brashness at Oxford.

"I see," I responded, and left it at that. "Is there anything I can do for you, Mrs. Hudson?" I proffered.

She had composed herself by this point. "No. I'm sure you know what to do, Doctor Watson."

"Then I shall go." I put on my hat, nodded to the mother and son and took my leave.

Outside, the mist had turned to rain. As I hailed a cab, I heard Christopher Hudson calling to me from the doorstep. I turned as he approached. "Dr. Watson, he will use Holmes's murder to beguile you. Be careful not to let him use this for his own purposes."

He turned and walked away as if no response needed to be given to his statement. He was correct. We both understood what he meant. A cab pulled up behind me and I got in.

• • •

The conditions at the Bethlem Hospital had improved considerably over the past twenty years. The age of patients naked, chained and put on display for visitors willing to pay a few pence to see the "loonies" was an unpleasant memory. Gone were the barbaric therapies of binding patients in icy sheets and feeding them emetics and purgatives. These practices were replaced with "occupational therapy," beneficial drugs and something called "psychoanalysis" introduced by the famous Austrian doctor Sigmund Freud. I had often discussed Dr. Freud with Holmes, who found the doctor's theories to be overly complex and unsupported by any real physical evidence. I myself had read some of the Freud's works and thought them to have merit, particularly his book on dreams. I found that fascinating.

As I mounted the steps of the institution and passed through the stately columns of the domed building, I recalled my last visit to this hospital that had been nicknamed "Bedlam" centuries ago. Ten years before, I had come to see a cousin, Thomas Callaghan, after he returned from the Boer War. He was suffering from profound melancholia and sleeplessness. He would lapse into a stuporous state and remain fixed and rigid for hours at a time. He was finally committed to hospital when he awoke one day and did not recognize his family. I've no doubt that these symptoms were residual from his experiences in that grisly African war. Once, in a more lucid moment, he confessed that his sleeplessness resulted from a vision of a battlefield strewn with dead. I do believe that the poor man had what I've observed as survivor's guilt. After a yearlong stay, he was released from Bedlam and sent home "uncured."

I entered the reception area and was greeted by a pleasant young woman who bade me to approach the desk and sign the register. "I am Dr. John Watson," I volunteered, and, as I picked up a pen, I heard a voice call out, "Dr. Watson. I was told you were coming."

A tall man, about sixty, with receding white hair and a similarly colored, trimmed beard hurried toward me. "I'm Chaplain Edward Geoffrey O'Donohue," he said extending a hand.

Chaplain O'Donohue's face was long, and the flesh around his eyes heavy, as if he were sleep deprived. He wore a very plain, dark three-piece suit with a watch chain hanging across the full width of his stomach. I thought it interesting that he wore no cross nor clerical collar nor any evidence of his occupation. There was kindness in his manner and a practiced gentleness in his voice.

"I'm sorry that Superintendent Smith couldn't be here. I have been appointed to accompany you," he said cordially. "What occasions this visit? Has some crime been committed?"

I hesitated, not wanting to say the words out loud. I motioned for us to move away from the reception desk to gain some privacy. This signaled the chaplain that my purpose here was one of great seriousness, and he leaned his ear toward me, hungry to hear what I had to impart. "It will be in tomorrow's papers. Mr. Sherlock Holmes has been murdered." I communicated this with as little emotion as possible.

The chaplain raised his head and blinked at me as if poleaxed. "Oh my word," he stammered. "Villainous…This is terribly shocking… .I will take you to him at once."

As if on a mission from God, Chaplain O'Donohue quickly led me out of the reception area, through a heavy glass and wrought-iron door and into a long, spacious gallery with floor-to-ceiling windows facing the front lawn. Approximately a dozen female patients populated this "women's wing," attended by nurses in uniform. The room was furnished with paintings, potted plants, birds in cages, statuary and carpeting. It had the atmosphere of a hotel. All this was a product of the renovation the notorious hospital underwent in the late part of the last century. The heating was updated, hot water pipes were installed as were new water closets, and the unpleasant smells that had previously been attributed to the mentally afflicted residents of Bedlam disappeared as those effluvia had actually been emanating from the old, decrepit toilets and urinals.

Chaplain O'Donohue moved briskly through the room, paying not the least bit of attention to the patients as I trailed a few hurried paces behind him. One woman rocked back and forth in front of a window with a silly grin as if amused by her own reflection. A group of four women was gathered around a table playing cards, appearing as natural as any bridge club. Halfway down the long gallery, we approached a woman painting at an easel. Another female patient stopped to admire the painting. "It's so beautiful!" she declared.

"Thank you so much," the artist beamed. The admirer reached out reverently to touch one of the paintbrushes, and, with great swiftness, the painter slapped her so hard across the face that it sounded like a pistol shot. The admirer let out a wail of despair as nurses rushed forward. We sped by and I felt a bit as if I were chasing the White Rabbit.

At the end of the gallery, we came to a heavy, arched wooden door and the chaplain dug his hand into his pocket. As I waited for him to open the door, a female patient, wringing her hands and staring into a birdcage, caught my eye. For some reason she looked vaguely familiar to me. She was fair-skinned with long waves of ungroomed raven tresses. She must have felt my gaze, for she turned toward me and fixed me in a dull stare with the most haunted eyes I have ever seen. We held that gaze for a moment, and then surprisingly the corners of her mouth turned up in a slight smile, just as quickly that smile turned into an expression of near panic.

"Here we are," declared Chaplain O'Donohue. He pushed open the door and ushered me toward a stone stairway lit at intervals with old-fashioned, flickering gaslights. Together we descended.

"We plan to gut this entire basement wing when he's moved to the new Rampton Secure Hospital. It's scheduled to be completed this summer," he said glancing back at me over his shoulder. "I'll be glad when it happens. This place feels like one of King Henry's dungeons."

Indeed, this basement wing of the hospital did resemble something from the Middle Ages, cold and dark, with rough- hewn granite walls and floors and the sour smell of mildew.

After two flights down, we reached a guard sitting at a desk in an alcove. He was perhaps thirty years old, a bit too heavy for his blue uniform, with red hair protruding from under his cap. He was guarding a steel-sheeted door with rivets in it and passing his time with one of those weekly joke magazines geared to a fourteen-year-old mentality. The guard rose to his feet and nodded respectfully. "Afternoon, Chaplain," he said, in an accent that revealed a working-class, East London heritage.

"Freddy will attend to you from here," said Chaplain O'Donohue. And then, with a sympathetic hand on my shoulder, he continued, "I'm very sorry for the loss of your friend. It is a great loss to us all. If you'd like to talk about it…" He gave my shoulder another firm squeeze. I thanked the chaplain for his assistance and he departed.

Freddy removed a key ring from a hook on the wall. "Are you ready to go in, sir?"

"Yes, please," I responded anxiously.

Freddy nodded, unlocked the steel-plated door and pushed it open. Beyond was a short, dimly lit circular room with four wooden cell doors, each with three broad, tarnished iron bands bolted crosswise and a rectangular, barred peephole. All but one cell appeared to be empty. Freddy led to me to the furthest door and fumbled for a different key on his ring. I wasn't sure what to expect. Eight years in this dungeon could make a man a raving lunatic or a hopeless catatonic.

Freddy unlocked the door, and it swung open on creaking hinges. Inside the cell, his left hand manacled with a length of chain bolted to the granite wall, was Professor James Moriarty. He laid his sunken eyes upon me and rasped, "So it's true."

2

Eight years of rotting in this cell had done nothing to dull Moriarty's malevolence, both in appearance and character. Though now approaching sixty and slightly bent at the shoulders, Moriarty stood several inches over six feet. He had straight, heavy eyebrows above narrow, wolflike eyes. He was clean-shaven during his trial, but now had grown a broad moustache that turned down around the corners of his mouth. He was wearing faded dark pants, resembling tuxedo pants, a stained white shirt and, I guessed as an eccentricity, he was allowed to wear a cravat. He couldn't have been wearing it for my benefit since my visit had been unannounced. The manacle around his wrist restricted his approach to the door but allowed him to move around the cell comfortably enough.

The cell was more hospitable than he deserved. There was a small writing desk and chair, a bed that looked far more accommodating than the usual cot, a toilet, basin and a rug that reminded me of the ones I'd seen in Afghanistan during the war. Freddy brought me a chair and then quickly departed. Moriarty took a seat behind his desk.

"How was he killed, Doctor?" He asked with a tone that gave me the genuine impression that he did not know the circumstances.

"A blow to the head," I responded. Moriarty was fully aware of why I was here, but my intention was still to let him take the lead. If somehow he was behind this or knew anything of it, I wanted to finesse it out of him if possible. Letting egos as big as Moriarty's demonstrate their superiority is often the best strategy. I knew there would be no concealing my distressed state of mind from him, and he would take full advantage of that, so I concentrated on being the reactor and not forcing some false confession that would allow him to lead me off on some useless unicorn hunt.

"A blow to the head!" he said angrily, as if offended by the thought of it.

"And another to the chest," I volunteered.

He placed both hands on his desktop and exhaled as if trying to control his anger. "What does that stupid cunt Lestrade think?" he snarled. Despite his breeding and education, Moriarty often spoke like a whorehouse barker. During his trial, the judge had been forced to gag him more than once. He had shouted out threats to the witnesses, calling them all manner of vile names. Holmes had been convinced he was doing this for effect and even found it somewhat amusing. It was intended to intimidate and confuse. Everything that Moriarty did was thoroughly calculated.

"Scotland Yard is still investigating. I haven't spoken to Lestrade yet," I volunteered calmly.

Moriarty shook his head in disbelief. "Killed by a blow to the head. Perhaps it was a frying pan, eh? Perhaps it was that old cow, Mrs. Hudson?" he said mockingly.

"Look here, Professor, this act is wasted on me." I wanted to be forceful with him and get him to drop this pretense of sarcasm. It was a thin disguise for whatever his real thoughts were.

"Quite right, Doctor Watson. The gravity of this situation demands our best comportment." He opened a desk drawer. "Care for a cigar?"

He produced two cigars from the drawer. He could see my surprise that he was allowed such luxuries.

Moriarty smirked, "The guards do me favors in return for compensation. We'll all be here for quite a spell, so we've learned to get along." He held the cigar toward me.

"Thank you, no," I said curtly.

He lit his cigar, took a seat and puffed deeply, creating whirls of gray smoke in the cell. "You remember Colonel Moran, I assume?" He did not wait for an answer as there was no need. He was fully aware that, eighteen years prior, I had witnessed Moran's attempt on Holmes's life as Holmes and I crouched in the dark of the building across from the Baker Street flat and watched Moriarty's paid assassin put a bullet in the head of the mannequin that Holmes had placed as a silhouetted decoy. "He died last week in that cell right over there," he continued. "They determined it was a stroke. I was wondering why he wouldn't answer me that morning." Moriarty checked the ash on his cigar and tapped it into the sink. "His plan to kill Holmes, though flawed, had a certain elegance to it. Mind you, as I've said before, I did not authorize it. It was a totally renegade enterprise, but still I had to admire using a silenced air rifle to try and kill Holmes in his own world-famous Baker Street flat." He paused for a long moment as if considering Moran's death or some other thought that had flown into his head. "And now you tell me that someone has bashed in the skull of Sherlock Holmes. I won't have it!" he bellowed and slammed his free hand down on the desk with thunderous force.

I honestly could not tell if this was an act. Moriarty was unstable, to be sure. He had demonstrated these outbursts before. In this case, it might be premeditated to throw me off.

"With Colonel Moran gone, I have no company any longer, you see, Doctor," he said rather pathetically. "We were in the middle of a chess match."

His sudden change of mood put me off balance. "Yes, well, I'm told you'll be moved to Rampton shortly," I offered, though I have no idea why I had the urge to give this monster any comfort. "Perhaps when you get there, they will—"

"So you've come here for help," he barked, cutting me off and showing absolutely no sign of the sadness he had exhibited seconds before for his poor, departed friend, Colonel Moran.

"I came here because I thought you'd want to hear from me the circumstances of Holmes's death," I said calmly.

"Stop lying!" he shouted. "The man has been murdered, and you don't have a fucking idea who did it, even though there are scores who would be happy to see him dead."

"The vast majority of those are in prison," I responded.

"As am I, and yet, you seem to suspect me."

This exchange had been a misstep on my part. Both the clumsy lie that I'd come to inform him of the circumstances of the murder and then the pointed comment about the criminals in prison thanks to Holmes's efforts. He would see through the lie and take the second comment as a challenge to match wits with him, exactly the kind of conversation I wanted to avoid.

"You're quite right," I acquiesced. "I have come here for your help."

He was silenced by the abruptness with which I surrendered. It was a good strategy apparently. He let his eyes wander about the cell as he plotted his next move. He placed his cigar on the desk and fixed me in a level stare. "There are many things you don't know about Sherlock Holmes, Doctor."

It was a presumptuous statement, as if he knew more about Holmes than I. "There are many things we don't know about all men, Professor," I responded, betraying no resentment.

"That is quite true," he said with satisfaction. "Now let me ask you a question. The elaborate lie that Holmes created of our mutual death struggle at the Reichenbach Falls, did he ever explain that to you?"

"Of course he did," I responded.

"And what was his reason for that deception?" he asked slyly.

"It was to evade you and your murderous henchmen," I said with a hint of contempt that I trust he detected.

"And did you see me during this adventure with Mr. Holmes in Switzerland?"

"Yes. I saw you running toward our moving train in a failed attempt to catch up with us."

"Did you get a good look? Because I wasn't at the train station," he said silkily. "I was in Genoa involved in some other business matters during that time."

I had to admit to myself that I had been directed by Holmes to look at a man that he identified as Moriarty running toward the train that day. I'd never laid eyes on the professor before that time, so any taller-than-average commuter running for a train would have sufficed for Holmes purposes. Seeing Moriarty several years later, my memory could have easily transposed his face onto the man at the train station.

Moriarty watched me mull this over for a moment before he continued. "For the first year of Holmes's so-called 'death,' I assumed he was trying to draw me out into the open. Why else would he include me in this deception? Obviously this was a conspiracy to get me to come out and disprove this fraud." Moriarty yielded the trace of a smile. "This is the vanity of genius; I thought I knew what was happening, and it taught me that one must always dig deeper into the dark recesses of the human mind. You see, it finally occurred to me that Holmes understood my psychology even better than I realized. I used the rumor of my death to full advantage by receding further into the shadows. I could transact my business without any meddling from the authorities. I did exactly what Holmes anticipated I would do. And, when all the facts were in, I understood why he had included me in this scheme. He was giving me an out as well. You see, Holmes was a selfish man, and if he couldn't have me, no one would." Moriarty exploded with a huge laugh. "He knew I would exploit my supposed death. I must say, it took me a while to piece it all out." He gave me a look of rapture. "He wanted me all to himself."

I remained speechless. Not just because Moriarty seemed to be lost in some half-mad state at his recollection of that period more than twenty years ago, but also because I didn't want to say anything that might dissuade him from venting what was on his mind. I waited for him to speak.

His face darkened as he seemed to be organizing his thoughts. "I will help you find Holmes's murderer on one condition, Doctor," he declared.

"I will consider it," I responded steadfastly.

"I want to attend his funeral," he said flatly.

This took me totally by surprise. I tried to quickly decipher what his motive could be. Perhaps he thought it was another ruse and Holmes wasn't truly dead. Perhaps it was the first step in some escape plan. I would have understood a trade for improvement in his living conditions or a shortening of his sentence, which was impossible since he was serving three consecutive life sentences, but this request to attend the funeral...Holmes was a respected and beloved citizen of London. It would be a huge event with royalty and dignitaries from all corners. Granting Moriarty's request would be like inviting a cobra to a christening, yet, I was convinced that Moriarty was indispensable to my objective. I believed this was an earnest negotiation.

"I will propose it," I said with as much frankness as I could muster. If I could get Lestrade to grant the proper security, I would fulfill my end of the bargain and hope that Moriarty would fulfill his end.

I heard a faraway screaming from the ward above. I turned toward the open cell door and could see across to where Moriarty indicated Colonel Moran had recently died. The screaming abruptly stopped and there was a sudden, ringing silence in the basement cell. I turned back to Moriarty and saw him sitting eerily still in his chair, as if a wax figure. He seemed to be done with me. I rose from my chair and moved to the door.

"Dr. Watson..." I turned back at the sound of Moriarty's voice. Cigar smoke curled out of his mouth and he studied me for moment with a malicious stare. "Are you prepared to look into the darkness?"

"I'm looking into it right now," I responded as I stared back fiercely, and I walked out.

I dragged myself down the front steps of Bedlam. I was emotionally spent from the day, and I still was scheduled to meet young Hudson at the coroner's in an hour. I resolved to refresh myself at the Northumberland Arms and then proceed to the morgue. The rain had begun to fall again and thankfully a horse-drawn four-wheeler approached up the driveway.

• • •

The roads were wet, but the rain was gone as I waited in front of the coroner's office for Hudson. I hadn't had much of an appetite when I stopped in at the Northumberland Arms but ordered a bowl of barley soup in an attempt to put something in my empty stomach. It made me feel marginally better, and it took a considerable effort to force myself to leave the warm, wood-lined comfort of the establishment.

As I waited in the afternoon chill, I heard a clattering sound approaching, and young Hudson coasted toward me on a motorbike. He was wearing small tinted goggles, a leather jacket of the kind that aviators wear, with a red scarf trailing behind him. He glided to the curb, cut the engine and hopped off the motorbike. The vehicle was steel-gray with whitewall tires and a placard beneath the crossbar with the name Harley-Davidson. He secured it to a railing with a chain and padlock and pulled off his goggles.

"I'm sorry to put you through this again, Doctor, truly I am," he said.

I was heartened by his acknowledgement of the effort he was making me extend. "One must face reality, Christopher. Holmes would be disappointed in me if I didn't look at this tragedy with a cold eye."

"Perhaps a younger set of eyes might help, as well," he added. This latest comment strained my patience again. "What did Moriarty have to say?" he probed.

"He said he will help if he is allowed to come to the funeral," I answered, not being able to think of any reason to conceal it from him.

"The funeral? Do you think that it is part of some escape plan?"

"There would have to be significant measures taken to make sure that doesn't happen."

We climbed the stairs and entered the building. "Do you think he is behind this?" he asked, continuing his interrogation as we approached the morgue desk.

"I don't know. I think he could be helpful as we move forward. If he is behind this, he'll relish a game of cat and mouse, and I believe his ego will slip him up. I must say, however, he seemed genuinely surprised that Holmes had been murdered."

"Maybe he was just surprised he succeeded," young Hudson speculated.

The coroner's clerk, a nice, plump young woman, looked up from the large oak counter that guarded passage into the examining rooms. "Good evening, Doctor Watson. Dr. Nolan told me you'd be back," she said pleasantly but with appropriate sullenness to acknowledge the circumstance of my second visit of the day.

"Good evening. This is Christopher Hudson." Christopher gave a polite bow of his head.

"Pleased to meet you, Mr. Hudson. If you gentlemen will kindly sign the log."

We signed the logbook and passed through the door that leads into that formaldehyde-laced, tiled whiteness. The bespectacled assistant met us at a cloakroom where Hudson exchanged his leather jacket and scarf for a rubberized coroner's apron. I would not need one as I intended to keep my distance from whatever proceedings Hudson was planning. I was already a little regretful that I consented to this. I couldn't see that an examination by a pending medical school student could do much good. Certainly this second visit to the morgue wasn't doing me much good. I had slept little and eaten little during the last twenty-four hours and was feeling a bit unsteady as we approached the autopsy room.

When we entered, the body was already waiting for us covered by a sheet on a porcelain-topped gurney. The coroner's file was lying on the sheet. I retreated to the corner as Hudson approached the gurney and picked up the file. The coroner's assistant exited without a word, but Hudson called after him, "Could I have a look at his belongings as well, please?"

The coroner's assistant poked his head back in the door, "Yes, sir. I'll bring them to you," he said respectfully and disappeared again.

Hudson scanned the coroner's report. The room was silent except for the rumble of the morgue's newly installed refrigeration system. From my vantage point I could see through the doorway into the main dissection room where a new body awaited the coroner's scalpel.

Finished with the file, Hudson put it aside and lifted the sheet. His confident, dispassionate manner dissolved in an instant. His mouth quivered and his eyes blinked back brimming tears. That moment reminded me what a towering figure Holmes must have been in the lad's life. He was no less than an uncle to the boy and perhaps even a second father.

The bespectacled youth returned with a canvas bag containing the clothes and belongings. "Thank you," said Hudson with a slight tremble in his voice. The assistant coroner hurried off again as if to other pressing business. Hudson placed the bag on the floor and then, having composed himself, bent over Holmes and inspected the damage to his forehead.

"He was undoubtedly killed by that blow to the head," I said trying to give him a running start and hence shorten our visit.

"Yes, I read that in the report," he replied quickly. "I'm confident the coroner has done an excellent job of medical examination. I'm not looking for injuries, I'm looking for evidence." As he said this, he withdrew a test tube and tweezers from his pocket. "See this speck here?" I drew closer and noticed a minute silvery speck at the edge of the indentation on Holmes' head. He collected it with the tweezers and put it in the test tube. His manner had become clinical, much the same way I had seen Holmes conduct himself when collecting evidence from a murder scene. "I'll analyze it at home," he said, pocketing the test tube and pulling back the sheet to reveal the crude, thick sutures that had been sewn across Holmes's chest, post autopsy. Suddenly, it was more than I could endure.

"I'll be waiting outside," I said as I lurched to the door. My queasiness had turned to full-blown nausea, and I felt as if in a swoon. I barely made it out into the hall, staggered into a chair by the cloakroom and hung my head between my knees. Presently, the nausea and disorientation passed. I picked myself up and resolved to wait outside in the fresh air.

Half an hour later, Hudson emerged from the building buckling his leather jacket and winding his red scarf around his neck. "Are you all right, Doctor Watson?" he asked, descending the steps.

"I hope that was of some use to you, because I have determined that I shall not be going back to the coroner's for some time," I responded sharply.

"Yes, well, may I say again that I'm sorry to put you through this, but I think I can be of great value in this investigation. I may have a couple new ways of looking at things."

"Yes, of course," I said softening. I wanted nothing more than to go home and lie down. It was almost dark, and a dome of clouds was threatening again.

Young Hudson whistled loudly and hailed a motor taxi. "I'll bring you up to date tomorrow."

I forced a smile. I was not particularly interested in being brought "up to date," and I regretted having indulged the young man at all. I bid Hudson good evening, shambled into the back of the cab and did my best to ignore the fumes.

3

A hot bath and large dose of brandy steadied me considerably. Sitting at my writing desk in my robe and slippers, I recorded the day's events in my journal. I documented only facts, not thoughts and feelings. It had been too emotional a day to recount all that. As I was writing, the sounds of merriment drifted up from Stafford Street. For the first time, I realized it was Saturday night and activity was swelling on these lively avenues of London. There was probably some event, a wedding or such, being held at the Brown's Hotel, a block away. The flow of people coming and going from large events hosted at the stately hotel often crowded my street.

I had resided in two apartments since Holmes and I vacated Baker Street. The first one was on Charing Cross Road, owing to my love of the theater. There I had a five-minute walk to no less than a dozen venues. I suppose this desire to live in the West End could be traced back to those joyous days I had spent with my dear Mary. We would attend the theater whenever possible, everything from Gilbert and Sullivan to George Bernard Shaw. Secretly, Mary harbored the dream of being an actress. She certainly had the looks for it, but I think she might have been an even better critic if she had chosen that pursuit. Her analysis of plot and performance were razor sharp. Over dinner she would evaluate every scene of the play. I would listen to her excited, musical voice and say nary a word. When she realized how much she had been twittering on, she would blush and ask if I didn't agree with her. I always agreed with my darling wife, the dearest soul who ever rose to heaven.

After Holmes retired to Sussex, I took the flat in the theater district, but soon the pace and population of the West End became too hectic for me. The idea was far more attractive than the reality, and attending the theater after Mary died often magnified my loneliness. I moved to my present apartment, on Stafford Street, less than six months later. I found the rhythms of Mayfair more suitable to my temperament. Everything I require is quite convenient, and, should I have the occasion and the companion to go to the theater, the walk to West End is quite pleasant.

As I closed my journal, there was a knock on the door. For the first time it occurred to me that whoever had murdered Holmes might well have a motive to do away with me as well. "Who is it?" I called out cautiously as my mind went to the Webley revolver in the locked drawer of my desk.

"It's Lestrade," came the voice of the Scotland Yard commander from the other side of the door. I made no attempt to make myself more presentable. Certainly there was no sense of formality between Lestrade and myself.

I had met the then Inspector Lestrade at the Baker Street flat a week after moving in with Holmes those thirty-plus years ago. Obviously, Holmes had been instrumental in his advancement through the ranks, and though Lestrade was often irritated by Holmes's condescension, he was as fond and surely as indebted to the man as any of us. I opened the door and, in a rather startling display of emotion, Lestrade threw his arms around me and buried his pointy chin into my shoulder. "How are you faring, Doctor?" he asked with deep concern.

"I am bearing up, Commander," I replied as I extricated myself from his awkward grasp.

Lestrade's spirit had grown more generous with age and success. When we first met, he was a sarcastic little rat-faced detective, and though age had improved his disposition, it had done nothing to improve his looks. His sallow complexion was now accompanied by deep furrows running down the length of his cheeks and across the width of his forehead. His dark eyes peered out from beneath folds of eyelid skin and, as the years had advanced, he began to remind me of a large-nosed proboscis monkey in a trench coat. Lest I seem ungenerous in my description, let me state that I had a legitimate affection for Lestrade. He was a faithful friend, absolutely trustworthy with any confidence imparted to him, and there was never a request within his power that he would not grant.

"Have you any new information?" I asked.

"I was out at that farm most of the day. I found no evidence in the granary and nothing the farmer says leads me to believe he has anything to do with it. Tomorrow, I'll have Gregson and his men question people in the town. Perhaps someone saw Holmes there." Lestrade eyed the decanter of brandy. "Mind if I have a little swallow of that, Doctor?"

I was exhausted and desperately wanted to retire. "By all means. Pour for yourself." It was more a plea than an offer. I didn't feel as if I had the strength to lift another finger. Lestrade poured himself an inch of brandy into a snifter, sat down in my leather armchair and gazed at me silently. I stared back at him blankly. After a few moments I broke the silence. "I don't mean to be rude, Commander, but if you have no news to tell me, I would be grateful if you would finish your brandy and bid a good-night. I am indescribably weary."

"I feel the same. I could fall asleep in this chair right now, but it was you who requested we meet here at this hour," he kindly responded.

It occurred to me that he was right. I had left that message for him by telephone at Scotland Yard when I was at the Northumberland

Arms. My brain was so dulled I had completely forgotten and only now remembered the reason.

"Quite so," I said somewhat abashed.

"Well, what is it you wanted to discuss?" he asked, sipping his brandy.

"I visited Moriarty today, as you know."

A frown appeared on his face. "How did he react?"

"It's hard to decipher. He seemed genuinely surprised and almost…" I searched for the right word, "…disappointed."

"So you don't think he had anything to do with it?"

"I wouldn't say that. Did you know that he has cigars and a rug and a bed with a mattress?"

"It's very difficult to avoid such things. You'd have to sack the guards every week. I say let him rot in his bed with a cigar in his mouth," declared Lestrade with the appropriate amount of contempt.

"It tells me that he's likely having contact with people on the outside."

"So perhaps he did order it. Moriarty still has tentacles in many dark corners of this town. You can be sure of that, Doctor. Even if he's been locked up in there for eight years, some of his gang took a blood oath. I believe there are a dozen men who, to this day, would do his bidding."

"And that is why I think he can help us. But in return he wants to attend Holmes's funeral," I said, bracing myself for the response.

"The funeral!" he cried. "That's unacceptable. He must be using it as part of an escape plan?"

"That was the immediate reaction young Hudson and I had when we heard it."

"Young Hudson," he said, surprised. "What does he have to do with this?"

"I told him he could assist in the investigation."

"How old is he? Fifteen?" he asked, incredulously.

"Not at all. He's just graduated from Oxford. Going into medicine or science…He seems undecided."

"Yes, yes…I remember the lad bobbing about in Holmes's apartment. Graduated from Oxford, you say? Good heavens. How old does that make us?" He marveled at the thought for a moment. "You know I disapprove of involving Moriarty."

Lestrade would have disapproved even more strongly if he had known what Moriarty had called him. "I believe I can handle him," I said, trying to sound confident.

Lestrade gulped down the last of his brandy and rose to feet. "Enough for today, Doctor. I'm leaving before we have two grown men weeping in here." He picked up his hat and shuffled to the door.

"I do believe that Moriarty could be instrumental," I urged him.

He opened the door, "Whatever it takes, Doctor. Whatever it takes." He put on his hat and departed.

4

The urgent knocking on my door woke me at seven thirty the next morning. I must have been sleeping for over ten hours and was glad of it. I put on my robe, crossed my living room and looked through the peephole. Young Hudson was standing on my doorstep. His hair was tousled and his state of disarray made it appear as if he'd been up all night. I opened the door and he barged into the room and launched a fusillade of information that he rattled off so quickly I could barely keep up with him.

"He wasn't hit with a shovel or the flat side of an axe. He was hit by a car. A French car of recent make. I have to do a little more research to get an exact match, but I believe it to be a 1912 Renault."

"A car you say. How do you know?"

"That metallic speck I found on Holmes's forehead…It's nickel plating. The same kind used on automobile bumpers. It has evidence of a sulfate-chloride process favored by French makers. The head and chest injuries are consistent with him being run down," he said with certitude.

I sank into a chair and couldn't help visualizing the event. "You seem quite sure," I said weakly.

"Because I *am* sure. Also, yesterday at the morgue, I took some soil from Holmes's shoes and compared it with his soil sample kit stored in the Baker Street attic. The soil came from the East End. Holmes had it labeled as Bethnal Green, but I intend to double-check that," he continued authoritatively.

"What was he doing in the East End?"

"Judging from the clothes he was wearing, I'd say he was meeting someone he knew. He had on well-worn walking shoes and a plain tweed suit with no tie. He didn't expect to go anywhere fancy, and he wasn't dressed to impress anyone, either. His attire and shoes were practical, but I would say not so casual as to believe he left his home unexpectedly without having time to change. He was there by appointment," he said with great confidence.

"My word! You have arrived at quite a number of conclusions," I said.

"We need to go out to Kent and see this granary," he demanded. "I'll drive. I have my mother's auto." He impatiently paced to the window and looked down at the street where Mrs. Hudson's automobile was parked. It was as if he was attempting to will us into the car and on our way.

"A minute, please. Let me absorb what you have said. Your theory is that Holmes went to meet someone in the East End with whom he had an appointment and was run down by a French automobile."

"A 1912 Renault, I believe." He turned back toward me.

"With nickel-plated bumpers?"

"Precisely, Doctor Watson." He paced from the window and stood over my chair.

"Precisely, indeed. You are advancing these theories with a surprising amount of precision."

"The theories match the facts. Can we get going, please?"

"How do you know that speck of metal didn't come as a result of a blow from a nickel-plated Webley revolver such as the one I have in my desk drawer over there?"

"I told you, because the process used on that metal was developed two years ago in France by Henri De Gard. Because the impression of the injury was long and flat consistent with someone being dragged under the front of a motor car and the head making contact with the bumper. I've been up all night confirming these facts, Doctor. I may be wrong in some particulars but not in general, and that is why we should leave now for that granary before the trail goes cold."

I couldn't help marveling at the reasoning the lad advanced, and I do believe Holmes would have been impressed as well. "I can certainly see you were listening very closely all those years sitting on the rug at Baker Street B."

He looked at me with all the intensity those blue-gray eyes could communicate. "I loved Sherlock Holmes, Dr. Watson."

There was no doubt from the timbre of his voice that this statement was true. "As did I, my boy." I replied quietly, putting both my hands on his shoulders. "Give me five minutes to get dressed."

• • •

Mrs. Hudson's car was a red, 1909 Daimler two-seater with a twenty-horsepower engine. It would be a ninety-minute drive out into the farmland in the middle of Kent, and at the edge of London, the decently paved streets gave way to a bumpy ride over the weathered country highway with stones and flints poking up through the tarry surface. It was comfortable enough inside the car, and Christopher appeared to be a very competent driver.

The *Herald*, *Mail* and *Daily News* were folded across my lap. I purchased all three newspapers to see how they had reported Holmes's death. The *Herald* headline read "Sherlock Holmes Found Murdered in Kent" and went on to state that Scotland Yard suspected Moriarty of being behind the murder. It additionally stated that an anonymous source reported that I, Doctor Watson, had gone to visit Moriarty at Bedlam, where he was being secretly held, and had tried to wring a confession out of him. It continued that there was no official cause of death disclosed as of yet, but sources tell the *Herald* that Holmes was murdered with an axe. "Where do they get this ridiculous information?" I said contemptuously.

"Some of it is true," said Christopher, glancing over at me.

"I wonder who the 'anonymous source' is who told them of my visit to Moriarty?"

"The same source who gets him his cigars, I imagine."

I threw the newspapers on the floor of car in disgust and watched cherry orchards and wheat fields soar past. After a few quiet minutes, I looked over at Hudson. There was a restless silence about the lad. It was as if his mind was always working out some mathematical problem. Maybe he was ruminating on this dreadful affair in which we were involved. In any event, I was happy to be chauffeured out to the location I had already intended to visit. This would save me the trouble of driving out with Lestrade. As I mentioned, Lestrade is a pleasant enough fellow, but when in an enclosed space with him for too long, he can carry on about such things as his bunions or office politics, which can get rather grating.

Young Hudson must have felt my gaze for he glanced at me out of the corner of his eye. "Are you all right, Doctor Watson? Do you need me to pull the car over?" he asked, as if regarding me as his feeble grandfather.

"I may be old, Christopher, but I am not so fragile that I cannot take an hour and a half drive out to the country."

"Right," he chuckled.

"That motorbike...? American made, isn't it?" I asked.

"Yes, it is," he answered with a sudden glow of enthusiasm.

"How did you come by it?"

"A chap from America, Rhodes Scholar, brought it over and sold it to me when he decided to go 'down under' and play Australian rules football."

"How many horsepower?" I asked.

"Four horsepower. Top speed of fifty miles per hour."

"Why didn't you get a Triumph? Show a little loyalty to your country," I said, teasing him.

"Because the Yank had a Harley-Davidson."

"Ahh, to be young again. Fifty miles per hour, you say?" I was glad to find a subject that cheered him. He seemed like such a serious young man much of the time, and we both needed a lighter subject.

"It goes every bit of fifty miles per hour, Doctor. I can vouch for that."

"I shan't tell your mother," I said with a conspiratorial grin.

We arrived at our destination, which was nearly the center of Kent. Had we driven another ten minutes, we would have been in Maidstone,

one of the larger cities in the county, with a pub on High Street that serves excellent bangers and mash. I felt guilty that my appetite had returned, but I've little doubt that my dear friend would have forgiven me. I could imagine Holmes's voice saying, "My dear Watson, we must not spend one second on useless emotion, only cold, intellectual observation will speed us to our purpose."

There was a metallic rural mailbox with an address painted on it at the entrance to a dirt road. We made the turn and a quarter of a mile down we found a substantial farmhouse in the shade of some ancient oak trees. There was a Scotland Yard police car parked in front of the house. Opposite the house was a red barn and granary with a high-pitched roof and second-story loft window. Beyond those two structures was a field of barley, half harvested, with a petrol-powered tractor parked in the middle of it.

Hudson stopped the car a hundred feet short of the house, quickly got out and began examining the area leading up to the granary.

I got out and watched him wind his way to the building, bent over, with his nose to the ground.

"Useless! Bloody useless!" he complained. "The place has been trampled." He went to the door of the granary, peered in for a moment and then disappeared inside. I followed him but, before I reached the door, he reemerged and resumed his search of the grounds.

"Here!" he said excitedly. He got down on one knee and gingerly poked around the edge of a tire track. "See this narrow, block-tread tire print? That is from a French Michelin tire."

I stood over him and looked down at the track. It appeared approximately the same size as those of the police car though it did create a distinct cross-tread impression in the clay-rich soil. Watching Christopher's determined demeanor, I was reminded how Holmes had always cautioned not to fit the evidence to the theory but rather the inverse. "We should check the tires on the farmer's vehicle," I urged.

"No need," he replied confidently. And he picked up a stray stalk of barley and used it to measure the width of the tire track. He broke the stalk to the exact width and compared it to a track made by the police car. The length of the stalk was clearly shorter.

"I believe, Doctor, you will find that this track comes from a 1912 model Renault, and that someone drove down that road, backed up to this barn and deposited Mr. Holmes's body inside."

"So you think the murderer drove that car?"

"Yes. But that doesn't necessarily mean that the person who murdered him is the same person who left his body here."

If Holmes were here he would have made the same comment as Christopher. I had jumped to a conclusion that the murderer and the person who left the body were one in the same. This could well be a conspiracy perpetrated by several people. The suspicion of conspiracy is what had led me to go see Moriarty as my first stop.

"Good morning, Doctor Watson," a gravelly voice called to me, and I looked up to see Superintendent Tobias Gregson walking our way from the farmhouse. Gregson still retained some of the flaxen hair of his younger days, though it had greatly receded. His tall, loose-limbed gait always looked to me as if he were trying to shake something out of the cuffs of his coat and pant legs.

Lestrade and Gregson started out as equals at Scotland Yard, and yet Lestrade had been advanced much more quickly than his colleague. It might have been because of Gregson's sometimes disagreeable manner. He was often perceived as snide and arrogant. Over the years, he had grown bitter about Lestrade's superior promotions. An additional irritant for Gregson was his constant position in the shadow of Holmes, and the fact that the famed detective had chosen Lestrade to be his closest contact at Scotland Yard. I never quite understood why Holmes opted for Lestrade. I know that Holmes thought Gregson to be the smarter of the two detectives, but from that very first grisly case at Lauriston Gardens, Lestrade had managed to cozy up to Holmes more successfully than his partner.

Gregson ambled toward us, shading his eyes against the morning sun. He was wearing a plain gray suit and had a scarf wrapped around his neck though it was not particularly chilly.

"A sad morning, Superintendent Gregson," I answered gravely.

"That it is. I believe I'm still in shock. I'm sure we all are," he said. "Who is this young man with you?"

"I'm Christopher Hudson, sir," answered Christopher, holding out his hand.

"Yes, yes. Mrs. Hudson's boy," said Gregson with a faint smile of recognition as he shook hands with Christopher. Gregson had only rarely ventured to Baker Street, while Lestrade had been a frequent visitor. I doubted that Gregson could conjure any memory of Christopher as a child.

"Christopher drove me out here this morning. He's recently returned home from Oxford," I said completing the introductions.

Christopher got right down to business before I could stop him. "Superintendent Gregson, would you be so kind as to ask your officers to question witnesses as to whether they saw a new Renault two-seater in the area night before last?"

"A Renault?" said Gregson, giving me a puzzled glance.

"A theory of his," I said with a neutral air, trying to minimize anything Gregson might interpret as interference.

"You have theories, is that right?" Gregson said with an amused smile.

"I am formulating some opinions about the case," young Hudson replied confidently.

"Formulating opinions," Gregson repeated. "Well, we can always use the opinions of well-educated college boys." This was the kind of snide swipe that, to his detriment, Gregson could never resist. I felt bad that I had set Christopher up for the attack with the information about Oxford. It was unnecessary knowledge to impart to Gregson. Holmes had always taught me to disclose only information such as will advance one's purpose. Happily, Christopher seemed unaffected by the little dig.

"That tire track over there," he forged ahead. "It was made by a Michelin tire. That's a French company."

"We've taken casts of all the tracks around here already, lad," responded Gregson, showing unexpected tolerance.

"Excellent! Then I imagine it will be only a matter of days before you'll know that Mr. Holmes was run down in the East End by a 1912 Renault two-seater and then driven to this location and left in that granary," stated Hudson with a sarcastic smile of his own.

Gregson slowly turned to me and said, "An extensive theory, he has."

I smiled apologetically. Then Gregson burst out with a hoarse laugh. "I suppose the lad is bucking to make chief inspector by this afternoon."

Christopher seemed to be unconcerned by Gregson's ridicule. He smiled and nodded as if he were enjoying the joke as well. A young Scotland Yard detective exited the house with a leathery man in his late thirties, who I presumed was the owner of this farm. "Is he the one who discovered the body?" I asked Gregson.

"That's the one. Name's Tannyhill."

"What has he to say?" I asked.

"That he found the body. I've got to get back to London. You're free to talk to him if you'd like. Discuss theories and such," he said with a playful grin and then walked off to his car where the young detective was waiting for him. Before Gregson got in, he turned back around, "And, by the way, night before last, the local constable followed someone speeding down this road but lost him in the dark right about where it turns off into this farm. Maybe your Renault, hmmm?" Gregson climbed into police car and they drove off.

When I looked back toward the house, the farmer had been joined on the porch by his wife and eight-year-old daughter. They were all three gazing out at us. "Do you want to talk to the farmer?" I asked Christopher.

"No need," he said curtly. "Gregson is right. The man found Holmes in his barn and that's all he knows."

• • •

I was happy to learn that the pub on High Street was still in business. I ordered the bangers and mash and Christopher had the ploughman's lunch. The food was as good as I had recollected. I required Christopher not to discuss the case during lunch as I have always found that constant rumination on these investigations can lead to an unhealthy compulsiveness and cyclical kind of thinking that hinders progress. Giving the mind a few hours of peace a day is of immeasurably benefit. I discovered this from studying certain Eastern philosophies during my long convalescence after returning from the war. Lying in my bed for months on end, I learned not to dwell on the recuperation of my physical state and to improve my mental state by clearing away all the negative emotions. I likened my mind to a room that I would sweep clean every day, leaving it free of dust, dirt and cobwebs and filled with only the useful, orderly things required to pursue one's life.

During lunch, we talked about Christopher's interest in geology and the possibility that he might pursue a career in petroleum engineering. He said in the future there would be manmade islands on the North Sea pumping petroleum from beneath the ocean, that there would be huge transcontinental pipes carrying petrol to all ends of the world, that coal and coal mining would become extinct. The future, as always, was in new technologies and those on the cutting edge would reap huge rewards. The boy spoke like a true capitalist. I myself am no Bolshevik. I have always been a firm believer in the free-market system and equality for all. I even signed a petition in support of suffrage, although I think that some of the methods of the suffragettes are rather unladylike. I suppose, at heart, I am a Victorian gentleman, not as well suited to the twentieth century as to the nineteenth.

I continued the moratorium on further conversation for the ride home as well, in truth, because I wanted to take a nap, and that would have been impossible with young Hudson rattling on obsessively about French tires and automobiles.

• • •

When we returned to my flat, I found a letter had been pushed under the door. I opened it and found it was from Holmes's solicitor, Henry Pearson. He requested that I come to see him at my earliest convenience. I rang up Pearson, finding him available and anxious to see me that afternoon. I asked if I could have young Hudson accompany me, and he replied, "By all means. This involves him, too." This rather surprising response made me even more curious about the nature of the meeting.

Hudson and I made the fifteen-minute drive to Mortimer Street and the offices of Henry Pearson and Associates. As far as I could tell, Pearson had never actually had any associates. He had a secretary named Dora, who looked rather like a tortoise with big, sad eyes and an expressionless mouth. There was also a Bob Cratchit-ish clerk named Snodgress, who seemed responsible for the filing and billing.

Dora led us into Pearson's office where the stout, red-faced solicitor sat behind a massive oak desk. I had known Pearson from the Commonwealth Club and used him on a couple of real estate matters. I could not remember whether I had recommended him to Holmes or vice versa. I know that Holmes abhorred anything that included contracts or legal entanglements and could not recall a single instance when he was involved in any legal matter.

Pearson rose and ushered Hudson and me to a sitting area near a window that overlooked the street. "May I offer you gentlemen something to drink?" he asked.

We declined and he twisted around toward his secretary and reached out his hand, "Dora, would you please hand me the Sherlock Holmes file from my desk."

She did as asked with a tortoise-like deliberateness. "Thank you. That will be all," he said, and she sluggishly retreated to the outer office. He turned back to us. "Dr. Watson, I believe it will come as no surprise to you that you are executor of Mr. Holmes's will."

It came as a surprise to me that Holmes had a will at all, for as scrupulously careful as he was with every investigation, he was rather disorganized regarding his personal affairs.

"First, I want to offer my condolences to the both of you. Is what I read in the papers true?'

"The important fact is true," I answered. "Holmes was murdered."

Pearson shook his head in dismay. "I can't see that this fact demands I approach my duties any differently, however the circumstances of his death might complicate your job. Let me give you the major points and then tell you the specific reason I asked you come here today."

Young Hudson remained respectfully silent through all this. Pearson had said that this matter concerned him as well, or I would have asked the young man to excuse himself. I was considering doing that in any event when Pearson preempted my words by opening the file on his lap and launching into his presentation of the particulars.

"Mr. Holmes's estate is approximately one million, four hundred thousand pounds," he said without putting any particular emphasis on the figure. I was stunned. I knew that Holmes had often given his services to members of royalty and heads of state for large fees, but it never would have occurred to me that he could have amassed such a fortune.

"After all real estate and other assets are liquidated, Mr. Holmes directs that Dr. John H. Watson distribute one half of his estate to the orphanage or orphanages of his choice. One quarter of the estate shall go to his brother, Mycroft Holmes. All Sherlock Holmes's personal belongings, excluding those which Dr. Watson should wish to keep, are to be given to Christopher Hudson."

Even in death, Holmes continued to astonish. Could it be that he had anticipated Christopher's acumen for detective work even before the youth realized it himself? But how could he have predicted he would die at such a young age? If Holmes had died at seventy, Christopher would have been thirty-three and well established in whatever field he had chosen. Holmes certainly wouldn't have expected him to abandon a secure occupation to pursue a career in crime detection just because he was bequeathed a ballistics kit. It would make about as much sense as expecting him to become a boxer because he left the lad his set of boxing gloves.

For his part, Christopher appeared dumbfounded. He was as surprised as anyone by his inclusion in the will, and, for a change of pace, rendered speechless.

"And here is the specific reason I wanted to speak to you in advance, Doctor. Mr. Holmes makes only one more bequest; that being five hundred pounds and a stipend of fifty pounds a month to Delilah Church until her death. I was wondering if you knew who this person is. We have no information on Miss Church. We have done a cursory check of the phone books and birth records but have found no one by that name."

"I don't believe I know a Delilah Church," I responded. "I might want to look at my journals. Perhaps a case I'm forgetting."

"If I may ask," interjected Christopher, "what is the date of Mr. Holmes's will?"

"The will is dated June 17, 1910. It was amended a year later and witnessed by a notary in Sussex," said Pearson.

"And what was added?" Christopher continued with his examination.

"The bequest to Miss Church. I drafted the underlying document and the codicil was added by Benjamin Braxton, Esq., in Sussex."

"And I assume he doesn't know Miss Church, either."

Pearson nodded. "I suppose I will have to put a detective on this," he concluded.

"You have two on it already," said Christopher, self-assured.

"Right you are," said the solicitor with a smile.

"Have you a key to Holmes's house?" I inquired.

"Yes. I'll have Snodgress give it to you on the way out."

Before leaving, Pearson called me back into his office. He produced an envelope from his file with my name written on it in Holmes's hand. "This arrived with the amended will a year ago. Instructions were to give it to you upon his death."

"Thank you for your discretion, Mr. Pearson." I pocketed the envelope.

I left Pearson's office with the envelope, a key to Holmes's Sussex residence and another puzzle to consider, regarding Delilah Church. Christopher had his eyes on the pavement as we walked toward the automobile. "I feel quite flattered that he left his belongings to me," he said without looking up.

"You should," I responded. "Many of those items were extremely precious to him, particularly the ones that concerned his work."

He stopped and looked at me earnestly. "But I feel badly that he had no one closer to give them to."

"Perhaps he felt you were the best one to make use of them."

Christopher considered that statement.

"And by the way, he did say you could have only those things I didn't want," I added lightly, trying to ease his misgivings.

He forced a smile, still feeling slightly guilty about the bequest.

"Didn't you feel close to him?" I asked. "You spent quite a bit of time in Baker Street B."

"I did. But I was never sure it was mutual. He was always so… distant."

"That was his way. He didn't reveal his thoughts. One of the downsides of the trade I suppose."

As we reached the car, a ragged little boy and girl with a wheelbarrow selling kindling for "5 Pence a Bundle" rolled past. The boy wore coveralls with one strap broken. The little girl wore a tattered petticoat. Suddenly it hit me like a thunderbolt. Delilah Church. "Lilah!"

5

It would take twenty minutes in the insufferable London traffic to get to Bedlam. I knew I'd seen her face before, that dark-haired woman with the haunted eyes. She had called herself Lilah and had been one of the gang of street urchins whom Holmes referred to as the "Baker Street Irregulars." He often employed them for purposes of following suspects and gathering intelligence from every corner of the city. As Holmes put it, "They can go anywhere, see everything, overhear everyone." I did not know Lilah's last name. When I first saw her back in 1881, she was a wild-haired little child of seven. The Irregulars would swarm about the city directed by their sixteen-year-old leader, Wiggins, who ultimately used this early training to become a rather notorious crime figure in the East End.

Lilah would be approximately thirty-eight years old now. I can't remember the last time I had seen her before my recent visit to Bedlam. I remember that as a teenager she was quite pretty despite the smudged face, layers of boys' clothes and kerchief on her head designed to conceal her long, dark ringlets. I imagine she wanted to pass as male in order to navigate the rough-and-tumble street life she had inherited. I could only guess what had transpired since her childhood to bring her to Bedlam. Even more mysterious was the reason for Holmes having made a provision for her in his will. Perhaps he had been informed of her present state. It would not be unlike Holmes to give assistance to those in need who had passed through his life, particularly the ones who had aided him in his professional efforts. He had always been quite generous to the Irregulars, and they returned that generosity with devotion. On numerous occasions they supplied us with a piece of information crucial to a case.

When we arrived at Bedlam, it had been roughly twenty-four hours since my last visit, and it felt as if there had been a year's worth of activity. This errand was a bit off the trail, but I wanted to resolve what I was almost certain was the case—that this fretful woman I observed the day before was actually the party named in Holmes's will.

A swirling afternoon wind stung my face as I remounted the stairs of the hospital, this time with Hudson at my side.

The same pleasant, young woman from the day before was stationed at the reception desk.

"Dr. Watson, I was not told to expect you," she said.

"Sorry about arriving unannounced. Something came up that requires I speak to one of the patients. Her name is Delilah Church."

"I can't authorize that, sir."

"Then would you kindly advise Chaplain O'Donohue that I'm here?"

"He's out in the field today. I can have you talk to Dr. Leeds," she offered.

"Yes, please. If that is procedure, then please call him for me."

A few minutes later, a squat, harried doctor in his white coat soon joined us in the reception area. From his attitude, you would have thought he was the only doctor on duty for the entire hospital.

"May I help you, gentlemen?" he said crisply and looked at me with faint recognition.

"Dr. Leeds, we would like to visit with a patient who I believe is named Delilah or perhaps Lilah Church."

"Are you a relative or have you been authorized for a visit?" he asked officiously.

"No."

"Then, as a matter of confidentiality, I cannot comment on the identity of our patients."

"This is a legal matter, Doctor Leeds."

"So is confidentiality," he assured me.

I refrained from pointing out that I could have Lestrade pull these records in a matter of hours, but I wanted to keep this nonconfrontational.

"Doctor, I am simply trying to determine if one of your patients is in fact the person named in the will of Sherlock Holmes."

Doctor Leeds's countenance transformed at the mention of Holmes's name. "I knew you looked familiar. You're Doctor Watson," he beamed.

"Yes, I am, and this is Christopher Hudson."

The receptionist piped in, "I told you it was Doctor Watson."

"I thought you said…No matter. I must have misheard." He shook our hands heartily, then added with great solemnity, "I cannot tell you how disturbed I was to hear of Mr. Holmes's death. I am a huge admirer. Has a funeral been scheduled? I would like to attend."

"A popular request," Christopher said under his breath.

"I will let you know," I said with a forced smile.

"As I have limited familiarity with the female patients, I will have to check the files. Would you please follow me, gentlemen?"

He led us to a file room with three walls of floor-to-ceiling shelves crammed with patient records. "Church, you said?" He moved over to the Cs, which occupied four long shelves near the top. Dr. Leeds dragged a stepladder over and climbed up.

"Yes. Delilah Church," I confirmed.

Flipping through files, he mumbled, "Childress…Christin…Chubb…Claiborne…Sorry, no Church."

"Perhaps, I could speak with the young woman. I saw her just yesterday. I could ask her if she's Lilah Church."

He came down from the stepladder. "These patients will tell you they're Marie Antoinette if it'll please you."

"I'd just like a moment with her. I'm quite sure this is the girl I remember from years back,"

"Hold on one moment. It's just possible…" His voice trailed off as he moved to a stack of folders inside a metal basket. He leafed through. "Success!" he declared and pulled out a folder, opened it and read, "Delilah Church, age 38, transitory catatonia, bouts of severe anxiety…" he droned. "Discharged. Uncured."

"Discharged!" I repeated in astonishment.

"Yes. This morning. That is why her file is in this basket."

"Discharged to whom?" I asked.

"To her son, Alexander Hollocks." He looked up from the file. "The same person who had her admitted."

"But her file says she has catatonia and severe anxiety."

"We don't cure them all," Doctor Leeds shrugged. "We don't even cure half of them. If he wants to take care of her at home, that's his right."

"Have you an address for her or her son?" I asked.

"None listed here," the doctor answered.

"What date was she admitted, Doctor?" asked Christopher coolly.

Doctor Leeds flipped back to the first page of the file. "April 18, 1911."

• • •

The dying light on the hospital grounds turned the trees to a murky green. As we descended the stairs of the hospital, weariness was claiming me again, and I had added a new task to my agenda—that of locating Lilah Church. Christopher had asked few questions of the doctor, but I could see the wheels were turning in his head. "What are you thinking?" I asked.

"Well, it occurred to me," he said, digging his hands into his back pockets, "that the date of Miss Church's admission into the hospital was followed closely by the revision of Mr. Holmes's will, which would indicate that he was keeping fairly close tabs on her."

"I think that's a reasonable assumption, but what significance does that have?" I queried, for other than the obvious fact that Holmes felt charitable toward an orphaned girl, I could not see what conclusion Christopher was reaching for.

"It seems notable to me that he singled her out."

"Yes, but he singled you out as well," I replied. "Likewise the orphanages"

"You make a good point," he sighed. "In any event, it's not a priority. I want to stop by Scotland Yard and ask Gregson if there's been a report of any stolen or recovered Renaults in London or Kent."

"Take me home first. I've had enough for the day," I requested wearily.

● ● ●

Twenty minutes later we pulled up in front of my flat. The sun had set and I was so exhausted I had actually dozed off during the ride back from Bedlam. "Thank you for the ride home," I said wearily as I reached for the door handle.

"Tomorrow we should motor down to Sussex and have a look at Mr. Holmes's belongings," Christopher said with his usual stridence. He seemed determine to drive me like an ox.

"Let's see what tomorrow brings. There may be other more pressing matters to attend to," I said gently.

I was on the verge of telling the lad that his zeal bordered on overstepping when he interrupted me.

"Doctor Watson, why don't you move back into Baker Street while we pursue the case? It would seem a more efficient way to proceed."

Several thoughts collided in my mind at once, the first being, of course, visions of Holmes and myself sharing that fabled space during all those years and all those extraordinary events. Second, it was true we had already formed a bit of alliance as regards the pursuit of this case, but up until now I had considered my actions as humoring the lad. Was he suggesting an equal partnership? He was a fine observer and possibly even a better chauffeur, but he certainly was not ready to step into the shoes of Sherlock Holmes, and I did not know if I was prepared to step back into mine. Perhaps he meant to pose the question as if I would be his mentor, though, thus far, this hadn't been his attitude, or perhaps thus far *he* had been humoring *me*. My hesitation in answering gave him pause.

"I'm afraid that may have been too forward a suggestion," he said cautiously.

"Not a bit. It's a natural thought, but I'm not sure I could bear it right now...the memories and all." I ended the discussion by getting out of the automobile and firmly closing the door.

• • •

Mounting the stairs to my apartment, I felt resentment welling up. This overreaching by young Hudson, the assumption that he would continue with me every step of the way, began to rankle me more with each stair I climbed. The audacity that he should invite me to move into a flat in which I had cohabitated with the greatest crime-solving mind of a generation was infuriating. I should not have allowed him to come to the coroner's office. I should not have indulged him at all.

I reached into my coat pocket for my key and felt Holmes's letter that Pearson had given me. I had wanted a good dose of brandy to accompany the reading of it, so I had decided to wait until I got home. A ringing phone greeted me as I opened the door to my flat. It was the prime minister's secretary. "Hold the line for the prime minister," came an authoritative female voice from the other end. Prime Minister Asquith was a rather urbane gentleman with a fine speaking voice, as most prime ministers possess, however he was known socially to have such ungentlemanly habits as looking down dresses and stroking female guests' thighs much higher than was considered polite. I agreed with most of his liberal stances except for his fondness for adding to the empire's fleet of battleships and his position against suffrage.

"My esteemed Doctor Watson," came a sudden, melodious voice from the telephone. "My condolences on the death of Mr. Holmes, a national hero to be sure."

"Thank you for your thoughts, Prime Minister."

"I wanted to inform you personally that our intention is to hold a funeral for Mr. Holmes in three days' time at Westminster Abbey. This gives the various dignitaries and heads of state adequate time to attend."

"Thank you, Prime Minister. That's very impressive and a great honor."

"Well deserved," he said sincerely. "I shall have Mrs. Bennett call you with the details."

"Thank you again, Prime Minister." I waited for him to hang up before I put down the receiver.

I sunk into a chair with my decanter of brandy, poured myself a double portion and placed the letter on the table. I stared at the familiar hand that had written "To My Dear Friend, Dr. John H. Watson" on the front of the envelope. I felt I had neither the strength nor the courage to read the contents of the envelope at that moment. However, Sherlock Holmes did not do things frivolously, so the assumption would have to be that if he left me a letter to read after his death, it was potentially of pressing importance. The envelope was sealed with red wax, and I carefully peeled it open and took out the single sheet of paper and unfolded it. It was written in Holmes's hand and read:

My Dear Watson,

Should I predecease you, this letter will serve as my final and most sincere communication. Know that you have been my greatest friend and constant support. You have saved my life on more than one occasion, and I'm quite certain no man could have as humble and considerate a companion as you. I admire you as much as any man I have ever known. You are an individual of unwavering moral character and insight, and for all these reasons I must impose upon you one last time. Please scrupulously carry out my wishes as detailed in my will. Please be so kind as to give my eulogy. There is no one who can speak the truth about my life better than my dearest friend. Like all men, I had my faults. I have tried to rectify my mistakes in life to the best of my ability. Whatever recompense I owe, I leave to my Maker.

Sincerely,

Sherlock Holmes

A sudden wave of emotion crashed upon me. I broke down weeping as I had not wept since losing my precious Mary. This letter had burst the dam. Mentally exhausted, my mind finally succumbed to the involuntary reflexes of my body, and I shook and sobbed with grief. I drank until I fell into a restless sleep and I dreamed of Holmes. I was following him. I was driving a car, but it was not running properly. Holmes was on foot accompanied by Lilah. She was both a child and a woman at the same time, as is only possible in a dream. They wound through the narrowing streets, his hand on her shoulder, guiding her. I tried to keep up with them, abandoning my automobile, which was growing wider and wider as the streets narrowed. They disappeared into a dark alleyway, and I found myself standing in front of Westminster Abbey. I entered and a funeral was in progress. Organ music played. The pews were filled with the many victims and villains from the cases that Holmes and I had pursued over the years. The prime minister, Lestrade, Moriarty and dozens of dignitaries were there. Holmes walked down the aisle with Lilah, who took a seat in a row beside her fellow Baker Street Irregulars, their young faces vividly recollected to me in the dream. Holmes continued to the front of the Abbey and approached the open casket. He looked in and then turned to me with concern saying, "It was a mistake. A terrible mistake." I nodded as if I understood. I suddenly bolted awake. Something akin to an electric charge surged through the muscles of my arms and legs. I was no longer tired. I realized I had another task to accomplish and it was a task that only could be accomplished at night.

6

CHRISTOPHER

Frankly, I was shocked to find that I had been included in Sherlock Holmes's will, and I had the distinct impression that Dr. Watson was displeased with this fact. For the last couple of days I felt I had been walking on eggshells with the doctor. I'm sure he viewed me as a bit of an upstart in his field and, maybe worse, as a meddler. My strategy had been to couch my observations as suggestions, but my inherently confident nature had already betrayed that plan in several instances during those first days. Watson was no fool, and he tried his best to accommodate me while concealing his annoyance, to which he was fully entitled. I had the utmost respect for Watson's intuition and powers of deduction. A man of his intellect could not help but absorb a lifetime's worth of knowledge in the company of the greatest detective of our time. But I knew I had a valuable role to play, and I wanted to prove my worth to Doctor Watson. After all, Holmes had left me all his belongings and there was no ambiguity in that. My hours of sitting on the floor and observing the legendary detective hadn't escaped his attention. Thinking back, I could remember occasions when I would take my hand-painted toy soldiers, which my father had brought me from Belgium, up to the flat and line them across Holmes's Persian carpet in a massive show of military force. Sometimes Holmes would even indulge my play by rearranging the pieces in what he told me would be the proper formation and then describe to me historic battles and the strategies used by the victors. Just as abruptly he would retreat back to whatever case he happened to be on or some other imponderable adult concern and brusquely shoo me out of the flat.

There is, however, one very vivid recollection that is certainly most pertinent to Holmes's bequest. I was seventeen and about to attend Oxford when Holmes took me to the Athenaeum Club for lunch. The Athenaeum is the most posh and exclusive club in London. I felt grown up and intimidated at the same time. This was a real man-to-man occasion with Holmes. He was several years retired by then, save the occasional exception when he was called in to consult on a matter of state importance. I assumed that he was in London for some other business and had fit me into his schedule, but, looking back, this might not have been the case.

"What do you intend to pursue at Oxford, Christopher?" he asked me casually after we had ordered.

"I'm interested in the sciences," I responded.

"A worthy pursuit," he said convincingly. "I myself have never been one for literature. I care little for philosophy and even less for politics, but much can be learned by observing the physical world." He paused as the waiter brought his gin and tonic. He took a sip and kept on with his thought. "Look at the men around this club… I recognize but two or three but can tell the majority of their occupations by simple observation. For example, the man at that table against the wall is a first-time guest of the man with whom he's sitting. If he had been here before, he would know that his attire is entirely too casual for the Athenaeum. He must have come here separately or else his companion would have informed him of such. I can tell from this distance that they are speaking English, though I cannot hear his accent, however when he passed I noticed that he has a deep tan and extremely rough hands, which makes me believe he is visiting from the Southern Hemisphere, probably Australia, and is either a wealthy farmer or rancher. Those two older gentlemen by the window were military men. I can tell by the cut of their beards and moustaches. The one on the right is a navy man, made obvious by the bottom of an anchor tattoo peeking out from his sleeve. The facts are borne out as well by the wind cap on his pipe, which is lying beside him on the table, a handy item when smoking on deck. The man at the table next to us is a surgeon. That is plain from the way he handles his knife." Holmes took another sip of his gin and tonic and was perfectly confident that his observations were correct. "Now you give it a try, Christopher." He checked the room for a candidate. "That man eating the Dover sole…focus on the details."

The man was two tables over. I turned discreetly and studied him, trying to see what Holmes might see, to look at him as Holmes might look at him. Holmes did not describe a man by facial features or hair color or height, although, in passing, he could tell you all those things about a man with only a quick glimpse. He saw all the details that make up the story of a man, not the description. The man dining on Dover sole had a receding hairline and shiny forehead. He had a round face and ruddy complexion that turned quite rosy at his cheeks. He seemed like a good candidate to play Santa Claus in a Christmas play. He wore a navy blue double-breasted suit with starched white cuffs and gold cuff links in the design of a small knot of rope. I could not see him from the waist down, but unless his shoes were extraordinary in some way, I assumed there was nothing to be gained from a fuller view. I watched him put another forkful of sole in his mouth and studied him. After another moment I turned to Holmes confidently. "The man is either a barrister or a judge. I can't be sure."

"Excellent!" chuckled Holmes. "Please tell me how you arrived at that conclusion?"

"On his forehead I could see the powder from the wig he was wearing in court this morning. Additionally, there are several long, curled strands from the wig on the shoulder of his navy-blue jacket."

Holmes nodded with satisfaction and what I might almost describe as pride. Hindsight makes me realize that he was grooming me. I can see clearly now that he was watering the seed he had planted when I was a young boy. Thereafter, we made a special occasion of having lunch at the Athenaeum every year on my birthday, which falls just before the holidays. At these lunches, Holmes would chart my progress at the university and discuss with me certain cases he was working on. Having been a chemist himself, he was always quite interested in hearing about my science courses. Geology, in particular, was of keen interest to him. He was fascinated by the ability to detect the position of hidden petroleum and gas reservoirs by the clues collected from the kinds of rocks and minerals that lay above and around them.

That first lunch was the most memorable. It was my initiation, and I remember feeling as if Holmes was treating me as a peer. Quite possibly that lunch may have been the only reason Holmes had come into London that day, and I remember every detail of it. I remember the waiter bringing us our first course, which was salmon mousse, and Holmes turning to the man next to us, the one who Holmes had speculated was a surgeon based on the precision with which he handled his knife. "May I borrow your salt, Doctor?" he asked.

The man turned to Holmes with a smile and handed him the saltshaker, "My pleasure, sir."

These memories steeled my resolve with the task at hand. I had retrieved much of Holmes's crime detection equipment from the attic and could say with a certainty that the soil I found on Holmes's shoes came from the East End, near the docks. Judging from the mixture of clay and silt, it appeared to match Holmes's samples taken from the area between Victoria Dock Road and Shipman Street. The passing years might have changed this composition a bit, and I would have to go to the East End as soon as possible to confirm my conclusion by taking a present-day sample.

I had also learned, from my evening visit to Scotland Yard, that a black 1912 two-seater Renault had been stolen from the home of a Nigel Loughlin in Kensington two days prior, confirming my theory regarding the cause of death of Mr. Holmes. I researched Mr. Loughlin and quickly concluded he was but an innocent victim in the matter.

I hadn't slept for thirty-six hours and still had several bloodstains to test from swatches I had cut from Holmes's clothes. I also intended to examine more carefully Lilah Church's file, which I had "borrowed" from Bedlam while Dr. Leeds was occupied with a stack I had "accidentally" knocked over. Then, quite unexpectedly, the telephone rang.

"I know it's late, Christopher," came Watson's voice from the other end of the line. "But I need you to accompany me on an errand, and night is the only time to accomplish this task. Please pick me up. We are going to the East End."

His voice sounded surprisingly energetic. When I left him earlier, he seemed to barely have the strength to make it up his stairs. Now he sounded twenty years younger and wanted to take a midnight outing to the most unsavory part of the city. At this time there would be no one but villains, whores and drunkards wandering those streets. No respectable person would be found in the East End at night unless they were seeking something unrespectable. It seemed to me an inspection of the area could wait until tomorrow. I had hoped to fit in at least a few hours of sleep. I learned to survive on very little sleep during my time at Oxford, but always found that two nights without rest diminished my abilities to function at top level. I pulled on my boots, locked up the flat and drove to Stafford Street.

7

WATSON

Waiting out front of my flat for Christopher to pick me up, I realized that my resentment toward him was purely a product of my grief over Holmes. The purging of emotions followed by the dream had made that more clear to me. Three hours earlier, when I entered my apartment, I found the evening air chilly and disagreeable, now I found it bracing and refreshing. I could hear Holmes's voice in my head saying, "Come, come, my dear friend, there is work to be done."

After a few minutes, Christopher pulled up in Mrs. Hudson's red Daimler and I climbed in. "Take us to the East End. I'll show you where," I instructed Christopher.

"Doctor Watson, I admire your stamina, but what is the mission which requires us to go to the East End tonight?" he asked.

"I want to speak to Wiggins, and he's a man who can only be found at night."

• • •

We parked on Butchers Road, a wide street lined with brick buildings. Most were crumbling structures that housed as many as ten families to a dwelling. Activity was sparse. A group of children was going through the pockets of a man lying drunk and unconscious in the gutter. They were scattered away by two men who dragged the victim into the shadow of a doorway for their own purposes.

Before we exited the car, I felt in my pocket for my revolver. I always found when visiting questionable areas it was advisable to cut short unwanted conversations by displaying a willingness to defend oneself. I had rarely had to use my Webley since leaving Afghanistan, but I would not hesitate if the circumstances required it.

I directed Christopher to a sturdy, well-lit, three-story brick building that a reliable source had told me was Wiggins's present headquarters. Wiggins had been leader of the Baker Street Irregulars and now, in his forties, was the head of the largest criminal network in the East End of London. He was a dangerous character, but had remained deferential to me. I had not spoken to him in several years, not since I had inquired about the whereabouts of a friend's daughter who had gone missing. Wiggins helped me locate her. She was in a flat paid for by a married barrister twice her age with whom she planned to run off. Unfortunately, he had no intention of running off with her. She was returned to her family and, within weeks, fled to the States with the first American she met.

I had intended to visit Wiggins about Holmes's murder and was frankly surprised he hadn't been in touch with me already. This visit became even more necessary in light of the Lilah Church situation. I was confident he could assist me in finding his former "Irregular."

We climbed three steps up to the building and pressed the buzzer next to an extremely thick oak door. Within seconds, a speakeasy swung open and a fleshy face peered out at us. "What's your business?" the face demanded.

"Please tell Wiggins that Doctor Watson would like to see him," I responded authoritatively. Without hesitation, the door opened to reveal that the owner of the face was a massive man wearing a pair of pants with such girth that you could have fit a barrel in them. He was wearing suspenders and an undershirt, which gave the impression of an overgrown child, however, the Colt .45 holstered at his side did not give that impression. He closed and bolted the door behind us and, comporting himself with a practiced manner worthy of a head butler, said, "Follow me if you please, gentlemen," and led us toward a sweeping stairway with a wrought-iron railing. This first floor of the building looked as if it were an abandoned factory. Where once there was some kind of heavy machinery, there were now stains and divots on the concrete floor. The place was empty except for a card game going on in a halo of light about fifty feet from where we ascended.

The second floor of the building consisted of a hallway lined with a dozen doors. Each of these rooms was a place of short-term business. At the top of the stairs sat a woman in her early thirties, in a rather elegant floral tulle dress. Behind her was a huge armoire. She was leaning back in her chair chatting with a young "employee" who was apparently in between her assignments.

Upon seeing me, the woman immediately leaped to her feet with a show of immense delight. "Doctor Watson, it's wonderful t' see ya!" She threw her arms around me and embraced me as though I were a long-lost relative.

"Good to see you as well," I said, a bit taken aback.

"You don't recognize me, d'ya?" she said.

Christopher smiled at me playfully, implying a colorful background for the two of us.

"And 'oly shit," she exclaimed with increased joy. "This is the Hudson boy. Am I right?"

Christopher's smile faded as soon as he became a participant and not observer in this little mystery. The woman's eyes flicked back and forth between us. "I'm Daisy. I was one of Mr. 'olmes's Irregulars. You couldn't 'a been more than six or seven last time I saw ya."

Our large escort interrupted. "Wiggins will be wanting to see our guests right away, Daisy."

"'E's been in an awful state ever since 'e 'eard the word about Mr. 'olmes," she declared, and she broke out crying.

Our escort ushered us away and up next the flight of stairs. "Good to see you again, Daisy," I called back to her.

"You as well, Doctor." And, as we ascended, I heard her tell the younger woman, "'e's a good man, that Doctor Watson. He used to give me 'alf a crown to feed me and my li'l brother, Matthew, when we was starvin."

That's when I remembered the little waif who used to stand at the back of the Irregulars holding the hand of her six-year-old brother. On the few occasions I recalled seeing them, it looked to me as if they hadn't eaten in days. This could have gone for all the little ones who were too young to fend for themselves. The recollection only served to make me feel that I could have done more.

The third floor was like the first, a wide-open space with pools of light. One of the pools illuminated a raised platform in the middle of the room with a figure seated on a satin armchair with matching footstool. This was Wiggins. Upon seeing us, he smiled and rose from his throne-like setting. Wiggins's front teeth were capped in gold. The others were brown owing to a lifelong habit of chewing tobacco. Stringy yellow hair hung down from beneath a black bowler hat, which he had sported since seeing it in a photograph of an American outlaw. He was wrapped in a smoking jacket with a fur collar and holding a silver, bejeweled goblet. It was a strange combination of things that he believed made him look fashionable and fearsome. Since his youth,

Wiggins had been a high-strung individual, but recent reports were that he was a dope fiend and quite mad. His appearance did nothing to convince me otherwise. He opened his arms wide in a display of brotherhood, tears running down his cheeks. "They will not make it to trial, Doctor," he said in his thick Cockney accent. "I promise ya that."

"So you know who did this, Wiggins?" His statement made me hopeful his network of informants had given him some intelligence on the case.

"I will soon," he responded with squinted eyes and clenched teeth, his grief suddenly replaced by a menacing fierceness. He stepped down from his platform and put an arm around my shoulder. He smelled of tobacco breath and body odor. "Good to see ya, Doctor." He patted his palm on my chest affectionately. "Good to see ya. I knew ya'd come."

Suddenly, a toddler in a diaper wandered out of the shadows. "There 'e is," said Wiggins gleefully. "Come 'ere, ya." He held his hands out toward the boy who immediately did an about-face and waddled off in the opposite direction. The child was suddenly intercepted by a young woman in a white nightgown who seemed to appear from nowhere. She swept him up, brought the squirming lad over to Wiggins and wrestled the child into his arms.

"Is he yours?" I asked politely. There was something disquieting about the way Wiggins handled the child. He pulled on the toddler's ears and rubbed his head as you would a puppy's.

"'E's one of five. Four different mums." He looked up with a sly wink. "That's what we do it for. It's always about the children, isn't it?" He abruptly put the lad back down on the floor. "Me back is 'urtin' again."

The woman in the nightgown rushed forward, grabbed the child and hurried off into the shadows. I heard the sound of a door closing.

"Late for him to be up, don't you think?" said Christopher matter-of-factly.

"Ahh...They never wanna go to bed." Wiggins said dismissively as he remounted his platform and sat down in the armchair. "So, Master 'udson, I'm told you are makin' quite a success of yourself in school."

Wiggins had given no hint that he recognized Christopher up until now, and Christopher was clearly surprised by the nonchalance of this revelation.

"I'm considering some options," Christopher answered warily.

Wiggins laughed heartily and pointed to his temple. "In my mind, I'll always be seein' ya 'iding behind your mum's skirt while the lot of us come trompin' up the stairs of Baker Street." He leaned back and smiled wistfully with those gold-and-brown teeth. "How many times? How many times? And Mr. 'olmes handin' out the shillins, sendin' us to all corners of this blessed town."

"What makes you familiar with my college career?" queried Christopher.

"Oh, one thing Mr. 'olmes taught me was to be a good observer. Mr. H taught me everythin' I know. We owe everythin' to Mr. H." He paused a moment for emphasis. "They say 'e was killed with an axe. That's a crock o' shite, isn't it?"

"It's not clear yet what killed him," answered Christopher quickly. His instinct to be mistrustful of Wiggins was perfectly justified, but, despite his disordered manner, it would be a huge mistake to underestimate Wiggins by thinking he didn't see through to one's true motives.

The unseen door opened and closed again and an efficient-looking lady in a very proper high-collared dress emerged from the shadows with a velvet pouch and walked purposefully toward us. She stepped up onto the platform, kneeled down and unrolled the pouch on her knee. From it she withdrew a ten-ampule box of Boehringer morphine hydrochloride. She broke the neck off the glass ampule and filled a syringe. Wiggins unshouldered his suspenders, undid his drawstring and dropped his pants. His legs and buttocks were covered with needle marks. She gave a brief exploration until she found a usable spot on his lower hip and then smoothly injected him. She wrapped up her bag and walked off into the shadows in the same secretarial manner as she had entered.

"Back problems," said Wiggins as he tied up his pants and spat his chewing tobacco into a spittoon. He peacefully sat down in his chair and ran his palm over the collar of his smoking jacket. "See this?...Russian sable. Most expensive fur there is." His eyelids began to sag noticeably as the morphine took effect and he began to ramble. "'Olmes was always special fond of ya, Master 'udson. 'E could see you were smart from the very first. Would ya like to spend a little time with one of my ladies? On the 'ouse. They can teach you things you can't learn at Oxford."

"Perhaps on another occasion, Wiggins, however I appreciate the hospitality," answered Christopher without any trace of bias toward the idea.

"We're always open," smiled Wiggins.

"We've come on a separate matter, Wiggins," I said, wanting to get down to business before the narcotics took their full effect. "We're looking for Lilah Church. Do you know where she is?"

"The madhouse I should imagine." Wiggins put his feet up on the stool and his hand down the front of his pants.

"So you remember her?"

"Certainly I remember her. Why should I forget her?

"She has a son you know."

"At least one. She may have more."

"He checked her out of Bedlam today," I said.

"I'm glad to 'ear she's feelin' better." Wiggins dug around in the pocket of his smoking jacket and pulled out a leather cigar case.

"Do you know his name?" I asked.

"I should think it's Mr. 'Somethin' Church."

"Does the name Alexander Hollocks mean anything to you?"

"That the name 'e goes by?" He bit off the end of a cigar.

"That's the name he used when he signed her out. Did she have a husband?"

"None tha' I know of." He lit his cigar and offered one to me. I declined but Christopher stepped forward and took it.

"I'll save it for later," said Christopher as he slipped it into his pocket.

"Do you know who the father of her son might have been?" I asked.

"Could 'ave been any one of us." Wiggins puffed serenely for a moment. "Do you know 'ow Lilah got the last name 'Church'?… She was left on the steps o' the church at one day old. She was raised there until she joined up with us when she was seven years."

"We'd like to find her," I said.

"Why's that?"

"She was named in Mr. Holmes's will," interjected Christopher, surprising me with his candor.

"And I wasn't, eh," said Wiggins jokingly. "I'll locate her for ya, Doctor. Shouldn't be too 'ard."

I leaned toward him confidentially. "What do you think about Moriarty?"

"I think 'e's still an extremely dangerous man," answered Wiggins matter-of-factly.

"Do you think he might have had a hand in this?"

He flicked the ash of his cigar on the floor and then squinted at me with a sinister reassurance. "I think you should go back to Mayfair, Doctor, and let me take care of 'ooever done this to Mr. 'olmes." He then called out, "Nurse! My back still 'urts."

The unseen door opened again, and I could hear the nurse's efficient steps clicking toward us. Our oversized escort emerged from the shadows signaling it was time to leave.

• • •

The streets were deserted on our way back. To our left the waters of the Thames ran dark and slow. The city seemed to have added grandeur in these sleeping hours. Even young Hudson seemed ready to surrender to a night's rest.

"I'm curious," I said breaking the silence. "Why did you volunteer the information that Lilah Church was in the will?"

"Can you think of a quicker way to find someone than to put out the word that money is waiting for him?" answered Christopher in a droll manner.

"True. But you were not so candid when Wiggins asked about the axe."

"Do you trust Wiggins?" he asked glancing over.

"I've unfortunately learned to trust few people."

"But Wiggins?" he persisted.

"No. Not completely."

"I think he knows more than he's saying about Lilah. And I think it's particularly curious that Holmes writes her into his will, and she disappears from the hospital the day after his murder," said Christopher.

"All the more reason to find her."

"I intend to, with or without Wiggins's help," Christopher said, determined.

"Wiggins is not a character to be taken lightly, Christopher."

"He made that clear," he said, without the slightest sign of intimidation.

I couldn't help admiring Christopher for his quiet bravado. I wanted to tell him I was sorry for my resentment these last two days, that all the misdirected rancor and spite had drained from me in that torrent of tears after reading Holmes's letter. Instead, I bid him goodnight and got out of the automobile.

8

I spent the next morning attending to arrangements for the funeral. Holmes had left his solicitor, Pearson, with no instructions as to how he wanted to be buried, so I became de facto arbiter of the event. I knew Holmes wouldn't have wanted the state funeral that had been offered by the prime minister. That would have been too much pomp and ceremony for a man who tended to loath rituals of these sorts. But I felt the public should have an opportunity to show their respects, and so I agreed that a ceremony at Westminster would be appropriate, but we would exclude the military procession and lying in state, which had been ruled out in any event owing to Holmes's head and facial injuries. Holmes's brother, Mycroft, suggested that his body be cremated and taken back to his cottage in Sussex. I was happy to have him take that decision off my hands, and so it was determined that following a public funeral at the abbey, Mycroft would see to the remains. Having consulted on the list of speakers, I went downstairs to wait for Hudson, who had eagerly called that morning and said he wanted to get started at nine o'clock. I told him to be out front at ten and the Daimler was patiently waiting when I walked out my door.

The plan had been to drive down to Holmes's cottage, start the process of going through his possessions and determine what information could be gleaned. We had been given permission by Lestrade to enter the cottage even though Scotland Yard had been unable to do a thorough inspection due to the abundance of bees that were swarming around the home when they had arrived the day before. Apparently, a few of Holmes's hives had been disturbed, and clouds of the former residents were angrily buzzing around the grounds. They called in a beekeeper, and he suggested it would be best to let them settle down before trying to investigate the cottage.

The drive to Sussex would take two hours, and, as we began, Christopher regaled me with the research he had already done that morning.

"I visited the Hall of Records," he said while weaving in and out of the Berkeley Square traffic. "There's no record of an Alexander Hollocks or Delilah Church, either. I did find a John Hollocks of Essex born in 1837, a William Hollocks born 1874 living in Middlesex, married to Louise with three daughters and a son, and an Arthur Hollocks born 1867 who served in the infantry in Burma, was medaled for valor, has a wife, Ellen, and is a childless Londoner."

"None of those sound too promising."

"No birth certificate, census information, license to drive for Alexander Hollocks or Delilah. Nothing."

"And that speaks to the manner in which a vast number of people exist in this city," I said, not surprised.

"Understood. It is logical that there would be no record of birth if you were left on the steps of a church as a newborn. But in the interceding thirty-some year…? Why no records at all? She doesn't appear to be an indigent. Where is the record of her son's birth?"

"You assume he is her son. That is only what this man 'Hollocks' stated to the hospital."

"Wiggins confirmed she had a son."

"True."

"And the hospital was willing to release her to his care."

"Also true, but she was there voluntarily. She could have left on her own accord."

"We should have asked around at the hospital for a description of this Alexander Hollocks," lamented Christopher. "Holmes would have thought to do it."

"There's time for that. I suspect Wiggins will find Lilah for us. Locating her is not our most pressing issue."

"Perhaps, but this whole affair about Miss Church troubles me. Too many coincidences."

"Maybe we'll find something at Holmes's place that can enlighten us."

Christopher continued to mull over the matter as we bounced southward again on the uneven road through Kent to Sussex. The drive felt more tiresome than the day before, the road rougher. Soon, Christopher resumed showering me with more predictions of the future. He said that the Royal Navy was changing over from coal to oil, another harbinger of the ascension of petroleum, and that the First Lord of the Admiralty had received approval to build oil-powered battleships. I had met the First Lord at a state affair recently. He's an earnest man named Winston from the illustrious Churchill line. He had a bit of a speech impediment and I urged him to take diction lessons if he desired to follow in his father's footsteps as a preeminent statesman.

At last, we arrived in Sussex with its narrow country roads. Holmes's cottage was down a mile-long private lane with overhanging elm trees that created a tunnel of gold and green vegetation. The lane opened up to reveal a two-story stone structure with a broad meadow sloping from the backdoor down to the chalk cliffs and turbulent English Channel. Holmes had always coveted privacy and here he had plenty of it. On various points down the coast a few more similar cottages could be discerned. Their inhabitants would look like no more than specks from this distance.

Christopher parked the car, got out and scrutinized the surroundings as if it might yield some immediate clues. The place looked just as it had on my previous visits. It was an enviable setting, though, being a devoted city dweller, I would not have chosen this impressive stretch of isolation for my retirement. Holmes, however, had been quite content here for the past years, and I was content to be his guest on a number of occasions.

A stray bee buzzed past my shoulder as I made my way to the door and produced the key that Pearson had given me. I unlocked the front door and we entered. The first thing that struck us was a vibrating sound, as if a large furnace was in operation somewhere in the cottage. We walked from the entry into the main room of the home and saw the source of the vibration. Hanging from a hat rack was a solid mass of perhaps five thousand bees. It was the size of a watermelon, and the creatures seemed untroubled with their new environment as they busily burrowed in and out of the thick cluster of fellow insects. I myself was not so comfortable with the situation. It would be hard enough sorting through Holmes's things, much less doing it while being careful not to arouse a swarm of bees. The next things that struck us was the abandoned torch lying on the carpet in front of Holmes's rolltop desk and the fact that the back door was left wide open.

The bees, however, were the first order of business. Within five minutes Christopher had donned one of Holmes's bee suits and returned with a pine needle–filled smoker. I watched through a side window as he laid a bedsheet under the cluster and then placed one of Holmes's square, three-tiered wooden beehives on the sheet. He carefully administered three or four puffs of smoke to the top of the cluster and a large clump of the bees dropped like liquid to the floor and then lazily crawled through the slots into the comforting darkness of the wooden hive. After fifteen minutes, the process was complete and Christopher carried the hive into the backyard and set it next to a dozen other hives, each perched on its own stump cut from a chestnut tree.

Christopher removed his helmet and walked over to me. "So shall we get down to business?"

"Absolutely," I answered. "You can start by putting that helmet back on and opening the safe."

On the back of the letter that Holmes had left me were instructions on opening a safe that was hidden in one of the stumps, beneath the middle beehive in the back row.

Christopher dutifully put the helmet back on and lumbered over to the hives once again. He had to sidestep the one fallen hive that had inexplicably landed in pieces on the ground and sent its inhabitants seeking shelter in the house. He carefully moved to the appropriate hive, lifted it off the stump and gently set it down on the ground. In the top of the stump was a notch that, when lifted, revealed a hinged section of the wood that flopped open. Hidden inside was a safe. Christopher opened it using the combination provided on the paper and extracted the contents, which consisted of an astonishing one hundred and ten thousand pounds in hundred-pound notes and numerous photographs and papers. He bundled it all in the bedsheet and we went inside to inspect.

"Perhaps this is what the murderer was looking for," said Christopher as he dumped the money and documents on the pine dining table.

"Perhaps," I responded.

"Was it typical for Holmes to keep this much cash around?" he asked.

"I cannot answer that with certainty. I never saw anything like it at Baker Street."

Christopher produced two pairs of gloves from his pocket and handed a pair to me. "The sequence of events is becoming clear to me now. Whoever left Holmes's body at that farm was in the process of driving him back here, probably in order to make his murder look like an accident. Perhaps he planned to stage a fall down the stairs or some other plausible cause of death. Unfortunately for him, he was forced to abandon that plan when he was followed by the police in Kent. He disposed of the body at the farm, yet he still came here."

"Which tells us what?" I asked. So far I was following his logic. I wanted to hear his entire theory before contributing.

"It tells us he had a second purpose in coming here. He was looking for something." He motioned toward the back door. "When he came in through the back way, he must have left the door open, and his torch attracted the swarm. He dropped the torch right there and fled. If the leaves weren't three-inches deep in the driveway, I'm sure we'd find the same tire tracks we found at the granary."

"So your theory is that he knocked over the beehive while stumbling around in the dark?"

"No. The hives are too far from the house for him to have knocked them over regardless of how dark it was, and it was quite dark that night. No moon at all. I checked the weather for the South Downs on the day that Holmes was murdered. A strong wind was blowing off the Channel in the early evening. You see that branch on the ground some twenty feet from the hives? It fell off the overhanging chestnut tree and onto that upended hive. Someone later dragged it aside. I'm not sure who or why."

"Impressive reasoning. I cannot find fault with it, except for the remarkable coincidence of it. I wonder what the murderer was looking for."

"I suggest we try and find out."

We put on our gloves and went to work. I looked through the paperwork in the rolltop desk and Christopher began sorting through the documents he had found in the safe.

After a few minutes, he announced, "Look what we have here." I turned to see him walking toward me from the pine table waving a document in his gloved hand. "This is a grant deed for this cottage dated May 31, 1903. The grantor was a Hermes Hollocks."

"Yes. I remember now that I asked Holmes who the former owner was and he said he had purchased it from a Frenchman who had returned to Brittany. I don't think he mentioned the name."

"That Frenchman seems to have been this Hollocks fellow."

"So what do we make of that?"

"I make of it more than a coincidence that this man and Lilah Church's supposed son have the same last name."

"What else did you find in that batch?"

"Not much. A couple of contracts for land purchases he transacted with Mycroft and some receipts for personal loans that he made. Did you know he once lent Gregson money?" asked Christopher

"No I did not. But I don't find it particularly surprising. They had a mutually beneficial relationship for many years and on a Scotland Yard salary I can understand how Gregson might come up short now and then. These are matters that Holmes would never have spoken of. He rarely discussed money."

"It was a five-thousand-pound loan. Pretty substantial."

I suddenly became uncomfortable with this conversation. I felt that Holmes's privacy was being invaded and like a reflex I felt that it was my job to protect it. "Why don't you go down to the constabulary and see if they have any information on this Hermes Hollocks? I will keep on going up here, and, if I find anything pertinent, I'll show it to you."

"The two of us can do both, can't we?" said Christopher earnestly. "I feel if there's questioning to be done, we should do it together. We have the time."

"Actually, we don't. I have to get back to London to take care of some arrangements this afternoon. When you come back around for me, I shall be ready."

Young Hudson stood there puzzling through my logic. He was obviously reticent to proceed without me or have me proceed without him. He hesitated long enough that I was about to tell him the truth; that I felt that these aspects of Holmes's world should still be kept a private matter and that I felt discomfort with his analytical peeping into his affairs.

"As you wish," said Christopher before I could turn my thoughts into words. "Certainly I defer to your judgment."

He laid the deed down on the dining table, quickly slipped out the back door and pulled off his gloves. "I will return for you before two o'clock."

I bid him adieu and moments later heard him drive off. I gazed out the window at the chalky cliffs and the windswept English Channel and thought about Holmes looking out at that view during all those solitary years.

I resumed my search of the desk. In the bottom drawer I found some photographs. Many were of Holmes and myself. There were photos of our walking tour of Spain, others at Lestrade's promotion party at Scotland Yard, the races at Ascot, a rugby match, a commencement speech at Eton. In the same drawer I found Holmes's checkbook and checkbook register. The records dated all the way back to 1907. There were only two parties to whom Holmes personally wrote checks during all that time. One was Mrs. Hudson. They were for thirty-five guineas a month, the rent on Baker Street B. The check was reduced to fifteen guineas in September of 1910, presumably because we hadn't lived there for years and used only the attic for storage. The second party to whom he wrote a monthly check, in the sum of twenty-two guineas, was someone named Beatrice Smithwick. For as long as I can remember, Holmes had an accountant in Marylebone handle his household financial affairs, otherwise those bills might never have been paid. Holmes had never been much for the banal details of day-to-day life, but these two drafts he had written faithfully on the same day of every month.

9

CHRISTOPHER

I was a bit surprised that Doctor Watson was sending me on this errand without him. I thought we were operating as a rather good team and should do all aspects of the investigation together. Apparently, Doctor Watson did not agree. I had the distinct impression that he wanted me out of the way while he investigated Holmes's cottage. During the last few days, I had sometimes been made to feel as if I was an intruder and, quite honestly, it hurt my feelings. It was a childish reaction and, admittedly, I had to bear much of the responsibility for my own status. I struggled to comport myself in the manner that Watson found appropriate, but occasionally I heard myself getting annoyingly chatty as I was taken with the exhilaration of being "on the case." Perhaps it was my youthful exuberance that gave Watson pause. Perhaps I was not demonstrating the proper gravity he thought required, but in all honesty, even with my most concerted effort, I could never be the staid Victorian gentleman that Watson was. I was born to the twentieth century, a changing world that would be documented in color and moving pictures. A world I believed would be less about manners and more about merit. In any event, I resolved to work harder to win Watson's confidence.

This matter of Church and Hollocks was getting even more mysterious. It was easy to jump to obvious conclusions, that this Frenchman Hollocks was the father of Lilah's child. Hollocks being a rather uncommon name, it would be a strange coincidence to run across two unrelated men by that surname. Still, that conclusion did not answer any questions. Hopefully, I would be able to get some information from the East Sussex constabulary and Hall of Records.

10

WATSON

After looking through Holmes's belongings for another two hours, I felt that melancholy descend upon me again. His violin, his scuffed Persian slipper with tobacco stuffed into the toe, his trunk filled with disguises, his boxing gloves, all conjured memories of those heady days. But I had to fight these feelings of nostalgia if I was to think clearly. Holmes was no longer here to do the sorting for me—Christopher was, and, though he had already proven his value, he was still inexperienced, and I had to consider his conclusions with caution. I thought his reasoning about the events of Holmes's murder sounded more than plausible, but did not address all the issues nor provide many answers. I decided to bundle up the cash and pertinent paperwork in the sheet and wait out front for Christopher's return.

Within a quarter of an hour, Christopher picked me up. I tossed my cargo in the back and we were off. Christopher had a wealth of information gathered from his journey into town, but instead of bursting out with it in his usual torrent, he asked me what information I wanted to hear first, and if I wanted to share with him anything about my inspection of Holmes's cottage. Clearly Christopher's behavior was a response to some signal I had sent him about the limits of this relationship, but I hadn't intended to dampen his spirit. It occurred to me that my recent moodiness might have created this less preferred, more mechanical Christopher. There was little to be done about it. In my present state, I couldn't control my every emotion or remark, and so this relationship would just have to evolve in whatever way nature took it. I didn't want to re-correct what I had already corrected and so I merely said to young Hudson, "Why don't you tell me about this fellow Hollocks first."

"Records show that Hollocks purchased the cottage in June of 1891 from an Elijah St. John, who was in the furniture business," he commenced. "I spoke to the chief constable, a William Gentle, who has been on the force for thirty-seven years. He remembered Hollocks, but never had the occasion to speak to him. He said he was a tall, thin-framed man with a dark beard, and he judged him to be in his mid-thirties at the time. Hollocks lived with his daughter and grandchild, who was an infant when they moved in. No sign of a wife. The only other person I could locate who remembered him was the lady who owns the bookstore. Her name is Elizabeth Acres. Hollocks came in and bought books on several occasions. Her description of him is similar to the constable's, and she said he had a significant French accent but spoke English tolerably well. The daughter, whom she said was no more than eighteen, came in to buy children's books for her son a few times."

"Did she remember the daughter's name?" I asked.

"No."

"Description?"

"Dark haired, thin. That was all she could say. The constable, however, also told me that, after the first year, he never saw Hollocks again. The girl and child lived there alone for a number of years, then one day the headmaster of the school came to the door and asked if the child shouldn't be in school. The mother said she would bring him when the school year started. They moved out of the cottage a week later and never returned. He said the cottage remained uninhabited until Holmes purchased it." Christopher glanced over for my reaction. "What do you make of it?"

"I think that running across two different unrelated men named Hollocks is quite unlikely. If we assume that this girl was Lilah and this Frenchman Hollocks was the grandfather, that means he has to have a son who was the actual father. There's no evidence of that. Another possibility is that when Lilah got pregnant, this man Hollocks for some reason took responsibility for her and the child."

"There's a third possibility," Christopher interjected. "Let's assume that this Frenchman Hollocks was actually the father of the child, but, for appearances, claimed to be the grandfather. That would explain the relationship more credibly."

"That's certainly also a possibility."

"But what's the connection to Holmes purchasing a cottage from Hollocks and putting Lilah in his will?" asked young Hudson, with brow creased as if straining to work it all out in his head this very minute.

"As Holmes would say, 'Once you eliminate the impossible, whatever remains, no matter how improbable, must be the truth.'"

11

Moriarty spent two hundred pounds on a custom-made suit for the funeral. According to his guard Freddy, when the garment was delivered for the final fitting, he slapped the tailor across the face, because he felt the lapel was too wide on his frock coat. All reports were that Moriarty was positively giddy about being allowed to attend the event. Lestrade had arranged for a special detail from Scotland Yard. Moriarty would be transported by armored police van to Westminster Abbey and accompanied by eight officers, who, upon seating him, would flank him two on each side and two in the rows front and back. For the entire journey, he would be shackled by his leg to Freddy, who looked to weigh easily fifteen stone. Naturally, as with all such events, there would be an abundance of security at all access ways to the abbey. With these precautions being taken, it was felt by all that Moriarty would have had a better chance escaping from the hospital than from his security detail at this event.

The two days prior to the funeral, I had been consumed by the arrangements. I was made arbiter of everything from flowers to seating assignments. We planned to set up four hundred chairs for the mourners in the abbey and had requests for five times that many. There had been inquiries from dignitaries as far away as Burma and Bulgaria. I hadn't the time or knowledge to prioritize them all, so I turned over all matters of protocol to the prime minister's office. The government had graciously offered to pay all expenses relating to the funeral, but still I felt that despite the growing grandiosity of the event, Holmes would have wanted something simple and brief. To complicate matters,

Holmes was a professed atheist, but one could hardly have a ceremony in Westminster Abbey without having a cleric speak, and so I gave that honor to Reverend Jonathan Goodsill, as warm and cordial a man as I have ever met. The other three speakers for the relatively short service would be, of course, Holmes's brother, Mycroft, the prime minister, who had requested to "say a few words," and finally myself.

I had managed to take the time during those few days to pursue the most curious item I had found in Holmes's cottage, that being the matter of the monthly check to Beatrice Smithwick. Through the bank I was able to trace Mrs. Smithwick to her home at 140 Warwick Road in Kensington. She was an elderly, wrinkled woman who conducted herself with a suggestion of aristocracy. She answered the door wearing a rather fancy hat with a veritable bouquet of silk flowers. She seemed to be the kind of woman who dressed for an occasion even if there wasn't one. I asked her why Sherlock Holmes wrote her a monthly check for twenty-two guineas. Initially, she seemed rather reluctant to answer. When I told her that matters related to her relationship to Holmes could be subpoenaed as there was an ongoing murder investigation, she relented and told me that the payments were for an apartment she owned on 422 Averill Street in Fulham. Holmes had been renting it from her for the last five years. When I asked her what cause Holmes might have to rent a flat on the outskirts of the city when he lived in Sussex, she became evasive again.

"I'm sure it's none of my affair what Mr. Holmes should want with the apartment," she dodged.

I was growing impatient with this woman. There was barely half an hour of daylight left, I had a myriad of things to accomplish for the funeral, and, at this point, I planned to make a visit to the apartment regardless. It seemed, however, that some background information would be helpful. I reiterated that I was now executor of all of Holmes's affairs and no one valued his privacy as much as I, and this was a matter that had to be tidied up one way or the other. I informed her that I wasn't going to continue paying rent for an empty apartment in Fulham.

"It's not empty, Doctor Watson," said Mrs. Smithwick with sudden candor.

"What is in it?" I asked impatiently.

"It's not 'what.' It's who."

"All right then," I said. "Who is in it?"

"Miss Church and her son. Mr. Holmes took them under his protection five years ago."

• • •

A thick fog had rolled in off the river when I arrived in Fulham. The sun was not completely set, but, given the light it provided, it might as well have been past dark. Four twenty-two Averill Street was an unwelcoming, three-story Gothic building that seemed quite at home in this thick gloom. I looked up at the windows facing the street. No lights shone from them. I walked up the stone steps and found the front door unlatched. I entered a cramped, dimly lit lobby with an apartment marked "A" to my left and a stairway in front of me. I mounted the steps and climbed to the second floor. There I found no sign that anyone inhabited this building. No light, no mats in front of the doors, no smell of cooking at this dinner hour. Indeed, the whole place had a stale, deserted smell. I ascended the next flight and arrived at a hall with two apartments, D and E, at opposite ends. I immediately had an intuition that someone was watching me. I stood still and listened. The building was absolutely silent. I moved to the door of apartment E and knocked gently. I could see a faint mist of light through the crack at the bottom of the door, but there was no response from inside. Holding my breath, I listened very carefully for any sign of life from inside the apartment. After a moment, there was the slight sound of creaking, like the shifting of weight on the floorboards. I knocked again, louder. "Is anyone at home?" I called, with unconvincing authority. There was something dark and unsettling about this building. I waited. Still no response. But I saw a waver in the light from the crack beneath the door, and I thought I smelled a faint whiff of perfume. Gardenia. I felt sure there was someone in that apartment.

"Who are you?" A voice shattered the silence. I whirled around to see a troll-faced woman standing in the shadowy hall, glaring at me like I was a trespasser. She must have come up the stairs behind me, or perhaps she came from the apartment at the other end of the hall. In either event, she startled me, as she resembled something you would encounter in the woods in a German fairy tale.

"Good evening, ma'am. I am Doctor John Watson, and I am looking for Lilah Church."

"No one lives in that apartment. And I don't know no Church," she said hoarsely.

I could see that neither my show of courtesy nor my authoritative introduction had softened the demeanor of this woman. "I spoke to the owner of this building, and she told me that Miss Church had a residence in this apartment," I said gently, determined to win over this old crone and imply that there were higher authorities than she that I had access to.

She lit a cigarette with a wooden match and the glow illuminated her wrinkled face. "I'm the manager of this building, and you've got no business here, Doctor John Watson."

"So you're saying I've been misinformed about Miss Church?"

"Say that if you'd like. Misinformed…yeah, you're misinformed. Now get going."

Inwardly, I had a deep desire to dislodge that cigarette from the old hag's mouth. "What would you think if I had Scotland Yard come down here and take a look around?"

"It wouldn't be the first time." She inhaled deeply then blew a white stream of smoke toward the ceiling.

Courtesy prevented me from telling the old woman how disagreeable I found her. This whole Lilah business had become extraordinarily vexing and what was even more galling was that she had been within an arm's reach only days before.

I took a last look at the door of apartment E and surrendered to more pressing matters. I walked past the old witch and down the stairs.

12

From above, the funeral must have looked like a mass of squirming humanity. Mourners clogged the entrance to Westminster Abbey, traffic choked Victoria Street to a standstill and the church bells rang forcefully, as if to emphasize the stature of the man who was being honored.

I felt a bit like a ringmaster at a circus. I stood in the midst of the throng in my black frock coat and greeted dignitaries, who were abandoning their limousines and taking to foot to make their way down the impassable street. King Ormstein of Bohemia, Lord Robert St. Simon, now ascended to Duke of Balmoral, and the prime minister himself all paid their respects and entered the abbey as the constables cleared the way.

Contributing even more to the commotion, the newspapers had all sent tripod-wielding photographers to document the event, and they ducked and dived about the crowd in an effort to catch photos of the notables in attendance.

An hour earlier, Holmes's body had arrived in a simple horse-drawn hearse. The coffin had been taken in through the side entrance, the same that would be used for Moriarty. Gregson would personally escort him along with his phalanx of Scotland Yard police. It was decided that handcuffing him would create too much of a spectacle, and so only his legs were shackled with an additional manacle connecting him to the right ankle of his guard, Freddy Carson. The chains were wrapped in black velvet to prevent them from rattling. He would be led in after all the guests were inside the abbey. This would not create a protracted distraction. There would be enough of a disturbance created by his presence as it was. It was decided that minimizing that time frame was the more desirable course.

Suddenly Wiggins emerged from the crowd and leapt to my side. He was wearing a stiff morning coat and top hat with his yellow scarecrow hair sticking down below his collar. In the daylight his skin looked exceeding pale with dark bags beneath the eyes. He furtively handed me a slip of paper and whispered, "'Ere's where Lilah lives." I glanced at the paper. It was the same address in Fulham that I had already located. I pocketed the address and thanked him. He put his hands on my shoulders and looked directly into my eyes, his own bloodshot eyes pooling with tears. "'E was a father to me. The greatest man I've ever known." He quickly moved off through the funnel of people shuffling toward the church door.

When the last of the guests had entered, scores of mourners still lingered on the pavement and lawn of the abbey looking forlorn and aggrieved. I thanked them for honoring Holmes and told them how much I regretted that there was not room for everyone to join us inside. With that, I turned and walked toward my grim task.

• • •

Funerals are designed to be comforting events. They are supposed to provide closure. But this event gave me a greater sense of discomfort and incompleteness. Holmes's murderer was still at large. Perhaps he was even in attendance, since, as Christopher had pointed out, the murderer very likely knew Holmes. Perhaps he was there in plain sight, inside the abbey, making a mockery of this ceremony with a secret sneer of accomplishment.

When I entered the abbey, the organ was playing a slow and somber version of Beethoven's Ninth Symphony. The ushers closed the doors behind me.

13

CHRISTOPHER

I was sitting in the eighth row with my mother next to me and my father on her other side. Mother wept freely, leaning into my father with his comforting arm wrapped around her shoulder. She had been bearing up well the last several days, but she melted again at the sight of Holmes's coffin draped with the flag and flowers. The last of the line of mourners were walking by the closed casket, paying their respects while the organist played Beethoven's "Ode to Joy" in a notably joyless way. Watson walked down the aisle looking distracted and melancholy and took a seat in the first row next to Mycroft Holmes and the prime minister.

    I know I am in the minority in this thinking, but I've always found funerals of dubious benefit. I know the ceremonies are meant to soothe the living and honor the deceased, but I find the over-glorification of the dearly departed to be a somewhat insincere and uncomforting practice. It seems to me that, with all the heaping of praise on the honoree, we are only encouraging bad behavior since all our secrets and shortcomings get buried with us without mention at such ceremonies. It would be more honest and preferable to sum up a man's attributes and deficiencies in order to accurately pay him tribute. "Old Joe drank too much and once slept with his wife's sister, but you could always count on him for a fiver when you were short before payday." That's the kind of eulogy I would like to hear.

I had been considering the funeral to be an excellent opportunity to gather information. I resolved to familiarize myself with the faces present and cross-reference them with the information collected from Holmes's cottage, the bulk of which I had managed to comb through over the past several days.

The mourners were generally seated in order of importance. The prime minister, Watson, Mycroft and heads of state were seated in the first two rows on the right side of the abbey. Next came the members of parliament, department secretaries, foreign dignitaries and notable celebrities. Then, in the eighth row, were my parents and myself along with leaders of London hospitals and charities to which Holmes had always generously, and anonymously, contributed. I knew of these contributions from records we had recovered at the cottage. One man in our row was Charles Grosvenor, president of an organization that ran three large orphanages in the English countryside where abandoned and delinquent children were raised and taught useful trades in order to be integrated into productive society. Grosvenor was a stout, round-faced man whose venous features spoke to an overindulgence of gin. I had heard nothing but good things regarding Mr. Grosvenor, who stood to gain from Holmes's estate if Doctor Watson so chose.

In the rows behind me were a few familiar faces along with dozens I had never seen. Many had been clients of Mr. Holmes. I recognized Reginald Musgrave and Major Murphy. Also in attendance was the French multimillionaire businessman Henri Roualt, who had found his Mexican-actress wife decapitated in bed one morning. Holmes had deduced that the expertise with which the butchery was accomplished pointed to the millionaire's Spanish cook, who it turned out had been having a lesbian affair with his wife. A year later, Roualt married a French stage actress, who was now seated in the chair beside him wearing a very tasteful black lace dress and fashionable hat I recognized as from a popular new French milliner named Chanel.

Others in the rows behind me were employees of Holmes's clients who had had a brush with the renowned detective and hence felt as if they had some special connection. Holmes had that effect on people. He questioned everyone at each case with such thoroughness, taking in every detail so thoughtfully, that people would often mistake his interest in facts for interest in them personally. I scanned each face, row by row, and tried to commit them to memory.

Those seated on the other side of the aisle presented far more interest. The first five rows were occupied by the top officers of the military and Scotland Yard, with a block of ten empty seats in the middle of the third, fourth and fifth row awaiting the arrival of Moriarty. Behind that came a slew of lords and ladies, including Lord Andrew Fitzroy, a powerful member of parliament, who was given to blustery speeches and unexpected and sometimes random political positions. Many thought his unwillingness to be consistent in his opinions to be a show of character. I considered his inconsistency to be a show of confusion or, worse, corruption. Beside him was his diminutive wife, Lady Emily Fitzroy, looking more like his son in her tuxedo pants and black jacket. Amidst this turnout of aristocracy sat Wiggins and several familiar faces from the Irregulars, including Daisy, Bales, Forest and one I remembered as Wiggins's main lieutenant, named Creed. Also amongst them, one I didn't recognize—a man in his thirties looking vaguely Latin with slicked-back hair. Wiggins sat glassy-eyed, staring toward the front of the chapel, probably contemplating his next injection. Beside him was his enormous doorman/bodyguard dressed rather comically in a button-busting white shirt, morning coat and top hat. With the instincts of a mongoose, Wiggins felt my gaze and slowly turned toward me and gave me a gold-toothed smile.

Just then, there was a stir from the mourners, and Chief Inspector Lestrade entered the abbey from the side, passed in front of the casket and strode to Watson. He bent over for a whispered consultation with the doctor and then moved to the end of the row and sat down. A few moments later a mixture of gasps and murmurs rose from the attendees as Professor James Moriarty entered the abbey, ankles shackled with a two-foot length of velvet-wrapped chain, escorted by his beefy prison guard Freddy, who had put on his best blue suit, and eight sizable Scotland Yard officers all overseen by Inspector Gregson. Very few had been privy to the fact that Moriarty would be in attendance. His villainous existence had been out of the public's consciousness for over eight years, but not totally forgotten. The straggling mourners walking past Holmes's casket looked up in alarm at the sight of the infamous criminal and scurried back to their seats.

With Gregson supervising, the group of officers shuffled Moriarty toward his row. The professor was immaculately dressed in his perfectly tailored, gleaming black frock coat and top hat with black hatband. Suddenly, Moriarty stopped and turned his head toward the casket. The first instinct of the group was to drag him to his seat, but Gregson halted them and leaned in to say something to Moriarty. The organ continued a strained version of Schubert as the murmuring from the congregation had ceased and all eyes were firmly fixed on Moriarty. He had become the main attraction, which undoubtedly gratified him. He said something in response to Gregson, whose stern expression changed to indecision. Gregson glanced over at Lestrade, who, like the rest of the assembly, was watching with curiosity to glean the content of the exchange. Undoubtedly, every move regarding Moriarty had already been choreographed, every possible escape scenario accounted for, but already Moriarty was trying to alter the plan. Gregson, however, seemed unfazed. As if to emphasize his mastery of the operation, he granted Moriarty's spontaneous request and directed his men to lead the professor over to the casket so he could pay his respects. The murmuring rose again. Lestrade leaned forward and looked down the row to see Doctor Watson's reaction. Though I could only see the back of Watson's head, he sat still and stoic, face turned toward the casket where Moriarty and his group of guards moved en masse. There was something obscene about watching Moriarty hover over Holmes's coffin, something unbearably offensive in the whole notion that this criminal had survived his heroic counterpart. I was angry at Watson for having made this indecent bargain with Moriarty, regardless of any possible benefit.

Moriarty stood head bowed and motionless beside the casket as though he were alone in the church. I could not see his face. He might have been praying. He might have been gloating. And suddenly, with one quick movement of his right hand, Moriarty yanked open the top of the casket, gazed down at Holmes's body, then emitted a primal, soul-searing howl toward the dome of the cathedral. The guards instantly ripped Moriarty away from the casket. Gregson slammed the lid! The group lurched Moriarty toward the exit, bewildered by what had happened and indecisive about what to do next. The horrified congregants gasped and gaped. Watson leaped to his feet to assist. He rushed over to the guards and prevented them from stampeding Moriarty out of the church. He grabbed Gregson, who was absolutely red-faced with rage at this violation, and looked as though he were about to strike Moriarty. The doctor managed to pull Gregson aside and pacify him and, in a matter of seconds, order was restored.

Watson instructed the guards to take Moriarty to his seat, and with the crisis seemingly over, they consented. For his part, Moriarty became somewhat docile. I could see him mouthing his apologies to Watson and Gregson, and then making as speedy work as he could to sit down and comply. As soon as all the officers were settled in around him, Moriarty turned around in his chair and gazed at the other guests with an unbalanced expression of sheer grief. I felt his behavior during those few minutes to be invaluably revealing. It convinced me that Moriarty had not had a hand in Holmes's murder and that he, as much as anyone, would not want Holmes dead, for who was he without his nemesis. He had lost his bright mirror, the only man by whom he could measure himself, the man against whom he had sworn ruthless vengeance, and now that opportunity had been robbed from him. Moriarty didn't want Holmes dead. He wanted him very much alive, so he could inflict punishment on him. It had been a legitimate howl of despair from Moriarty. He was howling about his loss. But, then again,

Moriarty was a master at manipulation, and he might have just put on one of the finest acting jobs I had ever witnessed.

Freddy, who was seated to the left of Moriarty, seemed to be the most unperturbed by everything that had transpired, undoubtedly being used to Moriarty's erratic behavior. He was busy craning his neck to get a view of the celebrities in attendance. His attention seemed to be most drawn across the aisle to Ellen McNeill, a wonderful stage actress and admirer of Holmes. At last the service started, and Freddy was compelled to face forward and stop ogling the luminaries.

The prime minister was the first to speak. He used the occasion to justify his push for "enhanced" militarization in what he termed an "increasingly dangerous and unstable world." He spent the body of his speech praising Holmes, but in the end found a way to assert that Holmes would have endorsed his policies and, on the way, sprinkled in a couple of quotes that I'm sure he hoped would be picked up by the papers.

I used the opportunity during the prime minister's speech to continue my inventory of faces. Behind Wiggins and the Irregulars came Holmes's solicitor, Pearson, his accountant, his shirtmaker, shoemaker and tobacconist, who procured Holmes's special blend from Africa. The rows behind them were filled with faces I'd never seen. A hundred seats were reserved for the public and those who wanted to pay respects had waited since early morning to gain a spot in these last ten rows. One of those mourners was a woman in a voluminous black velvet dress with a black lace veil over her face. She sat rigidly, betraying no sign of emotion behind the veil. From the appearance of her hands, fair and slender with nails painted red, I judged her to be a young woman. Beside her was a young man about my own age. His body language and slight lean toward her told me that he, in all probability, had accompanied her. The young man looked familiar though I could not place him. He had dark hair, brooding eyes and hawklike features. He was exceedingly lean and stared with clenched jaw at the pulpit as the prime minister expounded upon world affairs. While I was committing his face to memory, the lady beside him lifted her veil to dab the sweat off her brow. I immediately recognized her as Lilah Church. Her face looked pale and drained, and she was perspiring as if in a fever. Her expression was the same taciturn one that I had seen in the picture from her hospital file. I wanted to announce myself immediately, but it would have been indelicate of me to get up and climb over all the people necessary to get a word with her. I resolved to leap up as soon as the service was over. She dropped her veil and her head swiveled toward me. I felt as if she was staring at me through the lace mesh. There was a stirring as the prime minister concluded and left the pulpit. Many in the church took advantage of this pause to shift or cough, and I turned to watch him take his seat. When I looked back over at Lilah, she was facing straight ahead again, but the young man beside her had fixed me in a piercing stare. I assumed that he was her son, Alexander Hollocks, who had checked her out of the hospital. I nodded to him, and he broke off his glare and turned to listen to Mycroft Holmes, who had ascended to the pulpit.

Though Holmes frequently declared that Mycroft was the "brains" of the family, he certainly wasn't the personality. His speech was a fumbling but heartfelt tribute to his brother that referenced the firmament, Pythagoras and the table of elements. He likened the younger Holmes to the constancy and infallibility of immutably universal laws. Though he was always hard to relate to, there was no doubting Mycroft's emotions. He, like his younger brother, would not be classified as a warm individual, but both had the depth of intellect and character to be deeply empathetic with the human condition. Like Sherlock, Mycroft devoted himself to much selflessness and charitable causes, and, like his brother, tended to keep those things private. Mercifully, his speech lasted only a little more than five minutes, after which Mycroft dismounted the pulpit and retired his substantial bulk to his seat with his usual abstruse gravitas.

Doctor Watson rose from his chair and solemnly mounted the pulpit. For a few moments he gazed out at the congregation as if he'd forgotten what he was up there for, and then he proceeded to give a most splendid eulogy. He did not deify a man who had already been raised to Olympian stature. He spoke humorously of Holmes's shortcomings. His disinterest in literature and philosophy, his disorderly habits as a strange contrast to his perfectly orderly thought process, his expertise in violin, boxing and swordsmanship all wielded with a recklessness that sometimes resulted to the detriment of my mother's Baker Street flat. He spoke of a privacy that sometimes bordered on reclusiveness and a coolness that was sometimes viewed as misanthropy. He spoke of a man endlessly curious, frequently obsessed and steadfastly moral. He told a story of a time when he and his wife, Mary, tried to fix Holmes up with a woman, who by the end of the evening was informed by Holmes that she was allergic to cats, had an incipient stomach ulcer and quite possible a long-lost brother from her father's extramarital affair. All these things turned out to be true, and the woman was too embarrassed to ever face Holmes again. That was the last attempt Watson ever made to set Holmes up with a potential wife. During this, I glanced frequently at Lilah, who was staring motionlessly through her veil with her scowling son beside her. I glanced at Moriarty, who was leaning forward in his chair as if listening to the eulogy while he studied his perfectly shined tuxedo shoes.

In conclusion, Watson read a short passage from a personal letter Holmes had left him: "Like all men, I had my faults. I have tried to rectify my mistakes in life to the best of my ability. Whatever recompense I owe, I leave to my maker." I found that quote strange, as if a vague reference to something specific. Holmes was a man who rarely admitted to any personal failings, and he certainly was not religious. I supposed that in times of such introspection regarding mortality even Sherlock Holmes had felt an inkling of a higher power and a sense of his own imperfection.

Doctor Watson returned to his seat under the approving and misty gaze of all in attendance. The organist commenced a stirring rendition of "Nearer My God to Thee" and hundreds of voices joined in. It made me recall how my mother used to require me to go to church during my father's lengthy absences at sea, and so I was familiar with the words of this hymn. I joined in halfheartedly, remembering all those squirming Sunday mornings I spent in the pews of St Mary's Church. Two verses in, out of the corner of my eye, I saw Moriarty, singing fervently, then straighten up in his seat, raise his right arm and plunge a four-inch paring knife into his guard's neck! Absolute pandemonium followed.

I sprung from my seat, but being across the aisle and several rows back and with at least twenty guests and officers to climb over, I could not offer much assistance. I scrambled to get nearer the fray as Freddy slumped sideways, gurgling blood, and Moriarty blissfully continued to belt out the hymn while being pinned to his seat.

Chairs were thrown aside as Freddy toppled to the floor coughing up great volumes of blood. I fought to get to the center of the action as I heard an ill-advised voice above the shrieks and gasps direct people to, "Give him room!" The Scotland Yard officers stood back and foolishly allowed Freddy to mindlessly grab the knife and pull it out of his neck. This certainly sealed his doom as blood instantly gushed from the wound as well as his mouth. Doctor Watson rushed over and stuffed his handkerchief into the gash. Freddy's eyes were rolled back as he gagged on his own blood. The organ had stopped. People rushed to the exits. Moriarty was still singing at the top of his lungs, "Darkness be over me. My rest a stone," as a scrum of officers buried him, unshackled him from Freddy and wrestled him toward the exit with Gregson shouting instructions. Suddenly something occurred to me. I looked back to find Lilah. Her seat was empty. She was gone.

14

WATSON

The nuns were scrubbing the bloodstains out of the abbey's limestone floors when Christopher, Gregson, Lestrade, I and several other Scotland Yard investigators congregated the next day to review the disastrous events of Holmes's funeral. I had made a horrible mistake believing I could control or anticipate Moriarty's behavior. The barbarousness of the act was only matched by the apparent senselessness of it. Moriarty gave no reason for the murder. He was returned to his cell beneath Bedlam, leaving everyone to wonder what should be done with him next. I for one was in favor of an immediate hanging. I felt horribly betrayed by Moriarty, an admittedly foolish vanity to think his actions were directed at me personally. Moriarty is evil for evil's sake. His objective is always that which will nourish his black heart, and I, quite rightfully, felt to blame for allowing him to indulge his bloodthirsty nature.

The morning's papers were dripping with graphic eyewitness accounts of the funeral. None could explain how Moriarty got possession of the knife. Most accounts began with Freddy already writhing on the floor, therefore the group of us had assembled in the abbey to attempt to piece together the events of the previous day.

"We searched him thoroughly before leaving the cell and before entering the abbey," stated Gregson with the utmost certainty. "Somebody passed him that knife inside."

Gregson removed his scarf and I noticed an angry red boil on his neck. It didn't strike me as noteworthy, but Christopher immediately inquired, "What happened to your neck, Superintendent Gregson?"

"Damn bees at Holmes's place. This one's become inflamed," he said brushing it off. "Now, I know none of my men passed that knife to him. I was thinking maybe Freddy passed it to him thinking he was going to use it for something else. We know he was giving him cigars and newspapers and such back at the hospital."

During this conversation, Christopher had wandered eight or ten rows down the aisle of chairs, which had not yet been removed from the abbey. He crouched and eyed the floor beneath the seats as if doing some sort of calculation. He was wearing his leather aviator jacket, red scarf and American dungarees, which I had only seen on farmers and factory workers.

"What possible reason could this guard have had to give him a knife under such circumstances? Taking bribes to smuggle a man a few comforts in his cell is one thing. It's a huge jump to arming him in this situation and knowing you'll be the most likely suspect," offered Lestrade.

"I wouldn't give this guard that much credit. He didn't strike me as first in his class," responded Gregson while scratching the boil on his neck.

"Perhaps someone secured it to the underside of his chair," I posited.

"Impossible," Gregson shot back. "We checked that before any guest entered and then we stationed officers at the ends of the rows."

"Gentlemen, I have a theory." Christopher had gotten back to his feet and was standing in the aisle five rows back.

"About what?" asked Gregson tersely.

"How Moriarty got the knife. Does anyone have a pocketknife?" he asked. One of the officers produced an ivory-handled jackknife. "Yes, thank you, that will do," said Christopher courteously as he was handed the knife. "Now, can I get some of you gentlemen to take a seat in the rows directly behind where Moriarty was seated?"

The assembled Scotland Yard personnel blinked at Christopher as if deciding whether they wanted to participate in this parlor game from the upstart.

"It should only take a moment. Please."

After a few more moments of silence, Lestrade nodded for the others to accommodate Christopher. Gregson conspicuously stood his ground, not wishing to be a player in this reenactment.

Christopher directed half a dozen officers to occupy the three rows directly behind the chair where Moriarty was seated. He then guided me over to Moriarty's seat, sat me down and adjusted my feet on the floor with toes together and heels splayed. He walked to the row directly behind where he had arranged all his players and addressed the group. "Right before he murdered Freddy, I noticed Moriarty looking down at his shoes. Now I know why he was doing that." He sat down behind the three rows of officers and exactly four rows behind where I was occupying Moriarty's former seat. "Now the weapon was a lacquer-handled paring knife. I myself have only this pocketknife to use in the demonstration, not nearly so sleek as the weapon that Moriarty had."

Christopher bent forward and, with one smooth backhand, slid the knife along the floor beneath the seats into the little wedge I had created with my feet by sitting with my toes together and heels apart. I picked up the pocketknife and held it up. There was an appreciative murmur from the officers. Gregson remained stone-faced.

"During the hymn, no one would have heard the knife skid across the floor. Moriarty needed only to receive the knife, bend over and pick it up when he felt the time was right." Christopher walked back to me and retrieved his knife.

"But why did he kill the guard?" bristled Gregson, rubbing at his bee sting. Lestrade and I exchanged a look. Gregson seemed to be even more prickly than usual. Christopher seemed to bring this out in him.

"I have no idea," responded Christopher calmly. "I'd like to talk to him about that."

I asked the obvious question. "Who was seated behind him in those rows?"

"There was a scattering of lords and other elites including Lord Fitzroy, in addition to Wiggins and several of his crew," answered Christopher.

"Do you recall who was seated in the seat you were just occupying?" asked Lestrade having already warmed to the theory.

"Well, I would say this could have been accomplished from a range of the surrounding six to nine seats, but that particular seat was occupied by a dark-haired, Latin-looking man of thirty to thirty-five years of age. He was sitting next to Daisy, who was sitting next to Creed, who was sitting next to Wiggins." Christopher was perfectly clear on the arrangement. It seems, among his other attributes, he had Holmes's near photographic memory.

"So you think it was one of Wiggins's crew did this?" asked Lestrade.

"Seems most likely," answered Christopher.

"Why on earth would Wiggins want to help Moriarty murder his guard?" asked Gregson dubiously.

"I have no idea, but it was done, and I'm quite sure that's how it was done," answered Christopher confidently.

"Any other theories? I happen to favor this one," said Lestrade to the group.

"I'll go have a talk with Mr. Wiggins," declared Gregson.

My eyes shot over to Christopher. I could see by his expression that he wanted the opportunity to speak to Wiggins first, but he had the good sense not to suggest it. This was official police business and even Holmes would not presume to interfere with the activities of Scotland Yard. Contrary to the beliefs of some, Holmes never withheld information from the authorities or interfered in any way with an investigation. Frankly, it mattered little to Holmes what Scotland Yard did when he was on a case or what they knew or didn't know. Occasionally they were a convenient bludgeon and could be used to leverage some situations with the threat of their authority, but, Holmes generally left them toddling behind him as he single-mindedly pursued those minute details that only he could discern and that would ultimately yield the truth. I was beginning to see a bit of this attitude toward Scotland Yard in young Hudson.

15

A visit to Moriarty was certainly in order. A fierce debate had already commenced in the streets and in the Parliament about what to do with him. If tried, it would be a speedy trial with the outcome certain, and most voices were calling for just that, but Lord Andrew Fitzroy called for a full investigation of the circumstances of Moriarty's imprisonment and relationship with the victim. I always considered Fitzroy a bit of a glory hog. He enjoyed chiming in on any subject that was getting attention from the papers. Sometimes he was for the suffragette movement, sometimes against, at first in favor of Irish home rule and then against. The rather rotund Fitzroy traced his lineage to Henry Fitzroy, First Earl of Wharton and illegitimate son of Charles II. The illustrious line included William Fitzroy, Sixth Earl of Wharton, nicknamed "Bobbing Bill" for his habit of shifting from Tory to Whig and then back again during his tenure. Lord Andrew was already giving interviews to the *Post* about how, "Justice can only be served by a thorough investigation of the event." Never mind that a hundred people saw Moriarty bury a paring knife into Frederick Carson's neck. Surely he had an excellent reason and, of course, "Justice must be served." The sodding windbag.

I met Christopher in front of Bedlam at two thirty in the afternoon. I felt he was entitled to participate in this visit to Moriarty. Undoubtedly his version of how the professor procured the knife was correct. His keen observations during the emotional upheaval of the funeral would have made Holmes proud. I, conversely, could barely trust myself. I was still in a most hostile state. I was obsessing about the events of the day before. I had let Moriarty turn the occasion into an opportunity to showcase his villainy. This interview could not wait, but I needed someone there who could observe coolly.

When Christopher and I descended into the musty chill of the basement cells, we found two Scotland Yard officers stationed there. They were two of the same men who had escorted Moriarty to the abbey, and I'm sure they were dispirited by what they considered to be a failure on their part. I placed my hand on their shoulders in turn, shook their hands and asked their names.

"Roberts," said one.

"Dobbs," said the other.

"The failure was mine, gentlemen, not yours," I assured them. They nodded unconvincingly and led us to Moriarty's cell.

There had been no changes to the cell since the last time I had visited. Moriarty still had his comfort. While the debate and furor raged over his gruesome act, his life remained essentially unchanged. He was sitting behind his desk sketching a view of the inside of the abbey as witnessed from his seat at the funeral. There was remarkable detail, down to the flowers adorning the altar and the expression on my face as I delivered the eulogy. His wrist again was loosely shackled to the wall and he was wearing his funeral attire sans the jacket. He addressed us without looking up. "So you've brought a friend. Christopher Hudson, is it? Pleasure to meet you."

I nodded for the officers to leave us alone and they withdrew. Christopher and I sat down in the two chairs across from the desk that had been readied for us. I glared at Moriarty, seeing him with different eyes for the first time. It was one thing to see evidence of a man's crimes. It was another to have watched him commit a murder with his own hands. "I'm here to ask you what you've gained from this senseless act."

Moriarty looked up, rubbing his chin in mock thoughtfulness. "You're right. Maybe I didn't think this through properly. Now where will I get my cigars?" He reached into the drawer and pulled out a fresh cigar. "My last one." He put it between his teeth and returned to his sketch. "I'm grateful to you for coming today to straighten out my thinking on this matter. How is it going with the investigation?" he added casually.

"That is no longer any of your concern," was my quick retort. Christopher was silent keeping his eyes glued on Moriarty. Moriarty acted as if Christopher were not there and continued with his sketching.

"What, Doctor? Has this event created a rupture between us? I'm feeling quite warmly right now toward you. You arranged for me to attend the funeral, and I had a splendid time." He was also having a splendid time trying to goad me, and it was hard not to take the bait.

"You have destroyed any trust. Any gentlemanly understanding we had is dead."

"Now you're hurting my feelings," he said, forlorn.

"I don't give a damn about your feelings. I'd just as soon see you hanged."

"They won't hang me," he said confidently.

"They might."

"They won't."

"And why not, you dishonorable sack of shit!"

This epithet made him abruptly stop his sketching. He looked up at me with a particularly menacing expression. "Because they have secrets," he hissed.

"Who?"

"Not your concern."

"I would like to know."

"Would you really like to know, Doctor?"

"Yes," I said firmly.

"Here's something you wouldn't like to know. I had your wife killed. That maid…I believe you called her 'Annie'…her real name was Rose Sullivan. She was a prostitute who had worked in one of my whorehouses. What you thought was heart failure was merely a lethal dose of mercuric cyanide in your beloved Mary's tea. I was hoping it would draw Holmes out of hiding, but apparently he didn't care."

Before I could think, I had lunged across the desk to throttle the bastard, but he was expecting this. He blocked me with a taut section of his chain across my throat, looped it around my neck and snapped it tight. His grip was remarkably powerful and I could feel the veins in my head bulging as I fought for air but could not summon a single atom of oxygen into my lungs.

With an incredible smoothness and economy of motion, Christopher thrust aside the desk, kicked the chair out front under Moriarty and planted his heel on the professor's throat. I heard a choking sound from beneath me as the chain slackened and I was released.

The two officers rushed into the cell, having heard the clatter of furniture. Christopher calmly backed up a step and the officers pulled

Moriarty to his feet and held him with his back against the wall. A smile curled across his lips. "You were never cut out for this work, Doctor. But the boy might be."

"Are you all right, Doctor?" asked Dobbs.

"I'll be fine, Officer Dobbs. Thank you," I said, massaging my throat. "We haven't concluded yet."

"I would be more comfortable if we stayed."

"No need. A small mishap," I said blithely.

Christopher said nothing but followed my lead by shrugging as if this had been an insignificant skirmish.

"If you say so, sir." The two guards relented and reluctantly withdrew once more.

Moriarty rubbed a bruise on the back of his head and then proceeded to dust himself off. "Rose Sullivan is buried in a shallow grave outside of Derby. Botched abortion." Moriarty righted his chair and sat back down in it. "I would have had your wife stolen away from you, Doctor, but that would have been a long process. Instead I decided to kill her."

Christopher gave him a vicious backhanded smack across the face. I believe he did this to co-opt me from doing even worse. My mind was a whirl of emotions. I knew I could no longer endure being in Moriarty's presence. Nothing productive could come of it in my present state. I gave him one last feeble glare and walked out of the cell convinced that the next time I saw him he would be standing on the gallows.

16

CHRISTOPHER

Moriarty was tall and more powerful than most men but seemed to have no formal training in any of the fighting arts. That coupled with the fact that he was shackled did not make for a particularly formidable opponent. I was a bit stunned that Watson would attack him, but his story of the Doctor's wife's death had a ring of truth, and I could easily see how it would be extremely difficult to control oneself after such a revelation.

"You're an interesting fellow, young Hudson. Maybe I should have paid more attention to you," Moriarty said after Watson had stormed out. He looked around the floor for his cigar and found that it had rolled up against the wall. It was nearly split in two. "Pity," he said as he picked it up, removed the broken half and placed it back in his mouth. He dragged the desk back in front him, put his elbows on it and leaned toward me. "Many think I was well-born, because I have given that impression. No, I am the son of a workingman, just like yourself. Not so worldly as a merchant captain, my father was an accountant with the railroad. He worked for the Canterbury Railway in Leeds and then it was swallowed up by George Stephenson and his South Eastern Railway. Stephenson decided that, given the way he ran his affairs, it wouldn't do to have accountants looking over his shoulder, so he sacked my father with one day's severance. That was a year before South Eastern went under. Stephenson plundered the company by paying himself a huge dividend out of the operating capital. All the graft and wild speculation led to the complete collapse of the industry for nearly a decade. My father was unable to find employment. He hanged himself in our attic. I was the one that found the simpering weakling. My mother went to work as a maid. She was caught stealing food and was imprisoned for a time." He turned his eyes toward the ceiling and mused for a moment. "I was thirteen."

Whether these things were true or not, there was a method to this disclosure. This battle with Moriarty would not be fought hand-to-hand. The battlefield on which I would have to better him was a psychological one. He had information to impart. He wanted to impart it, even if he was going to do it by trickery and riddles. He had a reason for killing Frederick Carson. Either Freddy *did* something or he *knew* something. This was not a random act. He might have killed any number of other people to greater effect. Gregson, for example, might have been a likely target.

"I had no wish to distress the doctor so, but did you hear what he called me?" said Moriarty coming out of his reverie. "I'll not have that. I have shown him proper respect. As you witnessed, I did not strike the first blow. There are rules for men like us. Holmes understood that. I think you do, also."

I studied him trying to determine the best way to approach my objective.

"You speak, don't you, lad?" he said, as if issuing a challenge.

"Yes, quite well," I responded.

"And you have come here, why? To find out the reason I dispatched that slovenly simpleton?"

"Among other things." I chose every word very carefully.

"You know all you need to know."

"Meaning the information I already have should lead me to Holmes's murderer and the reason you killed your guard?"

Moriarty smiled cryptically. "We considered kidnapping you, you know...when you were a small child. I myself have never had much fondness for children and made the assumption that Holmes didn't, either. That was my oversight."

"And I suppose my good fortune. Why did you kill Freddy?"

"Why would I kill a cockroach in my cell?"

"You compare it to killing a cockroach?"

"Have you read Nietzsche's *Beyond Good and Evil?*"

"Yes."

"And what do you think of it?"

"I think it has some merit."

"Do you!" He was delighted. "Give me your thoughts."

"I think there are certain arbitrary religious and social norms imposed on the individual to keep him...controlled."

"Yes, yes..." he said excitedly. "Long ago I freed myself from all that moral prejudice. That was Holmes's shortcoming. He was never able to free himself from that false morality. It led to his demise."

"How so?" I asked matter-of-factly.

He started to say something and then stopped as if realizing that he had already said too much. "Have you made a timeline, Mr. Hudson?"

"I have, yes," I answered, trying to exude confidence.

"Then if you have made a proper one, you and Watson know everything you need to know."

This was a very powerful statement, indeed, and it made me hesitant to question him any further. I did not want to let on that I knew less than he assumed, and it was quite possible from his words that I knew more than I was aware of. I had a timeline, but it was in my head. What was he referring to exactly? The chain of events that had led to Holmes's murder? Freddy's murder? Or was he trying to mislead me? I didn't think so, but I wanted to review all the facts I had gathered before speaking to him again. "I must leave now, Professor."

"Stay awhile. We can discuss philosophy."

"I'm sorry, I cannot. I will come again soon." I thought to myself how strange and cordial this last exchange was.

He nodded with resignation. "I suggest you be very careful. You are quite clever and therefore you are in danger."

"Is that a threat, Professor?"

"You are in not danger from me, lad."

"I am glad to hear it." I got up from my chair and turned to leave.

"Please give the doctor my apologies. It's not true what I told him about his wife."

"Yes it is," I answered and exited the cell.

• • •

I found Doctor Watson, fists dug into his pockets, furiously pacing the lawn in front of the hospital. "Are you all right, Doctor Watson?" I asked gently.

"I want him hanged!" he said bitterly, eyes red from tears. "Why there should be any resistance at all, I can't fathom."

"Yes, you're quite right. He should be hanged," I said in a show of support. I thought it better not to question this reasoning at the moment, though, in all candor, Moriarty was far more useful to us alive and unburdened by the immediate prospect of facing the gallows.

"Why is Lord Fitzroy implying there might be some justification for this murder?"

In this morning's *Post*, bombastic Fitzroy had suggested that Moriarty was being abused by the guard and therefore self-defense might apply. This was a thin and dubious argument, but the tactic would allow for him to call for an investigation, which would inevitably lead to a panel of inquiry that would delay matters until all interest in the topic died. If Watson had been listening to Moriarty, he would know why Fitzroy was doing this. Lord Fitzroy had secrets and Moriarty knew them.

"I am going to call on Lord Fitzroy this afternoon," declared Watson.

"I think you should," I said, continuing to rally behind the doctor. "Would you like me to come with you?"

"No. I have some history with the man. A private conversation is what is called for." He seemed to be more in control of himself after he resolved to take his grievance directly to Fitzroy. "What did Moriarty say to you after I left?"

"That you and I knew all we needed to know to solve this case."

"He said that?" asked Watson, as if trying to confirm that he had heard correctly.

"He said, if I have a proper timeline, that we had all we needed. I would very much like you to tell me everything you can remember regarding your initial visit with him. Perhaps when he said 'you and Watson' he meant that each of us have part of the information."

"Yes, perhaps. We can deal with that later. I'll meet you back at Baker Street. First, I need to catch a cab to Chelsea." Watson marched single-mindedly toward Lambeth Road to catch a taxi.

I resolved not to relay to Watson Moriarty's apology or the professor's retracted claim of being behind the murder of the doctor's wife. I didn't tell the doctor, because I believed that Moriarty's revelation *was* true, and I'm sure Watson believed so as well. This was an uncomfortable piece of business. In that moment Watson had been laid bare and the rawness of his reaction both startled and embarrassed him. I don't think Moriarty had planned to make that disclosure, and I doubt he would have wanted me present for it, but, he, too, had lost his temper and used that long-saved bullet frivolously. This told me how Moriarty could be manipulated by his emotions and where the soft spots might be. I was struck by the sense of indignation he displayed when Watson called him a "dishonorable sack of shit." The professor did not take seriously attacks on his intellect or station, but the questioning of whatever twisted code of honor he felt he possessed seemed to wound him deeply. I would make use of that weakness to my best advantage.

I walked Doctor Watson to the road, and he hailed a cab. "Thank you for your assistance back there," said the doctor, with his eyes averted toward the approaching taxi.

"Not a problem," I said, trying to give the incident no emphasis. I was quite sure that is what Watson would have wanted.

"It was certainly impressive how you handled Moriarty," he said as the taxi pulled to the side of the road.

"I rely greatly on the element of surprise. No one expects it from me." I continued to downplay the event as I intended this to be the last we spoke of it.

"If you say so." He managed a wry smile and climbed into the back of a cab. I trudged back across the lawn to my motorbike as it started to rain.

17

WATSON

Lord Fitzroy lived in a ten-bedroom brick mansion situated on the Thames opposite Chelsea. It was built in 1732 and fourteen generations of Fitzroys had lived there since its construction. The rain had diminished to a drizzle when my taxi arrived. I rang the bell unannounced and a gray-haired butler named Phelps, who looked as though he had served at least three generations of the family, greeted me and led me through an entry hall with a marble floor and carved wood ceiling to an elegant living room, walls crammed with paintings of relatives and military figures who were quite likely relatives as well. I sat myself on one of the uncomfortable seventeenth-century couches and asked Phelps for some tea. The tea arrived before Lord Fitzroy. After approximately ten minutes, he descended from an upstairs bedroom wearing his smoking jacket. This delay made my temper even shorter than it had been when I arrived. He strolled into the living room and I rose from the couch to confront him.

"Lord Fitzroy, what motive do you have in advancing a justification for Moriarty's barbaric actions?" I asked, dispensing with any greeting.

"My motive is discovering the truth, Doctor Watson." He seemed surprised by my assault but ready to take up the battle.

"You witnessed the truth at the funeral," I continued indignantly.

"I witnessed the act, but that does not always tell the whole story."

"Moriarty's story is already well known."

"My dear Doctor Watson, I'm no fan of Moriarty, but the matter is larger than the man. Our criminal system must be fair from top to bottom. The man was being abused by this guard. It's tantamount to self-defense."

"Who told you that Frederick Carson was abusing Moriarty?"

"I cannot reveal my sources."

"Your sources are incorrect. Freddy was smuggling Moriarty cigars and other comforts. He had no stake in abusing him."

"Then why did Moriarty murder him?"

"Precisely!" I seized on Fitzroy's own words. "Moriarty *murdered* him."

This silenced Lord Fitzroy for a moment. Out the window, my attention was drawn to a young man walking across the grounds in full equestrian attire. A woman, also in riding attire, with short-cropped dark hair ran up from behind and surprised him. They both squealed playfully and twirled around in each other's arms. As the young man threw his head back in delight, I realized it was actually Lady Fitzroy, who, from this distance gave every appearance of being a teenage boy. The two women pranced off toward a waiting red roadster, giggling and shaking each other like schoolgirls. Lady Fitzroy got behind the wheel and the automobile skidded off down the gravel driveway.

"My wife and her friend are going to the country house for a few days to do some riding," said Fitzroy by way of explanation. None of that was of particular interest to me, but Fitzroy seemed eager to explain his wife's schedule.

"Well, isn't that nice for them," I said.

"Personally, I never liked riding the brutes. They scare me to death."

"I didn't come here to discuss horses."

"Then what brought you here, Doctor? What would you have done with Moriarty?"

"I'd have him hanged for this murder."

"You're being unreasonable, sir. The man is entitled to a defense."

"He'll offer none. And I don't want others with influence to offer it for him."

"And why would they do that?"

"Because they fear him," I answered pointedly.

He scoffed. "You attribute too much power to the man. Let justice take its course and he will end up hanged soon enough."

"The sooner he's at the end of a rope, the sooner we can all rest easier," I said hoping he would understand the implications of that statement.

He turned away and poured himself a drink from a cart arrayed with a colorful selection of decanters. "Doctor Watson, it is common knowledge that you lobbied for him to go to the funeral, and I understand how you could now feel responsible."

"That is true. I do feel responsible," I replied forthrightly.

"Well then, my dear Doctor, wouldn't it make you feel less to blame if you realized this guard was not totally undeserving of his fate?"

"It might, but I don't think that to be the case."

Fitzroy looked at me as if my lack of cooperation was beginning to bore him. "Doctor, I don't want to engage in an extended inquiry. My wife and I leave for the States on the *Titanic* in three weeks' time. I wouldn't want to have to cancel my trip."

"But you're going to insist on pursuing this notion that Moriarty was justified?"

"I'm going to pursue the truth," he said imperiously.

"The truth about Moriarty is already known. Maybe some other truths will come to light as well. Good afternoon," I said bitterly and departed.

18

When I arrived at Baker Street, Christopher had cleared everything off the north wall of the flat and created a timeline with string, a flurry of shredded paper and adhesive tape. The central event in his swirling galaxy of clues was the discovery of Holmes's body. All other information orbited around that. This was the first time I had visited the flat in several years. Christopher had hauled many of Holmes's belongings out of the attic, making the room not dissimilar to what he remembered from his childhood. The familiar confines of the flat had a calming effect on me. On the cab ride to Baker Street, I'd been able to collect my thoughts for the first time in several hours and realized that I'd been behaving like a madman. Moriarty's claim that he had taken the life of my darling Mary accomplished exactly what he wanted it to. It clouded my mind making all ability to divine the truth behind his lies impossible. I didn't want to ask Christopher's opinion on Moriarty's assertion. In truth, I didn't want to know. One thing was clear. I was no match for Moriarty. I was ignorant to think otherwise. Holmes had considered him an intellectual equal and that should have been all I needed to remember when believing I could manipulate him into helping me.

"Do you have anything to drink?" I asked Christopher wearily.

"There's an open bottle of Bordeaux there on the cupboard," said Christopher while adding another scrap of paper to his collage of facts. "My mother will be bringing us up dinner shortly."

In the cupboard I found the same wineglasses Holmes and I had employed for years. They were of the finest Irish crystal. I poured myself a glass almost to the brim and took a deep swallow.

"Would you mind relating what Moriarty said to you on your first visit?" asked Christopher as he stood back and admired his work. I could see that this timeline would be of no help to me. It struck me as a jumble of facts that gained no significance by committing them to paper and sticking them to a wall. Holmes kept all the information in his head, referencing and cross-referencing every clue in the compartments of his brain. It made sense that Moriarty, being a professor, would suggest this academic method. Perhaps he was trying to lead Christopher astray.

"Please give the wine a chance to work, Christopher. I can't bear to think about it right now." I flopped into my old armchair and made more of the wine disappear.

"I understand completely," he commiserated.

"By the way, this matter of Lilah Church still needs to be resolved. I meant to go back by there today but was sidetracked. Will you accompany me tomorrow?"

"We can go tonight if you'd like."

"No tomorrow will be fine."

"About Lilah, I was thinking…Don't you find it odd that Wiggins gave you her address after you had already visited the building?" he said turning toward me.

"He didn't know I already had the address."

"And you say the landlady tried to make you believe it was the wrong address."

"I would have pressed the matter, but I hadn't the time."

"Speaking of which, I should add this event to my timeline." He scribbled the information on some scraps of paper and triumphantly added them to his masterpiece.

A half hour later, Mrs. Hudson brought us a fine lamb stew and some bread. She gazed at the timeline quietly. "Moriarty is behind this." Mrs. Hudson said with certainty. "That guard must have known that, so he murdered him." This was the first time she had ever weighed in on a case.

"You may well be correct, Mother. But there are still details to be worked out." There was a certain amount of condescension in his voice that did not escape her notice. She studied him and seemed about to say something but refrained and withdrew from the room without further comment.

In a short time, we had finished Mrs. Hudson's stew and opened a second bottle of Bordeaux.

"What were you saying about Wiggins earlier?" I asked, now mellowed by my third glass of wine.

"About finding it odd that he gave you an address when you no longer needed it?" Christopher had resumed scanning his timeline with his glass in hand.

"What were you suggesting?" I rose stiffly from the dining table and settled back into my familiar armchair.

"It seems to me that Wiggins has a line on everything, but not only does he not produce the address in a timely fashion, but he also doesn't seem to be aware that you had already tried to visit the location. I wonder where he suddenly got the address. Scotland Yard had no record. You were only able to obtain it through Holmes's obscure business records. Wiggins would not have that same information. I know that he could not have obtained it from the hospital, because they had no idea of her whereabouts. This brings up the likelihood that Wiggins knew all along where Lilah was, but only revealed it to you after you had discovered it for yourself."

"You're saying he gave me the address after I already knew it in order to cover up that he had been concealing it."

"That's a reasonable conclusion. He wants to continue to make you believe he's being helpful even if he's not."

"But she showed up at the funeral for God's sake. How was he going to conceal that?"

"All the more reason why he decided he might as well give up her location. And by the way, if she hadn't lifted her veil, we might not have ever known she was there."

"But why would Wiggins not want me to get in touch with Lilah?"

"I don't know." He gave a little flourish with his hand, the kind of gesture one makes after reaching the bottom of a second bottle of Bordeaux. "Perhaps I'm giving him too much credit."

"Tomorrow I'm going to return to that building and settle the matter," I declared while eyeing a dusty bottle of Madeira sitting alone in the cupboard.

"Why not tonight?" asked Christopher.

"Because I believe based on the conversation we just had, we are both drunk, and, before I open that bottle of Madeira, I am going to bed."

"I am perfectly lucid," said Christopher with a slight show of indignation.

"We will go in the morning. I am retiring to my old bedroom to get a night's sleep."

"Very well. I anticipated as much and had Mother prepare your room for you."

"You are a very foresightful, young man." I struggled to my feet. "Tomorrow we shall return to the building in Fulham. That was some excellent Bordeaux. Goodnight," I said and staggered out of the room.

The furniture in my bedroom remained the same as it had over a decade ago. I had taken with me my gramophone and Afghan War relics when I moved out, but nothing else had been removed or rearranged. I cannot fully express the comfort I felt climbing into the bed I had slept in for so many years. Undoubtedly, the wine contributed to this serene feeling, but so did every other sensation in my body, reminding me of the confidence and empowerment of those days with Holmes. I heard Christopher scribbling and taping pieces of paper onto his timeline as I fell into a peaceful sleep.

19

The next morning I awoke to a mild hangover and shuffled into the living room to find Christopher up and already dressed for the day. He was wearing those dungarees and an Oxford rugby shirt, blue with a white collar. His timeline was twice as crowded as the night before and he was studying it over the rim of his coffee cup. I myself never fancied coffee. I eschew the coffeehouses, where university students and intellectuals gather and debate matters of art and politics. I favor a nice, cozy pub where a man can get a pint and not hear a word about Russian novelists, German painters or those useless sods in Parliament.

I suggested to Christopher that we go to the Brown's Hotel for kippers and eggs as that would put us only a block from my flat, and I needed a change of clothes. I found breakfast at Brown's to be an excellent cure for hangovers, and the maître d', Edvard, always managed to find a table for me when I arrived unannounced.

We made the drive over, and Edvard seated us at a banquette by the window. Christopher ordered a cheese omelet and our breakfast arrived within minutes. I cut into my soft-boiled egg and let the yolk ooze over the two meticulously filleted kippers and soak into the thick bed of perfectly brown toast. I had barely put a bite in my mouth when Christopher said, "Tell me about that first discussion with Moriarty."

"Why don't you enjoy your omelet first?" I countered.

Christopher took a bite as if he had been ordered to do so by his schoolmaster. He looked across the table and gave me a sarcastic smile. "I'm eating. Now tell me what he said."

There was no discouraging this lad from his purpose. I put another forkful of perfectly layered toast, kipper and eggs in my mouth and chewed for a few moments just to demonstrate I would not be so easily cowed by his insistence. "At first I told him what I knew about Holmes's death."

"Right. You said that," he interrupted with his usual impatience.

"He asked what Lestrade thought, referring to him with a crude epithet."

"Yes, go on," he encouraged me.

"He spoke of Colonel Moran's death the prior week in a nearby cell. He reminisced about Moran's attempt on Holmes's life, and how he hadn't authorized it."

"What year was that?" Christopher hadn't touched another bite of his omelet. I took another mouthful of my breakfast.

"That would have been 1894," I said, thinking back.

"I see. Go on," he said, filing that fact away.

"We sparred a bit about why I'd come to him. Though I meant to conceal it, he knew I was looking for help." I struggled to recall the conversation. I had been in such an emotional state that it was coming back to me like bits and pieces of a dream. "Oh, yes," I recalled. "He asked me why I thought Holmes had created the hoax at the Reichenbach Falls where he and Moriarty had presumably gone over in a death struggle."

"And what was your answer?" Christopher asked eagerly.

"To avoid Moriarty's assassination attempts, of course."

"And what did he say to that?"

"Predictably, he made it about himself. I can't remember his reasoning, because it was so disordered, but it concluded with the pronouncement that Holmes engineered the entire affair because he wanted Moriarty all to himself."

Christopher put his chin on palms as if thinking very deeply about what I had just said. I waved to our waiter to refill my pot of tea.

"What year would that have been…? That incident at the falls, I mean," asked Christopher after having pondered the facts for another minute or so.

"It was 1891." The waiter arrived at our table and refilled my tea. I returned to my breakfast, as did Christopher, who remained deep in thought as he ate. I wondered at the abrupt conclusion of his questioning, but was happy to finish my meal in peace.

20

The plan was to take a quick stop by my flat in order for me to freshen up and get a change of clothes. When we arrived at the top of the stairs, I found my door had been pried open. Before I could reach to push the door fully open, Christopher grabbed my hand and gently nudged the door with the toe of his shoe. Neither of us expected the perpetrator to still be in the apartment. Undoubtedly, this burglary was done in the middle of night when the intruder had observed that I was not going to return home.

We stepped inside and took a visual inventory. The place had not been ransacked, though judging from the opened drawers and cabinets, it had been very thoroughly searched.

"What do you think he was looking for?" I asked Christopher.

"Where did you put the money?" he responded instantly.

I hurried to my bedroom closet. I had stuffed Holmes's hundred and ten thousand pounds in the pockets and lining of my heavy winter coat with the plan of taking it to Pearson's office in the morning and instructing him to add it to Holmes's probate.

My heart sank when I saw that the door to closet was open and the coat gone. I slouched back into the living room where Christopher was already sweeping the crime scene for evidence. "The money's gone, I take it," he said with a quick glance at my disheartened expression.

He moved to my desk where a drawer had been pried open. "He's also stolen your Webley revolver." The theft of the weapon disturbed me more than the theft of the money. It was a personal violation. That weapon had been at my side during the war and during countless cases with Holmes. The thief had taken a valuable memento worth far more than just the cost of a revolver.

Christopher removed a pair of tweezers and one of his test tubes from his pocket and collected something from the desktop.

"What is it?" I asked.

"A hair," he answered, taking it to the window to let the morning light shine through the test tube. "Black and most likely male. Do you have a pair of gloves? I foolishly forgot to bring mine."

"Yes, of course, in my dresser."

"Then I suggest you put them on, pick up the phone and have Scotland Yard come down here to take fingerprints."

• • •

Within fifteen minutes, Gregson arrived with his fingerprint expert. The man's name was Richardson and Christopher immediately began directing him around the flat, having him apply the dusting powder to those places he believed most likely to yield results.

Gregson, apparently irritated that Christopher had taken charge of his underling, stood in the middle of the room with arms crossed and face scowling. "What was he looking for?" he asked tersely.

"I suppose it was the hundred and ten thousand pounds we collected from Holmes's cottage," answered Christopher offhandedly. He took a moment to turn his glance away from Richardson, whose shoulder he had been looking over, as they moved from spot to spot. "And, unfortunately, he found it."

"You took a hundred and ten thousand pounds from Holmes's premises?" Gregson said in astonishment.

"Which was fully within my rights, as I am his executor," I responded, giving a weak defense of my blunder.

"But there's an ongoing investigation, Doctor," he said, admonishing me.

"Christ, Gregson, let's not stand on ceremony here. I am more distressed than anyone about this. I feel like a complete idiot."

"All right then, Doctor, but from now on I'd like to be kept abreast of anything you learn during your investigation."

"As soon as we have anything substantive, we will inform you, Inspector Gregson," answered Christopher for the both of us. He kept his hands carefully behind his back as he stalked the room for more potential fingerprints sites.

"That's very considerate of you, young Master Hudson. I will inform them down at Scotland Yard of your kindness."

Christopher arrived at a table near the window where I had placed Holmes's papers. "Judging from the scattering of these papers, I assume the intruder looked through them," he said while leaning over to take a closer look. "It would be quite cumbersome to look through them with gloves on. Richardson, would you please dust this tabletop for me."

Richardson obliged, and a slightly smeared fingerprint became visible an inch from the scattered pages.

"May well be Doctor Watson's," sniffed Gregson, not wanting to give credit too soon.

"That will be easy enough to tell," responded Christopher.

"And if it's not, all we have to do is search London and find the finger that made it. Maybe you can take care of that after your rugby match," sniped Gregson, referring to Christopher's outfit.

Christopher merely smiled back at him. "How's that bee sting, Inspector?"

"It bothers me less than you do." And he walked out of the flat.

21

Richardson collected fingerprints from me and Christopher and, with immediacy, concluded that neither matched the one on the tabletop. Whoever the culprit was, he had left that single print and departed with a fortune in cash and my valued weapon. I had not made a very good showing in the last several days in terms of judgment and this was starting to weigh on me. I believe that Christopher sensed my self-doubt and did not belabor the recent events. "We'll find your Webley soon enough, Doctor," was his last comment on the subject as we slid into the Daimler for a drive to Fulham and a second visit to the building where Lilah Church supposedly resided.

The day was already beginning to get away from us as it was nearly noon when pulled up in front of the building on Averill. The three-story Gothic structure did not look so dreary as the first time I visited. The sun was shining warmly, encouraging the hope of an early spring. We mounted the stone steps and entered the cramped, dimly lit lobby, which seemed to have the ability to willfully exclude any of the cheerfulness from the outside world. "It's on the third floor," I said pointing toward the stairs.

All of a sudden, the first-floor apartment door was thrown open and the trollish landlady came charging out us. "What do you want now?" she demanded.

Christopher eyed her, quite unfazed by her aggressiveness. "Initially, I should like you to have that ugly mole on your cheek looked after."

She produced a butcher knife from her apron pocket, and, with not the least concern, Christopher knocked it from her hand and pushed her against the wall with such force that her head snapped back against it with a thud. "You're a nasty little woman," he said holding her there. "Let's call Gregson and have her arrested for threatening us with that knife."

Again, there was something so economical and forceful about Christopher's movements that they seemed to be completed before one even had the time to process them. "Leave her," I said. "I'm sure she won't trouble us further."

The landlady looked up at Christopher fearfully, her formerly disagreeable demeanor fully drained from her. After a beat, he released her. "Get back in your cave, witch."

She gratefully scurried back to her apartment as Christopher bent over, picked up the butcher knife and buried it two inches into the wall.

We proceeded to the stairway and climbed to the third floor. Before we reached the hallway, I could hear music playing from our destination, apartment E. It was a raucous American tune that I had heard a number of times and guessed was called "Alexander's Ragtime Band" since the phrase was repeated over and over.

"Irving Berlin," commented Christopher as we approached the door. "Good taste in music, though I prefer Scott Joplin for ragtime."

"And I prefer Schubert," I responded with a frown. I found this song simplistic and childish, and it seemed to grow even louder as I firmly knocked on the door of apartment.

The door immediately opened and we were greeted by a tall, thin man in his early twenties with dark hair and sharp features. Christopher had already described him to me from his sighting at the abbey, so I knew this was certainly Alexander Hollocks. Instead of the brooding quality that Christopher had attributed to him, he seemed quite amiable. "Doctor Watson, how good of you to visit. Please come in."

He ushered us into a rather cheerfully furnished flat with yellow floral upholstered furniture and yellow walls covered with rather beautiful botanical drawings. The entire perimeter of the ceiling had been wonderfully stenciled with a grapevine pattern. Sitting in an overstuffed chair with her stare fixed on the fireplace was Lilah Church. She was made up like a painted bird. Her eyes were lined in blue with a shade of yellow powdered on the lids beneath her arched eyebrows. Her lips had a deep-red coating and some of that same red had been rubbed into the pale skin of her cheeks. On her head was a satin hat with a flurry of white feathers pointing straight back as if she were facing a strong headwind, and she was dressed in a white tea gown as one might wear to a garden party. On her feet she wore powder-blue ballet slippers. She was motionless and rigid and did not acknowledge our presence in any way. In her rather colorful appearance you might have thought she was a mannequin from a department store placed in that chair next to the fire.

"Mother loves this music," hollered Alexander as he hurried over and turned off the gramophone. She did not react to the sudden absence of music.

"This is Christopher Hudson," I said with a gesture to my companion.

"I am Alexander Hollocks, and this is my mother, Lilah Church," he said motioning to the unmoving, painted creature in the chair. He held out his hand to shake with Christopher.

"Forgive me, Alexander," I said politely, "but, although you recognize me, I do not remember ever meeting you."

He covered his mouth and made several thoughtful puffing sounds as if suddenly realizing the accuracy of this observation. "Quite right. We've never formally met, but being part of Mr. Holmes's outer circle, I feel I know you, Doctor."

The young man was beginning to puzzle me. "Perhaps you could describe what you mean by 'outer circle,' Alexander," I said. Christopher was observing him closely as I had by now learned was his habit when he felt the subject had pertinent information to impart.

"Perhaps you should describe it first, Doctor Watson, for Mr. Holmes always demanded discretion, and it is you who have come to us," he countered and gave a shrewd tilt of his head.

I decided to be perfectly direct. "I know that Holmes has been paying the rent for this flat for these last five years, and I would like to know the reason why."

A wave of relief seemed to wash over the young man and all evasiveness was dropped. "I am so glad you are aware of that. Now I feel free to answer your questions. May I speak freely in front of Mr. Hudson?" Alexander smiled apologetically at Christopher. "No offense meant, sir."

"Anything you can say to me can be said to Mr. Hudson with the utmost trust."

"Very well then. First may I offer you something? Tea? It might be a bit too early for sherry, or I have some excellent bottled wheat beer." His cordiality returned instantly, and I was surprised to find myself warming to this young man.

"Thank you, no," I said politely.

Our host turned toward Christopher, beaming. "The beer is made in Germany. You should really try it."

"Too early for me." Christopher smiled back.

"Come sit. I suspect we have a lot to discuss," he said cheerily and led us to one of the overstuffed couches, which were overflowing with finely embroidered pillows. Some were copies of the botanical images on the wall, and one was of the view of the grounds of Bedlam from the female patients' gallery. I glanced over at Lilah. She had not moved a muscle. I was tempted to start the conversation by asking about her, but trusted that explanation would come in the due course.

Alexander settled into an armchair across from us and took out a package of cigarettes. He offered us one and we declined. "Your landlady was not very inviting," I informed him. "On my first visit she told me no one lived here."

"Oh, yes. Old Miss McEwen can be rather protective of her turf. She can chase off wild dogs if she has a mind to." Christopher chose not to contradict him on this point.

Alexander lit a cigarette and blew out the match with a stream of smoke and settled back in his chair. He had a certain dandyish quality that I have always abhorred, but there was none of the petulance that sometime accompanied that sort of personality. He was courteous and frank, which I appreciated. "Let me start by saying that I consider myself a bastard. Not in the traditional sense, but in the sense that my mother and I were abandoned by my father when I was quite small. My father, let us say, *captivated* my mother when she was seventeen. He was a very worldly man. At least, that is what my mother told me. His name was Hermes Hollocks. He was a Frenchman who exported wines and delicacies from his home country. They met in London while my father was on business."

To my surprise, Christopher interrupted. "Is this narrative going to answer the question of why Mr. Holmes is financing your apartment?"

"Indeed, it will," answered Alexander with equilibrium. "But I must give you some context." This appeared to quell Christopher's impatience temporarily, and he sat back resigned to listen. "As I was explaining," continued Alexander, "my mother became pregnant quite quickly after their introduction. My father decided it would be best to move from his home in Brittany to a cottage in Sussex. That is where I was born. My mother was deeply in love with my father, and all seemed to go well for a year until he left us, never to return. He provided us with an allowance that arrived from Brittany by mail every few months, but, other than that, we were thoroughly abandoned. The reason for his leaving is unknown to me. I was little more than one year, and Mother was only eighteen herself. We lived in virtual isolation in that cottage for five years, at which time the money stopped arriving. During those years alone, Mother became more and more depressed and agitated. Believing that she could convince him to come back, she determined that we should go to Brittany and find my father. She took me across the Channel, and there we stayed for the next three years. She secured a job in a linen store in Rennes, and, in the evenings, she would search for my father, asking people if they knew of him and trying to trace him down through business contacts. Occasionally, she found someone who remembered him, but no one had seen him in years. I assumed he was dead. Finally, she gave up and we returned to England. We moved into a one-room flat in Harrow. Mother supported us by doing piecework and embroidery. I was able to get a job in a factory spooling thread. In 1899 we moved to the East End. The Marxists and radicals started to show up, and Mother participated in a worker's strike. During a protest she was badly beaten. It affected her eyesight for a time, and she could no longer work. Her mental state deteriorated until one day she showed up on the doorstep of Mr. Holmes at Baker Street. She was having delusions that Parliament was after her for being a French spy and wanted to execute her." Alexander began to tear up, and he stopped for a moment. "Mr. Holmes was so kind," he said stifling his tears. "Of course, you know that Mother was one of his Irregulars."

"I am well aware of that. I myself remember her as a child," I said with a wistful smile.

"Mr. Holmes more than generously arranged for us to have this apartment and has paid the rent ever since, asking us not to disclose the arrangement to anyone. A modest and righteous man, he is…was." His voice dropped off with the last word.

"Well, that's quite a yarn," said Christopher with a discernible edge of sarcasm.

"I'm sorry if I bored you," Alexander sniffed, sounding insulted.

"Not at all. I like a good story." There appeared to be a natural antipathy between these two young men. I had noticed Christopher to be rather clinical with most people at first meeting, but with Alexander he was quite engaged in an almost competitive way. "Why did you commit your mother to Bethlem Hospital?" Christopher asked pointedly.

"Because of the suicide attempt. She threw herself in the river. Fortunately, she was rescued by a port authority boat."

The fire crackled, and, looking over, I noticed that Lilah had moved. Her palms, which had been on the arms of the chair, were now on her thighs, and she was slightly leaned forward as if staring more deeply into the fire.

"And why did you take her out of the hospital?" asked Christopher without softening. It was as if he was accusing Alexander of exploiting his mother in some way.

"She called for me. She was so disturbed by Mr. Holmes's death that she wanted me to come get her. Frankly, for those few days thereafter, she was as lucid as I've seen her in years. She told me that you had visited the hospital, Doctor."

"I see. So she recognized me." I thought back to the cryptic smile she gave me that day. "May we speak to her?"

"As you can see, she is in one of her states. It could last many more hours. The doctors say it's a form of catatonia brought on by either depression or brain injury. She will not speak nor understand anything spoken to her."

"When does she come out of it?" asked Christopher.

"Eventually, she will sleep and then awake in a weakened state."

Christopher strolled to her side and gazed at her profile. There was absolutely no indication that the woman sensed anyone was there. "I'll have some of that tea now," declared Christopher.

Alexander seemed suspicious of this sudden request but remained outwardly gracious. "My pleasure. I'll put the kettle on. Doctor?"

"None for me," I responded. Alexander turned and disappeared into the kitchen through a swinging door.

Christopher had already noticed a sewing basket lying on a footstool by the hearth. He quickly retrieved one of Lilah's embroidery needles and brought it back to her chair. Bending over, he firmly poked the top of Lilah's slippered foot. She did not flinch nor move a muscle. I drew closer to observe. He poked the back of her hand. Still no reaction. He looked over at me. "Well, he isn't lying about that."

"Definitely some form of stupor," I confirmed.

Satisfied, Christopher returned the needle to the sewing basket, but not soon enough to avoid being seen by Alexander as he emerged from the kitchen.

"You mother does some excellent needlework," Christopher said as he pretended to rifle through the contents of the basket in admiration.

Apparently this ploy covered the deed adequately, for Alexander seemed unbothered and answered with pride, "She hasn't lost a bit of her skill."

Christopher straightened up with his hands behind his back and pasted on a smile. Alexander returned the same insincere smile and there was an awkward moment of silence.

"Let me tell you why we've come here today, Alexander," I said, growing somewhat uneasy with the apparent friction between the two men. "In his will Mr. Holmes left your mother five hundred pounds and a very comfortable stipend in the amount of fifty pounds per month until her death."

"In his will, you say? Mother…?" He seemed quite stunned by this information.

"Yes. As your story confirms, he had a long-standing concern for her. I am executor of the estate, and, therefore, it is my duty to come here and inform you of this and make all necessary arrangements."

"I…handle all of Mother's affairs," he answered in a fumbling manner that seemed designed to make him not sound too anxious.

"Of course you do, but I should like to have a conversation with her when she is…in a better state of mind," I said gently.

"And that is certainly as it should be," responded Alexander. The kettle whistled in the kitchen. He turned to attend to it.

"I think I'll skip the tea," said Christopher. "Doctor Watson and I have to be going. Isn't that right, Doctor?"

"Yes, quite true." I was more than happy to end this visit. "You should attend to your mother. Turn the music back on for her. Maybe you have some Chopin."

"Mother likes popular music," Alexander said as he hurried into the kitchen to turn off the stove. Within a moment, he whisked back into the sitting room. "Well, thank you for coming," he said, with hand extended. "It is certainly welcome news you have brought. A shame it has to come as result of such a tragedy."

"As they say in France, '*C'est des conneries complet,*'" responded Christopher and heartily shook Alexander's hand.

Alexander smiled back, "Yes, of course. Looking forward to your next visit. I will call you when Mother is back to herself." He led us to the door and closed it behind us. The ragtime music started playing again before we hit the stairs.

We descended to the first floor and saw that the knife had been removed from the wall leaving a small gash. Walking out the front door into the sunlight made me feel gratefully free of the building. Despite the bright furnishings of Lilah's apartment, there was something terribly oppressive about that Gothic structure. I did not look forward to visiting it again and resolved that my next visit with Lilah Church should take place in a happier setting.

"So what's your reaction to that bunch of lies, Doctor?" asked Christopher pointedly before we even reached the sidewalk. Even for Christopher this was a very blunt reaction.

"You seemed to have had an immediate antagonism toward that young man," I said.

"I don't trust him. There's an unctuousness and false humility." We climbed into the automobile. He started it up and let the engine run.

"He seems to care very much for his mother," I said not having any particular reason to defend him.

"It would appear. However, I have my doubts as to the fact that she is his mother," he said, staring forward across the hood of the Daimler.

"Why should he lie about such a thing, and how could he have come up with that whole story about Hermes Hollocks? We certainly know the man existed and lived in that cottage with the girl and the child."

"And then he disappeared into thin air."

"What are you suggesting? That they murdered him? The boy was one year old and she was eighteen." Christopher was letting his personal feelings interfere with his logic. A dangerous trap which one should stay alert to at all times.

"I don't know what I'm suggesting except that we have only a small part of the story with many inconsistencies," he said, softening a bit. "Let me ask you this question. Don't you think that a child who spent his formative years across the Channel would know some French?"

"I would expect so."

"The French phrase that I spoke to him, do you know what it means?"

"I don't speak a word of French."

"I said, 'This is complete horseshit.' Alexander's response was to smile and shake my hand."

"Perhaps he was merely being polite in not pointing out your lack of command of the language." I knew this was a rather flimsy argument, but I felt an urge to make it. Christopher's reasoning seemed so far afield that I didn't want to let it go unchallenged.

"He claims they spent three years in France but they have not one single French item in the room. Not one single memento." He looked over at me as if expecting a counterargument. I didn't offer one. Assuming some sort of victory from my silence, he pulled away from the curb. "*Honk!*" A bus roared by, swerving to avoid us.

"Mr. Hudson, you are on the verge of getting yourself fired as my chauffeur." Christopher looked over at me, chastened by the near miss, then carefully pulled into traffic.

"You're suspicions are superfluous, Christopher. We've accomplished our purpose for today, that of informing them about the bequest. We shall speak to Lilah when she emerges from this... condition."

"I would like to administer some diethylbarbituric acid and question her," grumbled Christopher. "That might help get at the truth."

"Now you suspect *her* of something? For goodness' sake, the woman has been in a lunatic asylum for over a year."

"Too many unanswered questions and too many coincidences."

"Well, you can add them to your timeline."

"I shall," said Christopher with finality.

22

When we returned to my flat, a carpenter and a locksmith were in the process of repairing the door. My elderly landlady, Miss Margaret Courtright, had arranged for it. Miss Courtright had none of the maternal charm of Mrs. Hudson. She was a willowy and finicky woman who fretted everything and insisted on perfection in her building. Nothing went unattended for more than twenty-four hours, as witnessed by the prompt repairs to my door. Certainly, this is not the worst quality in a landlady, however occasionally she would worry things to the discomfort of her occupants. One time I had a broken window latch in the sitting room and she insisted on having it repaired while I was laid up in my bedroom with the flu. If she saw a piece of wallpaper peeling, you were sure to have a paperhanger knocking on your door at seven the next morning. Undoubtedly, last night's burglary had driven her to near hysteria. There is nothing more unsettling as having one's home invaded. Earlier that morning I had Gregson reassure her that the culprit was not of the violent sort and was looking for something very specific and business-related and would not return. Seeing as how the intruder had made off with my gun, this assurance seemed a bit hollow, but Miss Courtright appeared mollified.

Having heard Christopher and I return to the flat, she came upstairs and informed me that my telephone had been ringing every five minutes for the last half hour. Our intention had been to go to Scotland Yard and meet with Lestrade, but just as Miss Courtright reported, the phone rang right on its five minute schedule.

"Doctor Watson?" asked a vaguely familiar woman's voice from the other end.

"Yes. To whom am I speaking?"

"This is Mrs. Beatrice Smithwick. We spoke several days ago regarding the flat in Fulham." Her tone was much more congenial than it had been on that first visit.

"Yes. Oddly, I just returned from there," I told her.

"Doctor Watson, I have something very important to show you. It concerns Mr. Holmes," she said in a hushed tone.

"Might you tell me what it is, Mrs. Smithwick?"

"I think it would make more sense to show it you. Can you meet me at one of my buildings? It's in Marylebone…478 Weymouth Street, in half an hour? I'm in apartment 407."

I was reluctant to delay our meeting with Lestrade, but this woman had kept Holmes trust for five years and that certainly spoke to her credibility. "I will be there in half an hour, Mrs. Smithwick," I said and hung up the phone.

"Mrs. Smithwick wants to meet in Marylebone in half an hour. She says it concerns Holmes."

Christopher was standing at the table by the window perusing the papers that I had brought back from Holmes's cottage. He looked up. "The woman who owns Lilah's building?"

"Correct."

"Do you want me to go with you?" offered Christopher.

"Might as well. Then we can proceed straight to Scotland Yard." Out my front window I could see the sun was about to surrender to a bank of rain clouds rolling in from the west. "Let me grab some umbrellas. We might be needing them."

• • •

Driving past Berkeley Square, people were scattering into the tony restaurants and shops as heavy raindrops started to fall. Inwardly, I wished I could join them. I felt as far from an answer to any of my questions as I had been at the beginning. I took comfort in the fact that Christopher did not feel the same. He expressed confidence that the answer was right in front of us. All we had to do was eliminate the impossibilities.

We took a right on Devonshire and arrived at 478 Weymouth precisely half an hour from when I put down the phone. It was a stately four-story brick building with high-domed windows on the top floor.

"Mrs. Smithwick is quite wealthy, isn't she," said Christopher, admiring the structure.

"Perhaps family money," I speculated.

"I shall do some research on her," declared Christopher as he got out of the automobile and opened his umbrella against the stiffening rain.

We hurried up the steps and entered a lobby that was under renovation. A debris chute extended down from the floors above into a huge rubbish bin on the lobby floor. The walls were open with the wiring exposed. I assumed there was some electrical work in progress, because there were no lights on. To our right was a stairway and directly in front of us was a wrought-iron elevator. Christopher shook out his umbrella, and we stepped into the lift. He raked the accordion door closed, pulled the lever and the car smoothly glided upward with a confident whirring sound.

As we ascended, we saw that the second and third floors looked as if they were in the process of being gutted. Walls were open, doors were off and bathroom fixtures were lying in the hallways. The elevator jerked to a stop on the fourth floor and we stepped out. There were six or more apartments on this floor and it had brand-new red carpeting. A sconce directly opposite the elevator was working and, though deserted, this part of the building looked quite habitable and even a bit posh.

"What was the apartment number?" asked Christopher.

"407," I reminded him. There was a mechanical clink behind us, and the elevator car descended into the dark wrought-iron shaft as if it someone had called for it. We walked to the end of the hall and located apartment 407. As we approached the door, I heard a distinct click.

Christopher grabbed my arm. "Run!" he commanded. We turned and ran just as the door burst open behind us. Christopher smashed the sconce with his umbrella, plunging the hallway into darkness. I saw a flash of muzzle fire and heard a gunshot. We reached the stairs as a second bullet slammed into the wall. Rattling down the stairway in the dark, my gamey leg nearly betrayed me. It buckled as we hit the landing on the third floor, but Christopher caught me. "This way!" He dragged me through the hall toward the debris chute. Footsteps pounded down the stairs behind us. Christopher virtually hoisted me headfirst into the canvas tube and dove in behind me. The chute bowed as we slid thirty feet to the lobby and were dumped into the broken plaster and empty cement bags in the huge trash bin. With a push from Christopher, I scrambled out of the bin, and he bounded out right after me. We rushed to the front door to find it was key locked from inside. The footsteps were rapidly approaching down the stairs.

Christopher ran back to the elevator and forced open the door. The car was hovering above on the second floor. "Hurry!" he called to me in an urgent whisper. I shot to his side. There was a twelve-inch-deep recess in the floor at the bottom of the elevator shaft where the pulley housing protruded. The footsteps grew louder. Christopher prodded me and I leaped down into the shaft. Christopher hit the call button and leaped in beside me. The elevator car began its decent from the second floor and we lay down flat on our bellies not knowing how much room would be left when the lift reached the bottom. The floor of the shaft was slick with graphite. The car creaked downward. I felt a pressure on my back as it descended on us. It was equivalent to having a three-hundred-pound marble slab placed on top of me. It pinned me to the floor and I could not fill my lungs. Fortunately the lift had completed its descent. The footsteps arrived on the marble floor. My face was turned toward Christopher, but, in the darkness, I could not see anything. I could not hear him breathing. I could hear only the footsteps slowly approaching across the lobby. I took a last shallow breath and held it. The footsteps stopped. There was a significant silence. Then the footsteps receded slightly as if in confusion. The front door rattled as if the gunman was making sure it was locked. After another quiet moment of confusion, the footsteps approached the elevator and stopped. I needed air. I slowly exhaled and silently drew as much oxygen into my lungs as the crushing weight would allow. The elevator door rattled and the gunman stepped inside the lift, making the car bounce slightly above us. Again, there was silence as if he were trying to work out how Christopher and I could have vanished. The elevator door rattled again as he stepped out. There was silence once more. Suddenly, with a loud clank, the elevator motor whirred into motion. The gunman had pulled the lever and the car droned upward. The relief of the crushing weight lifting off me was overwhelmed by the fear of imminent exposure. As the elevator rose, the light filtered over the edge of the recess revealing the gunman's shoes and then his legs, his waist…There was only one option now. I was about to lunge at him from the darkness when a gunshot rang out! It exploded in the empty lobby and set my ears to ringing. I looked over at Christopher in the rising light. He was confused as I. Had he been shot? We looked up as the gunman's face was about to come into view. His body listed, collapsed on its side and hit the floor. He stared into our faces with lifeless eyes.

23

CHRISTOPHER

Just before the gunshot, I had arrived at the only solution possible. Watson and I were going to have to leap out at the gunman as soon as the elevator allowed enough clearance. One bullet, even to the torso, would be survivable. I could launch myself at him, absorb the shot, and, hopefully, with Watson's help, subdue and relieve him of the weapon. One thing was assured: lying defenselessly at the bottom of that shaft was certain death. As the car was rising, I had glanced at Watson and his expression was determined as mine. The old soldier was certainly not going down without a fight, and there was no one with whom I'd rather go into battle. Later I told him so.

The solution I hadn't considered was that someone would shoot our assailant in the back. The bullet was expertly aimed to penetrate his heart. It did that and more, exiting through his chest and creating such a pool of blood that it dripped into the recess under the elevator and gave the lobby a pungent, metallic odor.

After the gunman toppled over, I scrambled on top of him and wrested the weapon from his limp hand. I scanned the shadows for his killer, but he had already fled. I rolled the gunman over on his back and immediately recognized him to be the Latin-looking man who had been sitting with Wiggins's group during the funeral. My mind raced through the implications of this fact.

"Do you recognize him?" asked Watson, sensing from my expression that our assailant was familiar to me.

"I recognize him, but I have no idea who he is. He was sitting with Wiggins and the Irregulars during the funeral."

"Well he certainly knew who we were," said Watson as he bent over to take a closer look at the dead man's face. "I don't think there is much question about his intentions."

"But now there are many other questions." I rose to my feet. "One of us should inform the police while the other stays with the body."

"You take care of the police. I could use a rest." Watson sat back down on the floor with a groan and leaned up against the cage of the lift. "I don't think this one is going to be too hard to keep an eye on."

"I'll return as soon as I can. There must be a back entrance to this building." I wandered off toward the stairs and beyond I found a hallway that led straight back to an unlocked door that exited onto the mews behind the building. This was undoubtedly the escape route that our elusive rescuer had used. By now he could be half a mile away in any direction. I walked up to Weymouth Street in the hopes of finding a payphone. When I got there, I found a police officer standing on the corner of Harley and Weymouth lecturing a young man about the perils of crossing the four-lane street in the middle of the block. I approached calmly, trying not to raise his excitement level. "Officer, may I have a word with you?" He was wearing a rain slicker, and a steady drizzle was still falling. He was a tall and stout man with muttonchops and a heavy moustache.

"Yes, sir. How may I be of service to you?" I took his arm and guided him away from the young man, who was more than happy to be relieved of his company and who quickly faded around the corner.

"There has been a shooting at 478 Weymouth." I said evenly, trying to be as low-key as possible.

"A shooting, you say!" he blurted loudly. "At the brick building?"

I would have called it a murder had it not been for the fact that the shooter seemed to be defending the lives of Watson and myself. "Yes. And a man is dead. He was trying to kill me and my companion."

"And what is your name?" he demanded.

"I am Christopher Hudson. And what is your name, sir?"

"I am Sergeant Archibald Hayes, Archie that is."

"Sergeant Hayes, would you please call and inform either Commander Lestrade or Superintendent Gregson of this situation and then meet us back at the building to take charge of the body."

"Lestrade or Gregson?" he said, impressed. Archie had a bit of a lisp owing to what sounded like some ill-fitting false teeth. "Yes sir, Mr. Hudson. I will do so immediately...You say this man was trying to kill you?"

"The details will be explained to you when you join us in the building. Please it's quite urgent." By this point, it probably would have been easier and quicker for me to find a payphone on my own, but I was eager to get back to the scene and examine it.

"Right away, sir," said Archie dutifully and hurried off down the block.

I returned to the building to find Watson still seated on the floor rubbing his sore back. "Did you call them?" he asked.

"I found a police sergeant on the corner of Weymouth and Harley. I wish I could get some more light into this blasted place," I said as I examined the lobby for any potential evidence. Our rescuer was as stealthy as our attacker was reckless. I doubted he had left any clues to his identity. The gun was certainly a revolver as there was no sign of a casing and I hadn't heard any brass hit the marble floor. However, the bullet had passed through our Latin friend, so the slug was somewhere in this lobby. Unfortunately, the dimness of the area made it quite impossible to determine where that might be.

"Do you think Wiggins wants us dead?" asked Watson almost mournfully, for I believe the doctor considered Wiggins a friend.

"I am not ready to venture that. I know that this man was in his company and that is the only time I've ever seen him. I know for a certainty that *this man* wanted us dead," I said, hopelessly scanning the area. "I'm going up to that apartment and take a look. Do you want to come?"

"Thank you, no," the doctor said, wincing as he shifted around on the floor. "I'll let you have at it."

I trudged up the three flights to the fourth floor and entered the wide open door of apartment 407. The room was unremarkable and unfurnished. It was ready to be occupied, with a new coat of paint and some attractive mahogany wainscot. I checked the bedrooms, kitchen and all the closets. All were empty and it seemed the flat would yield no evidence without a very close inspection.

As I descended into the lobby, Sergeant Hayes bustled in through the back of the building. "Mr. Hudson, I have informed Scotland Yard of the circumstances," he declared proudly. "Lestrade and Gregson are said to be in a meeting and will attempt to get here within a half hour's time. I also called for the coroner." He joined me at the bottom of the stairs.

"Good thinking, Hayes. Thank you."

"Oh my! We have quite a situation here, don't we?" remarked the sergeant as we approached Watson and the body lying in the pool of blood.

"Sergeant Archibald Hayes, this is Dr. John Watson."

"Dr. Watson!" the sergeant said in awe. "We've met before. I was a young officer on that case at Thor Bridge with that South American governess."

"Oh, yes. Maria Gibson," recalled Watson.

"Like many, I'm a great admirer. And when I heard about Mr. Holmes—"

"Yes, thank you," said Watson, cutting him off. This was a refrain he would have to hear for many months to come, and I could see it was getting no less painful each time.

"Do you have a torch, Sergeant?" I asked.

"Sorry, sir. Don't bring one when I'm working the day shift." His rain slicker was dripping water and contaminating possible evidence wherever he stood. I considered mentioning this fact to him, but decided the damage was probably minimal. There certainly was no question as to who had tried to murder us, and I planned to return later to gather evidence on who might have murdered our would-be murderer. Until there was some light in this place any careful examination was impossible.

"How are you feeling, Doctor?" I asked, looking down at the fifty-nine-year-old as he rubbed at his lower back and grimaced.

"Not as young as I used to," he said good-naturedly. "Anything interesting upstairs?"

"Nothing. I think we should leave Sergeant Hayes to wait here for Scotland Yard as you and I have someone we need to visit."

"Yes, I thoroughly agree," answered Watson as I extended a hand and helped him up off the floor.

"I assume that's all right with you, Sergeant," I said.

"That's my job, sir," the portly policeman answered amiably. We hurried off, leaving Sergeant Hayes to his task.

24

Both Watson and I were anxious to get over to Kensington to have a word with Mrs. Smithwick. What motive she would have had to set us up for this ambush was hard to divine, but she, without doubt, was in a position to answer many questions, and we were anxious to speak to her before anyone was aware that the plot had failed.

When we pulled up in front of her house on Warwick Road it occurred to me that a weapon might be appropriate in case there was someone in the home in addition to Mrs. Smithwick. It was entirely possible that she had been compelled to make the misleading telephone call. As I walked around to the boot of my mother's auto to find what might be useful, I resolved that from now I would carry my switchblade, which I had procured in Marseille during a trip in my freshman year at Oxford. I remember spending the rest of that summer indulging in the notion of becoming expertly practiced in it, so that with one movement I could produce the blade and hit my target. I pursued this ambition for many hours and thus made a ruin out of my dormitory wall.

I opened the boot and found the contents to be a pair of my mother's dirt-caked hiking shoes, an old blanket, the spare tire and a two-foot tire iron; not a very handy weapon to walk around with but usable for this occasion. I grabbed the tire iron and closed the boot.

"What's this?" asked Watson when he saw the item.

"We no longer have the use of your Webley, and I don't intend to walk into another trap defenseless," I responded.

"Quite right. And if there's no trap, we'll beat the truth out of the old woman with a tire iron," he said with no small measure of sarcasm.

"If that's what's called for," was my rejoinder. "I'm not in a very charitable mood."

Watson slouched up to the front door with me at his side. It was then that I noticed our disheveled state. Watson, very uncharacteristically, had his shirttail out, his coat and forehead smeared with graphite and his hair in a disordered, whirlwind shape. I myself had blood smeared on my clothes and shoes. I knocked on the door. As expected, there was no response, but lights in both the upstairs and downstairs windows made me confident that someone was home.

I decided it was best not to waste time and wedged the tire iron between the frame and the door. A panicked female voice instantly called out from the other side, "Go away or I'll call the police!"

"The police, I'm sure, are the last people you are likely to call. Now open the door," demanded Watson.

There was no reply to his directive. I gave two firm yanks on the tire iron, the wood splintered and the door surrendered. I kicked it the rest of the way open and found the diminutive Mrs. Smithwick rapidly backing up in her hallway with absolute terror in her eyes at the sight of Watson and his young, blood-spattered, tire iron–wielding companion. She stumbled onto her rear end on the oriental carpet, took one last look at us coming toward her and fainted dead away.

"I'm going to see if anyone else is in the house," I told Watson, feeling my lack of compassion for this woman could be excused by the fact that she attempted to lead us to our death earlier in the afternoon.

I went upstairs and took a look around and concluded that Mrs. Smithwick was quite alone and apparently did not expect a visit from us.

When I came back downstairs, Watson was crouched over the still-unconscious woman with an expression of genuine concern. "I'm afraid this is more serious than a fainting spell. We need to get her to hospital. I fear it's her heart."

"She better not die on us. She has some questions to answer," was my retort.

"Call an ambulance unless you want to carry her to the car and take her there ourselves."

"I'll call the ambulance," I said walking toward the telephone. "I want to search the place in the meantime."

It took approximately fifteen minutes for an ambulance to arrive from the Charing Cross Hospital, during which time I thoroughly checked all the drawers on both floors of the home. The woman had very little documentation regarding her properties or business affairs. There was no question she was well off. The value of her jewelry, which she carelessly kept in the top drawer of her vanity, was easily five thousand pounds. There were pictures of her and her husband, who was of indeterminate occupation but might have been an architect or builder, suggested by the drafting table in the background of one photograph. They had traveled to Greece, Turkey and Italy. There appeared to be a son, who would be in his early fifties by now. The most interesting item I found was a photograph of her at a groundbreaking with Lord Fitzroy in attendance. It seemed to be the christening of some large construction project in some indeterminate part of the city. It struck me as a bit of a coincidence, but beyond that there was nothing to indicate that Mrs. Smithwick was other than a wealthy widow who led a perfectly traditional, privileged life.

Watson and I stood out front as they wheeled Mrs. Smithwick, who was growing more ashen by the moment, to the ambulance. Watching the van recede into the gloom, it occurred to me that today was the vernal equinox. The sun had set six minutes ago, at exactly six o'clock, and there would be equal night and daylight. All things being considered, I should have figured out by now who Holmes's murderer was, but I had only suspicions. I barely knew the identity of the man who had tried to murder us hours before and no idea who had murdered our assailant and why. Either someone wanted us alive or someone wanted him dead, perhaps both. It seemed Baker Street was our logical next stop as Watson was in no condition to continue the investigation tonight. He groaned as I helped him slump into the passenger seat of the Daimler. The first stars were winking in the half-moon sky as we made the silent twenty-minute drive back to the flat.

25

When we arrived home, Watson could barely stand. I directed him to lie down on the couch in his drawers and lit some moxa, which is an ancient Asian remedy of dried mugwort molded into the shape of a cigar. When the end is lit, the glowing ember radiates a penetrating heat which, when held close to afflicted areas, relaxes the muscles. As I warmed the meridians of his back with the mugwort preparation, I couldn't help noticing that the doctor's fondness for three meals a day was becoming evident in the form of at least fifteen to twenty excess pounds.

"That smells like the worst cigar anyone has ever lit," he complained. "What is it?"

"It's moxa. A Chinese classmate introduced me to it. It helped me overcome a tendon injury I sustained playing rugby." I placed the smoldering stick of moxa in the ashtray and took out my acupuncture needles from the doctor's bag that my parents had given me as a Christmas present. "You're going to feel some slight pinpricks on your back, Doctor. Do not be alarmed. It is called acupuncture, and the Chinese have been using this method successfully for centuries."

"Pinpricks?" he repeated with a high degree of skepticism. "And that's supposed to cure my back? Maybe you should get out some leeches as well."

"I know you're irritable, but give a try. There's no harm in it," I said reassuring him.

"I've had my back go out on me before," he declared. "This will require at least two days of bed rest, which I don't intend to have. I'll take a snifter of brandy over Chinese medicine to make this feel better."

I inserted the first slender needle into the gan shu point, which is on the left side of the spine just below the shoulder blade.

"First I'm shot at and now I'm turned into a pin cushion?" he complained.

"Just give it a chance, Doctor. This should relax you." I tapped in two more needles along the meridian.

"I don't find this the least bit relaxing. How many of those needles do you intend to jam into me?"

"I would estimate enough to make you shut up and let me help you."

Watson heaved a sigh of resignation, and I proceeded to place another twenty-five needles along the proper meridians. As I was preparing to apply heat to the needles, my mother knocked on the door. "I've some dinner for you two."

I opened the door and she entered with a tray of pork chops, applesauce and a Yorkshire pudding. She placed our dinner on the table and her eyes came to rest on Doctor Watson.
He was face down on the couch in nothing but his drawers. With a muffled voice he said, "This is most undignified...Do I smell pork chops?"

"What happened to Doctor Watson?" my mother asked in astonishment.

"He took a bit of a tumble," I answered, not wanting to alarm her with the truth.

"What did he tumble onto? A pin cushion?"

"No, no. This is a treatment I'm giving him. It's called acupuncture."

Mother noticed that my medical bag was open. "Ahh…You're using the medical bag we gave you," she said, looking very gratified.

"You'll have to excuse us, Mother. Thank you so much for dinner." My mother was used to being shooed out of this apartment, so she gave me a peck on the cheek and quickly retreated. When I turned back around, Watson was snoring. Though I was hungry, I decided to add the recent events to my timeline and wait on dinner until the doctor awoke. Even if it turned cold, I thought it would be more pleasant for us to eat it together.

• • •

Two hours later, Watson was still sound asleep. I had taken the needles out and placed a blanket over him. The time had passed quickly as I had been working diligently on my timeline. Now that Watson and I had become targets in this case, I placed notations on the wall for our relevant activities from the day we entered. I annotated those items on the timeline with details that I put in the blank pages of an old college notebook. I recorded every particular of my conversation with Moriarty, Wiggins and the others we had interviewed. Finally, I succumbed to hunger and ate my dinner while standing over the table and studying the flurry of paper scraps on the wall. It was all I could do not to eat Watson's share of the Yorkshire pudding. Glancing at the clock, I was surprised that we hadn't heard anything from Scotland

Yard regarding the crime scene on Weymouth Street. I telephoned the station, and was greeted by the watch commander, a Lieutenant Mansfield.

"Hello, this is Christopher Hudson. Are Commander Lestrade or Superintendent Gregson there?"

"They've left for the evening," came the world-weary voice on the other end.

"Could you give me some information about the incident on Weymouth Street?" I asked politely.

"What incident on Weymouth Street?" His voice suggested indifference.

"There was a shooting. A man was killed. I left Sergeant Archibald Hayes in charge."

"I know nothing about a killing on Weymouth or a Sergeant Archibald Hayes."

"He goes by Archie…Archie Hayes," I said, hoping to move things along.

"Archie or Archibald, I'd know him if there was anybody by that name."

And suddenly something to occurred to me. A feeling of dread instantly welled up in my chest. "And what about the killing?" I asked fearing the answer.

"Sir, if there had been a murder on Weymouth, I would know about it."

"Thank you, Lieutenant." I hung up the phone. I felt a thickening in my throat. What a terrible blunder I had made. How could I have been so easily deceived? The urgency of the moment had made me drop my defenses. Clearly "Sergeant Archie Hayes" had been an impostor and, in all likelihood, the very man who had killed our would-be assassin. I had to admire the cleverness of his operation, but, at the same time, I was disgusted by my own ineptness. The muttonchops, moustache and police uniform were all an elaborate disguise. What I mistook for false teeth were certainly stage teeth. In my state of confusion I had been an easy mark. Now my mind was spinning, trying to remember every detail of the encounter. I had to regroup. This was no time to compound my failures. I had to get hold of myself and salvage whatever evidence I could. I dashed off a note to Watson and put it beside his dinner plate. Throwing on my aviator jacket and scarf, I hurriedly retrieved the hand-carved ivory box, which my father had brought me back from one of his journeys around the Cape of Good Hope. In it I kept my childish valuables: a gold-plated medal I received for winning the hundred-yard dash in grade school, a sapphire tie tack given to me by my grandmother, my Oxford freshman pin, a ticket from the Louvre where I spent my eighteenth birthday and my switchblade. I pocketed the switchblade, secreted the box away in my closet, grabbed a torch and quickly slipped out of the apartment.

• • •

The hum of the Harley-Davison and the cold night air blasting against my face helped clear my mind. The vibrating solitude of the motorbike always brought me to a calm, internal place. It was as if every part of my being was involved in riding the bike except my brain, which would wander freely though whatever occupied it, finding solutions and posing questions. The traffic was sparse. I zoomed past a quarter-full bus carrying exhausted late-shift workers home from the factories.

Ignoring the traffic signals, I arrived at the building on Weymouth in twelve minutes. Checking the front door, I found it still locked. I drove around to the back and parked the Harley. The back door was unlocked. I stepped inside and turned on my torch, sweeping the area as I proceeded. There was no sign of life in the building and, dare I say it, no sign of the death that occurred earlier. As my beam shot across the lobby to illuminate the area in front of the elevator, I saw that the body was gone. Someone had even gone to pains to wash away any traces of blood. A recently scrubbed wet spot remained where the blood had pooled.

I walked to the rubbish bin, pulled myself up and shined the flashlight on the contents. As far as I could tell there was nothing of any evidentiary value that had been disposed of in it. I walked to the elevator shaft. The car was hovering on the second floor. Any blood that may have dripped into the bottom of the shaft had been cleaned. I positioned myself where our attacker was standing when he was shot. I placed the butt off my torch against my chest, trying to approximate where the exit wound had been on his body. He was shorter than me, so I adjusted for the difference, directing the light outward from the bottom of my ribcage so as to recreate the flight of the bullet. I swept the wall with the beam searching for the bullet hole and found it in the plaster behind the wrought-iron cage of the elevator shaft. I heard something stir from one of the floors above. I turned off the torch and listened. It sounded as if someone was dragging a heavy burden across one of the upper floors. "Rats?" I thought to myself. Often these sounds can be magnified in empty spaces like this. I have heard rats in the attic sound like polar bears moving around when the night is still. I continued to listen, and the stirring stopped. I turned my torch back on, stepped into the empty elevator shaft and found the bullet hole in the wall. I clicked open my switchblade and dug it into the hole. Suddenly I heard a snap and a squeal! It rattled me momentarily, but confirmed my suspicion that the stirring had been rats and it seemed as if a well-placed trap had accomplished its purpose.

I resumed digging around in the plaster until I had hollowed out a one-inch diameter hole. The slug was not there. Someone had already extracted it. Whoever had done this job had been very efficient. I saw little reason to investigate further. I could have checked all the floors in the hope that either the body or some evidence had been left behind, but that seemed more than unlikely. I could find no further evidence of the crimes that had been committed only hours before. It was half an hour to midnight, I was out of answers and there seemed only one logical place to go to get them.

26

The streetlights along the entire length of this block of Butchers Road had been intentionally smashed. This served two purposes. First, the faces of those respectable members of society could not be so easily discerned when they came to visit Wiggins's establishment. Secondly, predators who roamed this stretch of the East Side could more stealthily prey upon the victims who haplessly wandered into their territory.

I coasted to a stop in front of Wiggins's building and cut the engine. Immediately, three dangerous-looking characters emerged from behind a clutter of large, wooden packing crates and squinted into the glare of my headlight. "That's a noice motah bike, you 'ave there, lad," said one as he walked a circle around me with the other two watching and licking their chops. The one who spoke I supposed to be the leader. He bore the earmarks of a life spent on the streets. He had a deep scar extending from above his left eyebrow to the corner of his mouth. He had a cauliflower ear and flat nose suggesting he'd seen some time in the boxing ring. Several of the joints of his fingers were permanently bent and swollen, also giving evidence of time in the ring. "That's a noice jacket you got as well," he added after making a full revolution around me and my bike. His two cohorts took a few shuffling steps toward me. It was time to consider my options. It would be folly to try and hold them off with the switchblade. Retreat was an option, but it would require starting the engine and getting up to speed before they caught me, pulled me off and beat me to a pulp. I could negotiate. I had twelve pounds in my pocket and their leader seemed to covet my jacket. I was loath to give it up, but it was replaceable. Under no circumstances would I give up the motorbike without a death struggle. I could shout for help or make a dash to Wiggins's door and pound on it, but if no one responded within seconds I would surely be dragged into the shadows and beaten senseless. "This is a bad place for a young man loik you to be gettin' lost with a fine motahbike and jacket loik that," said the leader as he leaned into my face tauntingly.

Just then, the door of Wiggins's building burst open as if it might come off the hinges. Wiggins's enormous, suspendered, gun-toting doorman glowered down from the top of the stairs. "What's this?" he boomed. My tormentors froze in place. "I 'ope I'm not seein' wha' I think I'm seein', Fogel," the huge doorman snarled in an uncharacteristic cockney accent. "You're not botherin' Master Hudson, are you?"

"No, no! We were not botherin' Master Hudson," answered the street tough with great anxiety. "We was merely discussing 'is motahbike. That's all it was, Sir Patrick." The hoodlum grinned obsequiously.

"I 'ope I don't 'ear different. If it was Wiggins what saw you botherin' 'is friends out 'ere he'd be feedin' you each others' testicles." Something about his inflection made me believe this was not a figure of speech.

"No need to bothah Wiggins," said Fogel with an urgency that bordered on panic. "We was tryin' to be 'elpful to the young man."

"Come over 'ere, Fogel," demanded the massive doorman as he pointed to the step in front of him.

Fogel stood cringing like a frightened child not wanting to take his whipping. The doorman glared down at him.

"I'm sure Mr. Fogel is sorry for any misunderstanding," I interjected. "No harm done."

The doorman sniffed and seemed just as happy to forego the physical retribution. I believe he knew his point was made. "*Entrée*, Monsieur Hudson," he said with a sweep of his hand and a perfect French accent.

"Thank you, Sir Patrick," I said gratefully. "Let me lock up my motorbike first."

"That won't be necessary," he said. "Mr. Fogel will watch out for it, and I assure you it will be here when you return."

"You can be certain o' that, sir," said Fogel, as if he were now my best friend. "Safe as the crown jewels it is with me."

I handed over the motorbike and followed Sir Patrick into the building. "Get yer 'ands off of that motahbike else I'll cut 'em off," I heard Fogel say to one of cohorts as the massive door closed behind us.

A great deal of furniture had been moved in to this first floor of the building since my last visit, and it was taking on the feel of an exclusive gentlemen's club. These new furnishings undoubtedly accounted for the discarded packing crates out front. There were rugs, velvet armchairs, leather couches and a magazine rack with the latest periodicals and newspapers. There was a temporary bar consisting of a table with various brand-name liquors. A very elaborate mirrored and hand-carved bar was under construction. No doubt this was to be Wiggins's premier brothel. The lighting was still discreet and the other thing that remained was the poker game way off on the other side of the first floor in a smoke-filled haze of light. "We weren't expecting you, Mr. Hudson," cooed Sir Patrick. "We'll be meeting Wiggins on the second floor."

"Thank you. May I ask why they call you Sir Patrick?"

"Because that is my name," said the massive doorman as if there could be no other logical answer. He led me up the sweeping staircase. Despite Sir Patrick's graceful comportment, the runners creaked loudly beneath his substantial weight, giving fair warning to anybody above. We reached the business floor of the building, and Daisy, seated behind her little reception desk, lit up when she saw me. She shot up from her chair and gave me a motherly hug. "Christopher, how good to see you again. Come to visit Wiggins?"

"In part," I said with a warm smile.

No sooner was Wiggins's name uttered than he came clomping down the stairs to greet me. He was wearing cowboy boots and a holster with an antique-looking gun. His straw-blond hair was tied back in a braid and his clothes consisted of dirty dungarees and a long-sleeved undershirt with three buttons below the collar. He held out his hand and smiled with narcotized eyes. "'Udson, 'udson, 'udson…welcome, welcome."

"Good evening, Wiggins. I'm in the mood to take you up on your offer of one on the house," I said enthusiastically.

"That's the spirit!" Wiggins slapped a hand on my shoulder jubilantly. "That's what I love about the younger generation. It's all about what's between the legs. Daisy, line up some company for Mr. Hudson."

"Right away, sir." Her floor-length skirt and petticoat rustled as she quickly moved off down the hall and disappeared into one of the rooms.

"Did I say on the 'ouse?" Wiggins gave me a doubtful stare. "Of course it's on the 'ouse!" He roared with laughter and slapped me on the back this time.

If I claimed not to be frightened by this addled character, I would be lying. Watson told me that Wiggins was not to be trifled with. He had grown up on the streets and was afraid of nothing. He had survived by sometimes being the rat and other times being the ratcatcher. I had to be very cautious in my probing of Wiggins and how I presented the topic of this afternoon's attack, but that was the subject I came to explore and there was no doubt that Wiggins had the most to offer. I would have to get around to it subtly though.

"So take a look at this, Christopher," Wiggins blurted as he pulled the gun from his holster and twirled it on his finger. "This was Jesse James's gun. Had it on 'im when 'e was killed. One of 'is best friends shot 'im in the back. Do you know who Jesse James was?"

"He was an American outlaw. Shot in the back of the head by one of his associates named Robert Ford, who was hoping to collect a five-thousand-dollar reward." I had read a good deal about American outlaws in my youth.

"If you can't trust your partners…eh?" he bemoaned. Then that lament quickly passed and he proudly brandished the weapon. "I bought it at Christie's, this gun. It's been authenticated. Forty-five-caliber Colt. How much do you think I paid?"

"I can't even hazard a guess," I answered.

Sir Patrick stood against the wall observing impassively. For such a large man, he had an uncanny ability to make himself inconspicuous.

"Thirty-six 'undred pounds. The underbidder was Lord Walpole." He laughed heartily and his thick East End accent got even thicker. "Imagine me outbiddin' a lord 'ose title goes back ten generations. And me not even knowin' my real father." He spun the cylinder, and I could see the gun was fully loaded. "A piece of 'istory this is."

"Very impressive," I said, trying not to sound too patronizing.

Wiggins mused about the irony of outbidding a lord as he admired the gun in his hand. "Let's get down to business then!" he said suddenly, holstering the weapon. "Have you 'ad a look at the menu?"

"I can't say as I have."

He grabbed a sheet of paper off Daisy's desk and handed it to me. It was indeed a menu of services offered at this establishment and described with very little ambiguity all manner of sexual activities in ascending order of price. "See this one…" said Wiggins pointing to a particularly pricey item on the menu which included a whip and goose quill. "Personally, I think that's overpriced at six pounds, but it's simple supply and demand around 'ere. Whatever the market will bear." He said this as if he were merely an innocent bystander to the activities of the brothel. He shook his head as he took out a pouch of chewing tobacco and put a plug of it in his check. "When Englishmen get older, they get quite perverted." He said this with an edge that implied the menu might only scratch the surface, and then chuckled to himself as if reviewing in his head some of the more deviant activities of his clientele. This seemed like a good opportunity to get to my real purpose.

"I thought you should know," I said matter-of-factly, "that someone tried to kill Watson and me this afternoon."

"What you talkin' about!" he exclaimed. His reaction seemed positively spontaneous and sincere. "Who was it?"

"I did not recognize him. We were asked to have a meeting in a building on Weymouth Street, and this man rushed out of the apartment and started shooting at us. He chased us down to the lobby where we hid in the elevator shaft. He seemed to have us cornered but instead, someone shot and killed him, then disappeared."

"This afternoon! On Weymouth Street!" He seemed quite flabbergasted by the account.

"Yes," I said flatly. I didn't want to reveal to Wiggins the fact that I'd recognized the attacker as having been in his company at the funeral. That would have been too accusatory. I wanted to see what information he attempted to elicit, for that might give me a clearer picture of his involvement.

"And the police, did they identify the man who tried to kill you?" he asked calming himself.

"Unfortunately, I left the body with a police officer who later turned out to be an impostor. In all probability he was our savior. He and the body disappeared."

Wiggins's face became a mask. He stared through me as if trying to put the pieces together in his head. "Well, that's a rather harrowin' story," he said after a few moments of silence.

Daisy returned with three young women who had "freshened up." Their faces were powdered and they had rouged red cheeks and deep red on their lips. One was blond, one brunette and the last was redheaded. They lined up and smiled at me ingratiatingly.

Wiggins did not even seem to notice they were there. "Obviously, you need to be very careful, young 'udson," he said with his voice lowered. "You are dealin' with adults now."

"Moriarty said the same thing to me," I responded.

"He's a wise man," he said, shaking his finger as if to reinforce that assertion.

Creed, Wiggins's main lieutenant since they were street youths, came down the dark stairs from Wiggins's third-floor abode. Creed was blond, muscular and rarely spoke. I remember from my childhood that he had a rather severe speech impediment. I now realize it was probably due to a cleft palate. Back then, Creed whispered his information to Wiggins who would pass it along as he saw fit. He quickly moved to Wiggins's side and whispered something in his ear. Wiggins's reaction indicated this was business that needed to be attended to immediately.

"I must go now," he said, then quite unexpectedly took my head in his hands and leaned forward until our brows were nearly touching. "You believe I'm your friend, don't you?" he added earnestly.

"Absolutely," I answered without hesitation.

He released me and the cheerful, carefree Wiggins returned. "Take any of 'em." He meant the girls. "All three if you want." He nodded to his trusty doorman. "Patrick, come with us." He hurried back up the dark stairs with Sir Patrick and Creed in tow.

I turned to Daisy and the three young women, who fluttered their eyelashes at me demurely.

"Who would you like, Mr. Hudson?" said Daisy in a professional manner.

"I choose you, Daisy," I responded with a gentle smile.

Her businesslike comportment dropped and the brothel hostess became quite flustered. "Wouldn't you like a younger girl?" she said blushing.

"They don't know as much you," I said slyly.

The three working girls tittered. Daisy fiddled with the pleats of her gingham skirt. Her hand moved up to the collar of her frilly white blouse. "If that's your pleasure, Christopher," she said gathering her professionalism. "Julia, take the desk please." Daisy took me by the arm and led me down the hallway to the great amusement of the other three girls.

We entered a room halfway down the hall. It was actually quite a bit nicer than I would have expected. There was a large bed with a feather comforter, a dressing table and bureau for the girls and a lavatory shared with the next room. I suspect that many of the employees lived as well as worked in these rooms. It seemed quite clean, and, if you raised the shade on the windows, the room could be tolerably bright during the day.

Daisy chatted nervously as she sat down on the bed and unbuttoned her blouse. "So how have you and your mother been getting along since you returned from university? She's such a nice woman, your mum."

While she anxiously babbled, I inspected the room for any potential peepholes or false panels where someone could spy on us. When I turned around, she was removing one of her stockings. "You don't have to do that," I told her. "I just want to talk to you."

"Oh…" she said with great relief. "I never would have guessed you were one of those, Christopher. Would you like me to start or do you like to talk first?" She pulled her stocking back on.

"Actually, I'd like to ask you some questions," I said.

"All right," she said cheerfully, re-buttoning her blouse. "What would you like to know?"

"Who was the Latin-looking man sitting with you and Wiggins's group during the funeral?"

Suddenly Daisy's relief was gone and her expression turned serious and quite vulnerable. "If I answer questions like that, Wiggins will 'ave me killed." There was no question that she believed this to be an actual possibility.

"Daisy, this afternoon that man tried to murder me and Watson and that man is now dead. I need to know who he was."

"He's dead," she said, horrified, as if trying to visualize it. "Please don't make me answer any questions, Christopher."

"Daisy, do you know who killed Sherlock Holmes? Was it Wiggins?" I asked firmly.

"No!" she answered reflexively. "Wiggins loved Mr. Holmes. He would never have killed 'im."

"Then you need to give me the identity of this man who shot at us. Daisy, either we're going to find out who killed Holmes or somebody is going to have to kill us before we do. You have to pick a side."

"I 'ave a side, Christopher. My own. If I sit 'ere and point fingers and give you information that I don't even know is right and Wiggins finds out I've been talking about 'is business, 'e will go very 'ard on me. I don't know who killed Mr. Holmes, and I don't want to know, and that's the truth." In her distress, her East End accent had returned. It was the voice she used as a street child and that scared child was certainly in evidence.

"You want to see justice done, don't you, Daisy?"

"I don't know what justice is, Mr. Hudson. Do I want to see the one who killed Mr. Holmes hanging from Tower Bridge? Yeah! And if I knew who it was, I would tell you."

It occurred to me that the justice argument had very little resonance if you lived in the East End. The concept of justice in Bethnal Green had been tested by the sweatshops and dock workers and found to be a scale that tipped cruelly toward those who could apply influence. Occasionally it was counterbalanced by those exploited individuals willing to exert pressure through painful sacrifice. Daisy had no union and nothing more than life and limb to sacrifice. For a resident of the East End, justice could only be gotten in exchange for blood.

"What if I could take you out of here, Daisy? What if I could arrange for you to have a different life?"

"What different life could you make for me, Christopher? Do you think I'm fit to 'ave tea at Claridge's? You think I could sit in a shop in Mayfair and talk to people about fine china or riding saddles and all that? I can't mix in your society. Your society comes east to this establishment when they want to do business with the likes of us."

"That's how it used to be, but things have changed. You can change your life." I waited for her to speak, but she merely stared at me as if I spoke a foreign language. "Daisy, I need your help."

She looked down at her hands as if she would find some answers there. Finally, she spoke up. "I could never live with it if any harm came to you or Doctor Watson. He is the kindest man I have ever known. I'm sure he don't even remember, but one year when I was twelve all the young ones got the measles, all got better but my little brother, Henry, who was only seven and it went to his lungs. We were sleeping in a stable on Huntsworth Mews and Wiggins said we 'ad to get Henry to Doctor Watson. So we show up on the doorsteps of Baker Street at eleven o'clock, the three of us, on a bitter-cold night with Henry in Wiggins's arms. And Doctor Watson sets up Henry on Mr. Holmes's couch and he gives him medicine and I sleep on the floor because Henry won't stay without me there, and Wiggins goes back to the stables because he had to see to the others. Doctor Watson took care of Henry for three days and your mum gave us toast and tea in the morning and Henry soup in the afternoons and you were just a little baby." Tears started to roll down Daisy's cheeks. "So I will tell you wha' I know and hope it will 'elp you, but you must never mention that we spoke about it."

I went to her side and put my arm around her shoulder reassuringly. "I promise you I will tell no one and no harm will come to you as result of anything you say."

She drew a deep breath. "The man you ask about called himself Sergio. I first saw him, I'd say, maybe two years ago. I never asked his last name or cared. He said he was from Spain and once went on to me about the mountains there. He was not a very interesting bloke, but believed he was quite irresistible to the girls and kept trying to get into their rooms for free. He would come around here and talk to Wiggins. It seemed like they were talking business. He was the…" she searched for the appropriate word, "…'companion' of a much older woman who lived in Kensington. She was widowed and quite rich. Wiggins never seemed to take this Sergio character very seriously, but he began talking to the old woman more and more. A few times she even came down 'ere, coming from the back stairs, of course."

"What did this woman look like?" I asked, thinking in all likelihood that this was the very woman who led us to the ambush.

"She was quite old. Her face was wrinkled. She looked like one of those old ladies who take their carriages through the park on Sunday. So Sergio is dead, you say?"

"Shot through the heart. And his lady friend is in the hospital."

"And all this has something to do with Mr. Holmes?"

"I have to believe so."

"Well, that's what I know about Sergio. Why would he want to kill Mr. Holmes or you and the doctor?"

"That's what I'm trying to figure out."

"Well if 'e's dead, then there's nothing more to it," she said hopefully.

"I believe there may be more to it than that. There might be someone else behind this," I said, disabusing her of that halfhearted supposition.

"I'm 'fraid you're right," she relented.

"Let me ask you," I said. "Do you know anything of Lord Fitzroy?"

"Plenty," she answered immediately.

"Tell me what you know."

"I know 'e's partial to young boys."

"And his wife?"

"I know nothing of her. But I can assure you he's never facin' her when they go at it."

"So I assume Wiggins uses this information to his own advantage with Fitzroy," I said delicately.

"A lot of 'em come down 'ere, and he blackmails 'em all. Not for straight-out money, but for favors…this and that when he needs it," said Daisy bluntly. "The fancy ones…they never want nothin' simple. That's why they come to the East End."

"What do you know of the relationship between Wiggins and Moriarty?" I queried.

"Moriarty's in jail," she said as if that were answer enough.

"Do you know if they have any contact?"

"No. I know that Wiggins isn't afraid of much but he had a healthy respect for Moriarty. Long time ago one of the Irregulars, named Hackney on account of we found him on Hackney Road stealing from a grocer, he left Wiggins and went to work for Moriarty. Wiggins told Moriarty he wanted him back and not to filch any of his crew and they had a fierce argument. Moriarty sent him back all right…in six pieces. Wiggins had Creed and Sir Patrick visit some of Moriarty's, and after that they had a pact. They stayed out of each other's business."

"I assume it wouldn't help to attempt to speak to Sir Patrick?" I asked feebly.

"Don't even try. I'm sure Wiggins told him you are to be respected, but 'e will never tell you anything. That goes for Creed, as well. If Wiggins ever goes down, those two will go down with him."

"Why do they call him Sir Patrick?" I asked, just out of general curiosity.

"On account of the way he speaks. He's well educated. Went to boardin' school," she said almost proudly.

"How did he come to work for Wiggins?"

"Wiggins got 'im out of a pinch with the police once. Some say it was murder, but I don't believe that. The thing you gotta understand about Wiggins is that he's a good man who's been in bad circumstances. And when he says he loves you and wouldn't 'arm you, he means it at that moment. But he's high-tempered, and sometimes that's what takes over." She looked up at me for affirmation. "You know, he's building flats for the poor…all around the city…for those tots like we were…for the next bunch of Irregulars."

It was oddly touching to hear her come to Wiggins's defense. Whatever could be said about Wiggins, he inspired loyalty, and it wasn't solely through fear. Many of his company had been with him since childhood and were bound by the shared experience of basic survival. They had only each other to rely on to make it through the day. There was something about that common denominator that built better character than many of the population of Kensington and Mayfair possessed.

I moved to the door. "You're wrong about one thing, Daisy. You are more than fit to have tea at Claridge's."

She blushed as her eyes turned downward. I slipped out of the room.

27

When I exited Wiggins's establishment, I found Fogel and his two companions warming themselves by a fire of old shingles and packing carton they had lit in an open trash bin. My motorbike was right at the bottom of the steps where I had left it.

"Hope they treated you all right in there, Mr. 'udson," said Fogel, warming his hands and elbowing one his of mates slyly.

"More than satisfactorily, Mr. Fogel. Thank you for watching my motorbike." I flipped him half a crown.

"'Appy to be of service," he answered gladly pocketing the coin.

At that moment, a black Renault two-seater came charging around the corner and sped right past the building. It was the very make of car that I had suspected was used in Holmes's murder. I jumped on my Harley-Davison, fired it up and immediately gave chase.

The Renault tore down Butchers Road and turned onto Dock Road as if making for the river. The roof and windshield were closed and the interior dark, so I could not see who was driving the car. I resolved to try and discreetly pull up beside the vehicle to identify the driver. I drew within a hundreds yards of the vehicle at a speed of forty miles per hour. Happily, it was well after one in the morning, and the streets were deserted. I eased out toward the middle of the street and opened the throttle, inching up to the level of the back bumper of the

Renault. I could see a dark figure behind the wheel but couldn't recognize whether it was a man or woman. I opened the throttle a bit more and pulled up even with the back tire. The driver was alone in the car, but the dark and fog conspired to thwart my view. I sped up a little more in order to pull up beside the driver's seat and get a full look at the profile. I gained a few more inches and suddenly the Renault turned sharply onto Narrow Street, heading away from the river. The driver must have seen me for he cut the headlights, and I heard him go full bore toward the marshland. I skidded to a stop, spun around and headed off after him.

The Renault had a two-cylinder, twelve-horsepower motor with a top speed of perhaps sixty miles per hour, which could put a good amount of distance between him and me if he got to the long stretch of Grove Road that cut a swath through the marshland.

At top speed I hit the roundabout at Mile End Road and saw the shape of the Renault up ahead careening onto Grove Road and the edge of the marshes. I headed after it, twisting my throttle as wide as it would go.

The marshes were a former hunting ground to kings and now home to a growing population of Eastern European immigrants. The buildings were humble and sparse and the bugs and wildlife plentiful. Several insects plastered themselves on my goggles as the wind rushed across my face at top speed and the engine whined threateningly. As I went deeper, the marsh mist blanketed the road, and I caught only glimpses of the Renault far in front of me as it passed in and out of the ambient light shed from the occasional building popping up on the roadside.

Clearly the driver of the Renault had altered his route in order to lose me, but his miscalculation was getting on a road with few ways off. If he didn't turn onto Roman Road, he would end up in the virtual dead end of Victoria Park.

I maintained a speed of fifty miles per hour and kept my eyes fixed ahead to my right where, about a half mile away, the Roman Road snaked off, lit by a string of streetlamps. I would be able to detect the movement of the Renault if the driver chose to take that route, otherwise he would have to slow down when he reached the park and give me an opportunity to catch up.

In half a minute I passed the intersection and determined that the Renault had not turned off. He had to be up ahead, though I could not see any sign of him. After another two minutes I arrived at the entrance to Victoria Park. I calculated that the Renault had been no more than a mile in front of me. At near top speed it would have arrived sixty to ninety seconds earlier. Either the driver had chosen to enter the park or drive around the perimeter, which would take him directly back to the entrance. If he had entered, this would be his only point of egress as the park grounds were encircled by an iron fence. The circumference of the park was 3.2 miles, so if he was driving at a manageable speed he would arrive back at my location between four and five minutes. If I entered the park now, I risked the chance of losing him if he had chosen to make the loop. If I waited for him to come back around, I risked the possibility that he would park either on the perimeter or inside the grounds and abandon the car. That seemed to be the less likely possibility, so I resolved to wait within sight of the entrance for the minutes it would take him to circumnavigate. If I did not see the car, I would assume he had driven into the park and would go in and find him.

I let my engine idle quietly and took this opportunity to clean the insect detritus off my goggles. It was nearly 2:00 a.m. The street was empty. The houses at the edge of the park were asleep and I could hear the frogs croaking to each other within the grounds. Victoria Park had been built in the middle of the nineteenth century in reaction to the growing population of the East End. It was believed that it would create a barrier from the squalor. There were fears that, with no open spaces, disease would spread from the stinking industries and slums of the roughly four hundred thousand East Enders to the rest of London. Used primarily for grazing and gravel digging, the land at this location was purchased relatively cheaply by the government. In 1841 Queen Victoria gave her blessing to the construction of the park within the Tower Hamlets, and, even before it was completed in 1843, East Enders started flocking to Victoria Park and enjoying its tranquil grounds. I was aware of this history because it was explained to me by my father, who used to take me here when I was a child. Having sailed to the Orient, he admired the Chinese pagoda that had been transplanted from Hyde Park, and, on occasional Sundays, would take me in a small rowboat to visit all three islands on the boating lake at the west end of the park.

After five minutes, I concluded that the Renault must have gone through the gate. Light was not plentiful on the grounds and it was too dark a night to turn off my headlamp and attempt a stealthy search. I turned my beam in the direction of the gate, revved the engine and entered Victoria Park at a steady ten miles per hour.

Grove Road bisected the park with small paths leading off it for foot traffic. To the left side was an open field with a scattering of elms. To my right was a play area with swings, slides and picnic tables. On weekends this area would be filled with families, but, presently, the only inhabitant was a sleeping beggar bundled in a blanket beneath one of the benches.

I rolled on, carefully scanning the area, and saw no sign of the Renault. Soon the trees on my left grew thicker and on my right a vast lawn sloped down to the boating lake. I could see the dark shape of the Chinese pagoda hovering above the water on the island. I continued to move forward, and the beam of my lamp grazed across some tire tracks in the lawn. They led down to the lake, and I felt confident of what vehicle had made them. I turned off my lamp and let the bike roll down the lawn noiselessly toward the water. The grass was slick beneath my wheels and I worked the brake gently so as not to gain too much speed. I scanned the area cautiously as I glided toward the footpath that surrounded the lake. I spotted the Renault parked like a ghost in the darkness of a stand of trees. I instantly stopped. The car's lamps were off and driver's-side door open. In all likelihood it had been abandoned. The driver could easily have climbed the fence and fled or could be hiding anywhere in the two hundred plus acres. I left my motorbike by the lakeside and warily approached the vehicle. Behind the windshield I could see only darkness. It had been almost fifteen minutes since I last spotted the vehicle, but the engine and radiator were creaking as if it had just been shut down. I considered the possibility that the driver was lurking somewhere in the shadows planning to leap out at me and attack. There was a multitude of places to hide around the lake. As I crept closer, my hand moved to the switchblade in my pocket. Suddenly the engine roared to life and the vehicle rocketed straight at me. The headlights burst on, blinding me, and I reflexively sprung into the air, landed flat on the hood and rolled off the fender onto the wet grass. I turned to see the driver's door slam closed as the Renault tore a swathe across the lawn and up to the road. I jumped to my feet and fired up my Harley to give chase.

My tires struggled to gain traction on the uphill grass and the bike skidded and wobbled, making me ease up on the throttle until I reached the road. I had seen that the Renault headed off toward the north gate, which I assumed would be locked. As I sped that direction, I did a mental inventory of my injuries. My knee hurt as did my shoulder but neither seemed to signal any major damage. Ahead of me in the dark, I heard the drone of the Renault. I heard the squeal of tires followed by a crash and, seconds later, I arrived at the north gate to see that the Renault had left the road and crashed through an old wooden section of fence separating the park from the Hackney Cemetery, which bordered it to the north. I bounced up onto the curb and followed through the gap in the fence. Off to my left I could see the automobile flashing along the road that wound through the ornate headstones and monuments of the old Jewish graveyard.

The Renault shot out through the gates and headed south toward Whitechapel Road. I reasoned he was making another run for the river, but going through the streets of Whitechapel and Spitalfields would give the maneuverability of my motorbike an advantage in keeping up with him. I hoped that if I could stay on his tail long enough, I would find an opportunity to pull even with him and learn the driver's identity.

The Renault took no heed of lanes or traffic signals as it hurtled through the sleeping streets. There was no traffic to speak of and only occasionally did I have to pass a lingering taxi or lorry crawling along the route with its predawn deliveries.

The chase wound us mercilessly back toward the Thames with the Renault's driver never taking his foot off the gas pedal. As we reached the old Whitechapel foundry, I tried to creep up on the flank of the car and the driver swerved violently toward my motorbike then swung a turn onto Dock Street, heading hard for the river. I skidded past the intersection then righted myself, rode up over the pavement, weaving between a mailbox and streetlamp, and resumed the pursuit.

When I had the car back in my sights, it was approaching the embankment road at full speed. Beyond I could see the full-shouldered width of the Thames with scattered lights on the opposite bank.

The Renault took a screaming left onto the Upper Embankment Road, and I arrived at the turn just in time to see it speeding head-on toward a hapless bakery truck. Horns blared and the Renault swerved hard, leaped off the road and tumbled out of control down the steep embankment with a tremendous crashing of metal and shattering of glass.

I sped to the spot where the automobile had left the road and looked down. I could see the outline of the car lying on its side on the stony shore with water lapping at it. There was no movement detectable. It had been a long drop down to a dark part of the bank and trying to reproduce it on foot would be too treacherous. I quickly rode to the path, a hundred yards beyond, leading down to the lower embankment. Not far off was Tower Bridge, lit up and powerfully straddling the Thames. I sped down to the embankment and parked my motorbike by a barge that was moored there. Crunching across the gravel shore, I reached the crippled automobile. I stepped up on the running board and peered inside. The car was empty. The driver might have been thrown into the river and drowned or thrown from the automobile on the way down and was laying on the incline. There was no way to tell in the darkness. I also had to admit to myself the possibility that he had escaped. Whether injured or not, he might have taken to foot along the river heading east. If that were the case, the choice would be to pursue him on foot in the pitch dark and risk leaving the automobile and having any evidence be contaminated, or stay with the car and do as thorough an examination as possible while waiting for the police to arrive and supervise their efforts as well. Given the variables, I opted to stay with the car and not make the same mistake I had made at the building on Weymouth. My instinct proved to be right, as a worker who had been sleeping on the barge came shuffling and squinting through the darkness to see what the commotion was about.

"There's been an accident," I told him as he approached me leerily. "I rolled my car off the road. Do you happen to have a torch?" I asked him, since mine had been shattered during the chase.

He took a look at the mangled automobile and another look at me and said, "You're lucky to be alive, man...Yeah, I've got a torch on the barge."

I offered him a crown for the use of the torch and his assistance in alerting the authorities. He gladly accepted and returned with the desired item posthaste.

28

Climbing around in a car that is toppled on its side on the banks of the Thames at two thirty in the morning is a bit of a challenge. I removed my shoes, brushed off my clothes as well as I could and left on my driving gloves. The passenger-side door was flopped open with that portion of the car facing skyward. I climbed in, being careful not to smudge any fingerprints. I wanted to do some evidence gathering before the police arrived. This would not affect their investigation as they would have no interest in the items I collected. Hair and soil samples held little interest for them, cigar and cigarette ash even less. I found all three in the vehicle. Wedging myself into the driver's seat, and careful not to touch the steering wheel or shift knob, I collected several black hairs from the backrests, some soil specimens from the floor and a miraculously almost intact cigar ash from the floor of the backseat. All these I put into sample tubes, which I had taken to carrying with me at all times. Unfortunately, one had smashed in my pocket during the chase, which later necessitated three stitches to my thigh. I hadn't even noticed it during the pursuit, but, in the calmness of my investigation, I started to become aware of the injuries from the night's activities.

I must admit that I probably did one investigation that should have been left to the police first, but I was disinclined to trust them to do proper analysis based on recent experience, and so I opened and examined the contents of the glove box. I found nothing unusual in it. The Renault, as I suspected, was indeed the one stolen in Kensington from a Nigel Loughlin, as confirmed by the registration paper. It also contained the owner's manual, a handkerchief and a penknife. Any fingerprint that might have been on the latch had probably been smeared by my probing, but I was confident that there would be plenty of prints to find when the police got there.

A bit more than an hour later Gregson arrived with his fingerprint man, Richardson, and two other officers in tow. The police superintendent seemed a bit dour and, frankly, I couldn't blame him since he had been pulled out of bed in the middle of the night. He had left specific instructions down at Scotland Yard to contact him if either Watson or I called, and, good to his word, he was on the case.

He strode down the shore, put his hands on his hips and eyed the wreckage of the Renault. "You can be awful annoying, Master Hudson, but you seem to be onto something."

"Yes, Superintendent, I believe you're looking at the murder weapon," I said motioning to the car.

"Then maybe you can inform me regarding the obvious questions. How did it get here and who was driving it?"

"I chased it from Butchers Road to Victoria Park and then down here. I didn't see who was driving. The car was empty by the time I was able to make it down to the shore. He may be laying dead up there on the incline for all I can tell."

He motioned to his two officers and pointed to the incline. "Sweep the hill as best you can. It'll be daylight soon, so don't go breaking your leg in the dark."

The officers turned on their torches and went about the assignment. Gregson turned back to me rubbing his chin. "So what was a fine young man like yourself doing on Butchers Road late at night?"

"What do most young men like me do on Butchers Road at night?" I answered.

"Well, most of them wouldn't dare to question Wiggins, but I suspect you did."

I gave him an innocent shrug and chose to leave it at that.

"Richardson, check the car," he said nodding to his fingerprint specialist. Richardson opened up his kit and set about his work.

"Mr. Hudson, you didn't happen to collect any evidence from this car before we arrived?"

"None you'd be interested in, Superintendent Gregson. Some soil and ash perhaps," I answered offhandedly.

"You know, Master Hudson, you're beginning to remind me of somebody," Gregson said with the smallest trace of a smile.

• • •

I chose to stay and observe the fingerprint collection process, during which time I explained to Gregson the particulars of the prior twenty-four hours. Instead of the expected chastisement, Gregson was quite supportive of my efforts. I did not reveal the name of our attempted murderer, as he would ask me how I knew it and I intended, at all costs, to protect Daisy's anonymity as a source. Even the information that I knew the first name of this character might get her in trouble somehow. I told him that I would come in and look through criminal-file photographs in order to identify our attacker.

By 6:15 a.m. there was enough light to finish the investigation. No one was found on the incline. No bodies were seen bobbing in the water. No trail of escape could be detected. I walked a mile eastward along the rocky shore as soon as the sun came up and found nothing of use. When I returned, the policemen were discussing with Gregson the strategy for towing the Renault from the river's edge.

The worker who had called the police for me had long since lost interest and returned to his barge to go back to sleep. I left his torch on the deck and decided to make one last stop before returning home.

• • •

I was utterly exhausted and the Charing Cross Hospital was out of my way, but I wanted to speak to this Smithwick woman if possible. The city was waking up as I rode along the Thames on the edge of Chelsea. The lorries were out and about making deliveries, workers were boarding buses as shopkeepers swept the pavements in front of their establishments. Everything appeared so normal and yet the last week had given me a glimpse of a dark and sinister world beneath the surface, where thieves and murderers roamed and even targeted me. Intellectually, I had always understood the duality of our society, and, more to the point, of the human condition, but something about staring down the barrel of a gun personalizes that intellectual exercise. Plenty of times I had been on the rugby field with opponents who would gladly break your arm or cripple your knee if that were their road to victory, but out here the contest was for one's whole existence. If this were to be my calling, then I would have to prepare myself to fight fire with fire. The gentlemanly investigatory practices of Holmes and Watson's day were faded. This was a new century with new and deadlier technologies, with higher stakes and shifting desires. This is not to say that the dark side of man had fundamentally changed since he walked out of the cave. Those same impulses drive him, but just as the new industries had fomented massive changes in manner and method to Queen Victoria's empire, the dawning of a new century and the ascendancy of machines that fly and others that speed along the earth with the power of 120 horses would change the nature and scope of the perils in our world.

I parked and locked my motorbike in front of Charing Cross Hospital and took the stairs to the second-floor nurses' station. There I waited to address two nurses who were changing shifts and updating each other on the patients' charts. The younger of the two finally looked up at me. "May I help you, sir?"

"Yes, I'm here to visit my grandmother…Mrs. Smithwick. She was brought by ambulance last night with some heart trouble." I tried to sound as concerned as possible.

"What's her first name?" asked the gruff older nurse, looking up from her chair.

I stared back at her totally stumped. I couldn't for the life of me remember the old bat's first name. I had looked through her papers and belongings, but, after the day *and* night I had experienced, my mind was too muddled to find it. "We just call her Grandma Smithwick," I smiled meekly.

The younger nurse came around from behind the station with a look of compassion. "I'm so sorry. Your grandma passed away," she said as she sympathetically took my hand. "Would you like to see her?"

I had no interest in looking at the corpse of the woman who had set us up to be murdered. At this point I just wanted to go to bed. "No. Never mind," I said dismissively. "But you've been very kind." The young nurse blinked at me, clearly taken aback by my callousness at the passing of my dear grandma. I turned and walked back to the stairs.

29

WATSON

When I awoke Christopher was gone and I had no idea how long I had been sleeping. I remembered Christopher poking me endlessly with needles, a mention of dinner and that was the extent of it. I sat up on the couch with the blanket wrapped around me. The pain in my back was much more bearable. On the table was my meal, and, next to it, Christopher's empty plate. I was famished. I rose from the couch, put on a robe and checked Christopher's room. He was not there. "Curious," I thought to myself. The clock said ten fifteen, and I couldn't imagine where he could have gone after the day we had suffered through. I put on some clothes and sat down at the table to have my cold pork chop and Yorkshire pudding when I noticed the note that Christopher had left for me. I could see it had been written hastily. It read:

> *Sergeant Archibald Hayes was a fraud. I'm going back to the building to investigate. Do not worry about me. Christopher.*

Well, he had certainly anticipated my reaction. I was concerned that my young friend was feeling a little overconfident. He was not experienced enough in our line of work to be out alone on a case while someone was trying to kill him. He did, however, know a thing or two about Chinese medicine. I stretched in my chair, and my back was much relieved. As I ate my cold dinner I pondered what Christopher meant by the police sergeant "was a fraud." There was little point in trying to track young Hudson down at the building and, in any event, I was in no condition to do so. I determined I had been asleep for roughly three hours and could easily use another seven hours of rest.

As always, Mrs. Hudson's Yorkshire pudding was excellent and I've never minded my meat cold, so, all in all, it was a very satisfying meal. I was in the process of inspecting Christopher's enhanced timeline, when there came a timid knock on the door followed by Mrs. Hudson's voice. "Doctor Watson, are you awake?"

I opened the door for her. "Yes, I'm awake, Mrs. Hudson. Please come in."

"I've come to collect the dishes," she said as she shuffled in wearing her slippers and Japanese robe.

"Thank you, Mrs. Hudson. The pudding was just as good as I remembered it."

"You're very welcome, Doctor," she said as she stacked the plates and placed them back on the tray. "It seems your back is feeling better."

"Yes, much looser," I said as I twisted side to side to test it.

"Christopher would make a fine doctor, wouldn't he?" she said, as if a prelude to something else that was on her mind.

"Yes, I'm sure he would be an excellent physician."

"Doctor Watson, would it be possible for you to have dinner with Captain Hudson and me tomorrow night?"

"Absolutely…if events permit. What time would you like me there?" This struck me as an abrupt invitation and likely something more than social.

"We'll be downstairs. Let's say between six thirty and seven."

"Splendid. If my schedule changes, I will let you know."

Mrs. Hudson picked up the tray and moved to the door. "Oh, and please don't mention our dinner to Christopher. I will tell you why later." She exited the room without waiting for an answer. I stared after her for a beat and then closed the door. I couldn't imagine what that was about.

30

After a fine night's sleep, I arose at seven thirty. My energy was good and my back felt splendid. I went into the drawing room and pulled aside the drapes. The dew was still fresh on the elms that lined the street. I opened the window and took a deep breath of the cool, damp air. I noticed that Christopher's door was closed. It had been open when I retired last night, so I quietly took a peek into his room. He was sleeping quite soundly on top of his covers as if he had come home, removed his boots and collapsed on the bed. I silently withdrew. I was anxious to get the whole story of his evening. Undoubtedly it was eventful, but I didn't intend to wake him as I didn't know what time he came in or how long he had been sleeping.

I went back to the drawing room and was considering lighting a fire when I heard a faint, irregular knocking on the door. I grabbed the fire poker and walked across the room. "Who is it?" I asked. The experience of the day before made me abundantly cautious. A garbled woman's voice could be heard from the landing. I cracked open the door and standing on the threshold was Lilah Church. The blue-and-yellow makeup on her bewildered eyes was running down her face in streaks. The red coating on her lips was smeared across her teeth and chin. Her hat was gone and her raven ringlets hung in disordered clumps down the sides of her face. Her powder-blue slippers and the bottom third of her white tea dress were caked in dry mud as though she had waded waist-deep through the marshes. "Doctor Watson, thank the lord!" She shot past me into the drawing room, and, fretfully wringing her hands, rushed to the window.

"What's the matter, Lilah?" I asked with alarm.

"They probably know I'm here," she said fearfully.

"Who knows? Who's after you?" I implored.

She turned and looked up at me with great agitation. "When I saw you at the hospital, I knew…I knew it was a bad omen…I couldn't stay…I knew they'd find me."

"Now calm down, please. Is someone trying to hurt you?" I gently put my hands on her shoulders. She was trembling fiercely.

"I've been walking all night." She folded and refolded her arms as if they were acting independently of her thoughts. "I was talking to the witch."

"The witch?" I said in confusion.

"The one with the stick and the ball." Then she whispered hoarsely, "She's got a dragon."

Christopher's voice came from across the room. "I believe she's talking about the Temple Bar monument. I'd hazard that she's in the midst of a delusional state." He was standing in his doorway looking disheveled and exhausted.

"She's got a dragon," repeated Lilah, as if to make sure that this fact was not ignored.

I could see that Christopher was correct. Lilah was in some sort of psychotic state. "Sit down, child," I said to her as I seated her in front of the hearth and proceeded to light a fire.

Christopher approached and gave Lilah a sympathetic but clinical inspection. "You probably went walking all over Westminster last night, didn't you, Lilah? Perhaps a little wading in Regent Park?" He flaked some of the mud off her skirt. "I'll analyze it later to be sure."

She smiled up at him and nodded eagerly as if all three of us were now in on some conspiracy.

"I'd like to try some phenobarbital," said Christopher. "It would certainly do her some good in her present state and perhaps we could get some logical answers from her."

I was in agreement. I picked up the telephone, called the apothecary and asked them to bring over a vial of the sedative. It would not only calm her delusions but act as a truth serum so that we could question her regarding her connection to Holmes.

While we waited, Christopher described his evening to me. I was positively stunned to find out about how we had been deceived by the fraudulent police sergeant, how he had chased the Renault all the way to the edge of the Thames, his conversation with Wiggins and the death of Mrs. Smithwick. All these pieces had been added to our puzzle. How they fit together was still a mystery. Certainly, Christopher had accumulated a wealth of new information for his timeline.

While we conversed, Lilah sat in front of the fire, alternately humming, mumbling and suddenly stopping with her head cocked as if to listen to some high-pitched sound. At one point she thoughtfully turned around in her chair and asked, "Dr. Watson, will Mr. Holmes be here soon?"

"Yes, Lilah, Mr. Holmes will be here shortly," I answered reassuringly.

She sat back with a peaceful smile that seemed to come from deep in her soul. A moment later, she abruptly rose from her seat and we watched uneasily as she walked across the room, and, to our relief, entered the bathroom.

While she was in there, the boy from the apothecary arrived with the sedative. I gave him ten pence and sent him on his way. Christopher retrieved his doctor's bag and prepared the hypodermic needle. Suddenly, it occurred to us that Lilah had been in the bathroom for quite a long while, and now we could hear the water running.

I went to the bathroom door and knocked. "Lilah, are you all right?" I called. The sound of water splashing into the tub continued. Christopher came up behind me. Both of us were becoming concerned. I tried the door, but it was locked. I knocked more loudly. "Lilah, please open the door!"

The door obediently swung open and Lilah stood before us fully naked with her hands at her sides and a beatific smile on her face. "Is Mr. Holmes here yet?" she said hopefully.

I averted my eyes. "Will you please put something on, Miss Church," I asked her gently. She made no move to do so, which, in this case, made more sense than my request since her clothes were wet and filthy.

Christopher calmly went to his room, returned with an oriental silk robe I presumed belonged to one of his lady friends and put it on her. I turned the water off in the half-filled tub and we guided her back toward her seat by the hearth. As we walked her across the room, she craned her neck, eyes searching the apartment as if expecting Holmes to jump out at any moment.

Once reseated in front of the warm fire, her eyes continued to dart around the room. "We're going to give you a small injection, Lilah," said Christopher kindly. "It will make you feel better, and it will make you a little sleepy."

"The needle, yes. It makes him feel better," she said knowingly. She watched as Christopher pulled up the loose sleeve of her robe, put the needle into her arm and pushed the phenobarbital into the muscle. He withdrew the needle and gave her arm a good rub as she started to hum a vague tune that I recognized as that "Ragtime Band" song.

Presently, her eyelids began to droop, her body relaxed and her chin dropped down toward her chest. She was breathing deeply and comfortably.

"Are you feeling more relaxed now, Lilah?" I asked her.

She nodded groggily. "Yes. I'm feeling much better." Her voice had a rather different quality than when she was in her state of agitation. There was very little East End in it. It had a lovely, musical lilt to it and was actually a touch refined. She could have passed for a shop girl in Knightsbridge.

"Why did you come here today?" I asked her.

"To see Mr. Holmes," she said dreamily.

"And you think Mr. Holmes is here?"

A tear rolled down her cheek, and she didn't answer.

"Lilah, why is Mr. Holmes supporting you and Alexander?"

"Because he loves us." She smiled warmly and wiped away the tear.

"And did you know you are in his will?"

"I shan't speak of it," she said suddenly becoming quite defensive. It didn't seem to be a response to my question regarding the will, but rather a reference to something else bubbling up from her unconscious.

"You must have been very special to Mr. Holmes. Do you know that?"

"I must never speak of it," she said, as if repeating someone else's directive.

"Speak of what?" I asked innocently.

She looked up into my eyes. There was a fear in them, but this time it was not the irrational fear she had exhibited earlier. It was a deep, dreadful remorse.

"Shall we give her some more sedative?" asked Christopher. It sounded more like a suggestion than a question.

"No. This dose has yet to take full effect…Lilah, what would you like to tell me?" I asked soothingly.

She did not answer.

"Lilah, you know who I am, don't you?"

"Of course I know you, Doctor Watson."

"And you trust me, don't you?"

"Mr. Holmes said there is no man that deserves trust more," she said with great sincerity.

"You must tell me what's on your mind. It might be of some importance in finding the one who…" I stopped before finishing the sentence. I didn't want Lilah to lapse back into a state of agitation. Christopher watched patiently. "Would you please tell me about Alex's father, Hermes Hollocks?" I asked, trying a different approach.

She looked across the room. "That's Mr. Holmes's chair." She was looking at Holmes's velvet armchair, where he spent many an hour contemplating cases or some piece of evidence.

"Tell me about Mr. Hollocks," I asked again.

"Hollocks," she repeated hauntingly. "Mr. Hollocks." Lilah looked up at me and swallowed hard. "What of Mr. Hollocks? He's gone."

"Tell me about the first time you met him."

"The first time," she repeated and looked back over at the chair, her voice drifting off dreamily. The drug had taken its full effect, and I was concerned she was going to fall off to sleep before we were able to get anything useful out of her. Her mouth moved, but no words came out. She seemed on the verge of saying something. Christopher and I waited. Her eyes were far-off, as if reliving an event. And then the words came. "He asked if I still had my virginity, and I said I did. He said he wanted to observe…that part of me, so I let him observe… Looking led to touching…I got astride him as I would a horse…He rocked me slowly on his lap…There was pain but then there was pleasure mixed in with it. I could see from his face that he was enjoying it, so I didn't interrupt his pleasure. I had nothing to compare it to back then, but now I know it went on a long time. After that, whenever I would come up to the flat, he would have a bath ready and wash me with a sponge and sweet-smelling soaps and pour oil into the water. The other Irregulars started to notice, particularly Wiggins. You couldn't get much by Wiggins. I said I was doing work for a rich lady and she wanted me to be clean and smell right." She paused. Both Christopher and I remained silent. "He told me I was with child before I knew it. He said he saw from my breasts. He went near mad that day.

I'd never seen him like that. He was always so calm, but that day he was fretting. I told him I wouldn't tell anyone. I would take care of his baby. I was proud to have it." She stopped and looked up at us doe-eyed with no trace of shame or regret.

"Bloody hell, what fools we've been!" exploded Christopher. "It's right in front of us!" He pointed to the names on his timeline. "Hermes Hollocks is an anagram for Sherlock Holmes."

By God! I wish Holmes were here to refute all I've written! Nothing has been more painful than to tarnish the reputation of a man I loved and admired so deeply. Not the blasted bullet in my leg, not even the death of my beloved. But Holmes was just a man, and he had faults. And they were deeper and more secretive than I ever imagined. Whether he took the seventeen-year-old girl during one of his cocainized states or yielded to some base, carnal moment, there was no excusing it. There was no overlooking the selfishness of the act.

Christopher and I stared at each other, the sheer weight of the truth silencing us. Finally, he spoke. "Who do you think knows about this?"

I couldn't find my voice. I could process the question, but could form no answer.

Christopher looked down at Lilah. "Does Alexander know who his father is?"

She was deeply asleep.

"Let her rest," I managed to say.

Christopher nodded, gently picked her up, put her in his bed and quietly closed the door. "Doctor, are you all right?" he asked when he returned. I must have looked quite shaken.

"Just a bit unnerved by it all," I admitted.

"I assume you're convinced of the accuracy of Lilah's story," said Hudson delicately.

"Yes I am," I responded gloomily.

"As am I," he said tersely, as if making no particular moral judgment.

My thoughts were cloudy. "Wiggins knows, to be sure. Moriarty knows, also." I mumbled, answering the question I was unable to articulate an answer to minutes before. "Moriarty alluded to it that first time I visited. I just didn't understand what he was referring to."

Christopher returned to his timeline to update it with this new information. "Do you think it's possible either of them was blackmailing Holmes?" he said while scribbling notations and taping them on the wall.

"It's possible," I said distractedly. "I have a few personal things to attend to Christopher," I declared abruptly. The truth was, I could not bear to discuss the subject any further. I needed to collect my thoughts.

"Of course," said Christopher, leaving off his cutting and taping and looking at me thoughtfully. "Please take care of whatever you need to. I will see to Lilah." He understood what I was saying and, this time, perhaps even how I felt. I quickly gathered my things and left the flat.

• • •

When I reached Oxford Street, I attempted to focus my jumbled thoughts and to evaluate my feelings. From whence did my outrage arise? Did I feel betrayed and hurt for not being trusted with this information about Lilah? Did Holmes fear a lack of discretion, or rather did he fear what my judgment of him may have been? Perhaps that was the answer. Holmes would have considered any flaw, any chink in his armor, to be a fatal one. He would have found it intolerable to be exposed to the judgment of his peers in any unfavorable light.

Walking past, I glanced at the stuffed mannequins in the window of a shirtmaker and caught my own reflection. How could I have been so blind? Were there things I was not allowing myself to see? Was I so enamored with Holmes that I unconsciously ignored what was right in front of my face? Holmes was a mere mortal, something I had barely considered when he was alive. He made a mistake and tried to rectify it as well as he could. Hadn't he done properly by this young woman? He made a generous attempt to live as a family. This was an enormous sacrifice given Holmes's disposition. But now was I merely rationalizing his behavior in my mind?

I turned the corner onto Bond Street, and there was some sort of commotion going on in front of one of the art dealers' establishments. A dozen suffragettes with signs saying "Votes For Women" were being rounded up by the police and they seemed to be putting up some fierce resistance as onlookers gathered. One young woman in tweed pants and blazer and long, dark, flowing hair was sitting on the pavement with her arms and legs wrapped around a lamppost while a policeman was beating her with his nightstick in an effort to dislodge her. I rushed over to intervene and leaped between the young woman and the stick-wielding officer.

"Stop this at once!" I demanded.

"Stand aside, sir," the policeman said warningly with his stick raised. He was tall and bony with the brushy sort of moustache that police seem to favor nowadays. His face was red from exertion and he had a barely contained anger in his eyes.

"Why? So you that you may strike this woman again?"

"This is a matter of the law, sir."

"We're engaged in a peaceful demonstration for our rights," the woman cried. Some of her fellow suffragettes shrieked their agreement as they tussled with the policemen trying to subdue them.

"Step aside, sir, or I'll have to arrest you, too," he warned again as he raised his stick a little higher.

"If you wish to arrest me for defending this young woman's rights, then proceed. I will have your badge and give you a lesson on law in the bargain."

"What is your name, sir?" he boomed impatiently.

"John H. Watson. Close personal friend of Scotland Yard Commander Lestrade, with whom I'm meeting later this afternoon."

There was an immediate change of attitude as he lowered the stick. "Dr. Watson..." he stammered, "...these women threaten to vandalize public property."

"Well, until they do, you have no cause to arrest them for this assembly," I declared.

"A rug dealer on Wigmore Street said they broke his window," he countered.

"Then have the rug dealer go down to the station to make a formal charge." I kneeled down beside the young suffragette who was still hugging the lamppost. She was quite pretty with narrow features, perfectly arched dark eyebrows and full lips. "What is your name, child?"

"Lilian Lenton," she replied. She was no more than twenty-one years of age.

I looked up at the officer. "There. Now you know her name."

The officer grumbled something under his breath, turned to his fellows and waved them off. They unhanded the other two women they were detaining from the group and grousily withdrew to their paddy wagon.

"Thank you," she said as she unwrapped herself from the lamppost and massaged her upper arm.

"Did you break that window on Wigmore Street, Lilian?" I inquired.

"Change does not come easily, Mr. Walton," she said ardently.

"The name's Watson, and I'll take that as yes."

"We have to make them understand it is impossible to govern without consent of the governed. Who are the people, Mr. Watson? We are," she declared, answering her own question. Two of her associates came over, helped Lilian to her feet and handed her a sign.

I admired the spunk of these women and thought they were one hundred percent right in their purpose, but not in their tactics. Some, like these, were accused of vandalism and even worse, arson and bombings. "I see," I said noncommittally. "Well, take care of yourself, Lilian."

"That I will do, Mr. Watson," she answered fiercely.

I walked off down Bond Street. The police were gone. The suffragettes gathered their signs and resumed their march. As I turned on Brook Street, I heard behind me the crash of a window and heaved a regretful sigh.

31

CHRISTOPHER

I don't even remember when I fell asleep. I was working on my timeline. The pieces of the story were now fitting together. In the early stage of pregnancy, Holmes had moved Lilah to Sussex, and concocted the scenario regarding the pursuit of Moriarty and his staged death so that he could disappear and live with her and the child. Holmes was an expert with disguises as well as accents, so, as long as he kept his distance, people would not recognize him as anything but what he claimed to be—a French importer named Hermes Hollocks. But, after a year, Holmes must have grown restless. He left Lilah and his child and, in all probability, did, as he claimed, travel to the Far East, but his conscience made him feel responsible for the young woman and the child she bore. Whether all this had anything to do with Holmes's murder was not certain, but it clearly explained his support of Lilah and Alexander and her inclusion in the will.

I knew the doctor was taking this revelation hard. His notions of what is proper condemned him to a certain mindset, but Lilah had been seventeen, and by all standards of full marrying age. She clearly was willing as evidenced by her own words. Granted, the consequences of such unplanned romances are many illegitimate sons and daughter, and that is unfortunate, but Holmes did more than most in this situation. He might have denied it. I do not believe Lilah ever would have betrayed him. He certainly couldn't have been expected to act as husband to the woman and, yet, he did.

It was clear to me now that Moriarty knew about Lilah. He had the advantage of knowing that he himself certainly was not dead during Holmes's absence, and, therefore, there was a reason that Holmes had created the ruse. How and when he came to know, I may never find out, but his statement during our discussion of Nietzsche, that "Holmes's false morality was his downfall," echoed in my mind. "Downfall" was the word he used, and I don't think he meant it figuratively. He was connecting the situation with Lilah to Holmes's murder in some way.

It was possible that someone was blackmailing Holmes. This information would have been valuable currency for someone's use. But blackmail hardly leads to murder. It seems to me the last thing you want to do to your blackmail victim is murder him.

I was pondering all these pieces when I sat down on the couch and must have dozed off. Not surprising, as I had slept for only an hour the night before. I was awakened by an insistent pounding on my door. "Doctor Watson! Mr. Hudson!" came the urgent voice from the other side. It was somewhat familiar to me, but I was still a bit disoriented and couldn't identify it. I glanced at the clock on the mantel and saw that it was a quarter past noon. I had been napping for over three hours.

"Who is it?" I called through the door.

"It is Alexander Hollocks," returned the urgent voice. "My mother is missing!"

I opened the door to find Alexander looking disheveled and literally beaten. "She's not missing. She's here."

"Thank God! I was hoping!" he cried and rushed past me into the flat.

"She's sleeping right now," I said and closed the door. "It will do her some good. I suspect she spent the night walking around London."

I did not mention the fact that we had administered her phenobarbital or that she was in a delusional state when she arrived at the flat. "What happened to you?" I asked. Alexander had a rather large bump on the right side of his forehead, a raw, red bruise on his right cheek, and had lurched in with a noticeable limp.

"I fell down the stairs," he replied.

"That's unfortunate," I said trying to sound sympathetic. "Why don't you take a seat? Your mother is fine for the moment, and I'd like to have a chat."

He sat down on the couch, calmed himself and to my surprise proceeded to tell me everything, completely unsolicited. "My mother, as you have obviously observed, is not well. She believes many odd things, and has told me different versions of the facts of my birth and childhood. She has probably told you that I am the son of Sherlock Holmes. This is in all likelihood true, for Holmes himself believed it." Alexander said this without prejudice, as if it was not an absolute fact and he was willing to consider any evidence that might dispute it. "I'm sorry that when you came to the apartment the other day I was coy about this fact, but I was not aware whether this information had been disclosed to Dr. Watson, and I knew that when he found out the circumstances of my mother's relationship with Holmes it might be…" he searched for the right word, "…difficult for him."

I was stunned by his very forthright recitation of the facts. I was expecting to have to pry to the truth out of him. There was no mistaking the resemblance between Alexander and Holmes—the narrow features, piercing eyes and hawklike nose. "I have no question that you are Holmes's son, Alexander, and I thoroughly believe what your mother told us this morning."

"Which was?"

"That your mother was indeed pregnant by Holmes, and he took her to live in the cottage in Sussex." I saw no reason to go into every detail of the disclosure. "Would you be so kind as to tell me your recollections? It may be helpful in our search for your father's murderer." It was so strange to refer to Holmes as "your father."

Alexander's eyes wandered to the scraps of paper on the wall. "I see you are making a timeline."

I was alarmed by the sudden realization that all my information was in full view. "I'm sorry. I must ask you not to look at that. Some of those facts are considered privileged and confidential," I said firmly.

"Forgive me, Christopher. May I call you Christopher?"

"You may."

"I'd like to be quite candid with you," he said, looking down at his lap as if in shame. He looked back up at me as if waiting for my approval.

"Proceed," I said evenly.

"You see, I'm a bit useless. You would think with such an illustrious father I would be better equipped. Not so. I have no more talent than the average factory worker. I am good at nothing…Not even caring for my mother. You see, Christopher, I drink to excess, and last night, while Mother was asleep, I went out and got quite drunk. When I returned home late, I found that she was gone. I staggered out of the apartment and must have fallen down the stairs, because there on the landing is where my landlady found me. That is why you see me in the battered state I'm in. This isn't the first time I've hobbled myself in a drunken stupor." Again he looked down in shame. "I'm disgusted with myself." He put his hand over his face and shook as if crying.

"I think it's healthy that you make such an admission. And be comforted by the knowledge that many other drunks have found rehabilitation. Perhaps there's a chance for you to turn around your state of uselessness." For some reason I could not muster a bit of empathy for this character.

"You see, that's just it," he exclaimed reaching across and grabbing my hand in a sort of gesture of desperation. "Let me help you find my father's murderer. That would be my redemption."

I studied him for a moment. I had so many questions for him. They might not even bear on the case, but I was fascinated to know about relationship between him, Lilah and Holmes. "Perhaps the greatest benefit you could be right now is to tell me about your upbringing," I said gently pulling my hand away.

"All right," he said willingly. He sat back on the couch as if settling in for a lengthy account. One thing I had noticed about him in our limited time together was that he liked to hear himself talk. "I have no memory of him from when I was a small child," he commenced. "From the first I can remember, I was told that my father was Hermes Hollocks and that he was forced to move away to France when I was small, but that he loved us very much and would always take care of us. As I told you before, we lived in virtual isolation at the cottage. I knew no different, so I was perfectly happy. I had one friend from the village. He was the grocer's boy and his father would let him stay and play with me while he was doing his deliveries. We used to throw rocks off the cliff for hours."

"Did Holmes ever come to visit you?" I asked.

"Not that I can recall. If he had, my mother would not have identified him as my father."

"And the story about going to Brittany and looking for your father, Hermes Hollocks, was a lie?"

"Yes, actually during those five years we moved to Manchester. The school headmaster in Sussex showed up at the door one day and asked about me. After he left, Mother became very anxious. She took me up to London and we stayed in a hotel. I can't remember which one as I was only five, but it was the most exciting thing that had ever happened in my life. I had never been outside a two-mile radius of the cottage. She bought me a tin of cookies and a jigsaw puzzle of the British Isles and left me alone in the room while she undoubtedly went to visit Mr. Holmes. A week later we moved to a flat in Manchester, and Mother took a job designing linens for the Havelock Mills. During our lives in Sussex, Mother taught herself to be an excellent embroiderer. She drew inspiration from those botanical illustrations on the walls of our flat."

"Bauer brothers." I was familiar with such drawings as they are exquisitely accurate and remind me of the exactitude of da Vinci's anatomical drawings.

"Yes, very good. You're a student?" he asked surprised.

"I have seen them in books. I presume those are authentic?"

"I believe they are. They were in the cottage since I was born. I assume Holmes purchased them originally."

"Yes, fine. Continue."

He pulled out a package of cigarettes, offered me one and then lit up. "When the mill closed, we did move into a flat in Harrow. The rest of what I told you before is essentially true."

"When did you find out that Holmes was your father?"

"The first I heard of it was when I was seventeen. When my mother was injured in the union riot, Mr. Holmes arranged for her medical care. She told me when she was in the hospital. She thought she was dying and believed I should know. I didn't believe her at first. She had already had bouts of disordered thinking. I asked her about Hermes Hollocks and she told me there was no such person. Later she withdrew everything she had told me that day, saying that she was not in her right mind. It was all quite confusing."

"Surely, you must have seen the physical similarities between you and Holmes. Didn't that make you wonder?"

"If you were me, would you have believed Sherlock Holmes was your father?"

"I might have, yes," I said instantly.

"Then I suppose you'd have to be me to understand how I think and feel," he responded with an unhappy smile. "After I first heard it mentioned, I thought it very unlikely. My mother had already shown a tendency to be…erratic, and make unfounded claims. Sherlock Holmes touched the lives of many people. I believed she was merely just one of them."

"Then when did you come to believe he *was* actually your father?"

"When mother tried to kill herself. He rushed down to the hospital, and there I met him for the first time. We had a long talk, and he apologized for not being present in my life, but as he put it, 'Fatherhood was not for him.'" Alexander fell silent and looked into my eyes as if trying to gauge my reaction. I remained impassive. His account was plausible enough.

"And what was your relationship like in the last two years?" I continued to probe.

"We were on excellent terms," he said, smiling as if reminded of some pleasant occasion. "He has shown great concern for my mother and me. However, it was always understood that confidentiality was of the utmost importance."

"Of course. He was a very private individual." I don't know why I said this. Obviously it did not speak to the reason for the confidentiality, but I felt compelled to agree once in a while in order to seem sympathetic.

"I thought Dr. Watson did an excellent job with the eulogy, didn't you?" he said with great earnestness as he crushed out his cigarette.

"I agree. Clearly, no one was more qualified."

There was an awkward silence as we gazed at each other. He was so like Holmes in countenance but totally opposite in character, unctuous and self pitying. Watson was right—I had a natural antagonism toward Alexander. Did I dislike him because he was Holmes's actual flesh and blood? Was it as simple as that? Was I jealous? "I shall wake your mother," I said, breaking the silence and rising from my chair. "You should take her home and let her rest."

"Yes, yes," he said most gratefully and sprung to his feet.

As I approached the bedroom door I glanced over my shoulder and casually asked, "Did you drive here?"

"No. I don't drive," was his immediate response. "I came here by cab."

I quietly pushed open the bedroom door. Lilah was sleeping peacefully. He came up beside me and smiled with relief. "Thank you, Christopher. Mother and I can make it home on our own."

My mother came upstairs, got Lilah out of bed and dressed her in a pair of my fencing pants and a flannel shirt. Thankfully, Mother asked no questions, as I had no time for explanations. I'd lost a good part of the day already. There were several things I had intended to pursue, and I was scheduled to meet up with Doctor Watson at Scotland Yard to confer with Lestrade and Gregson later that afternoon.

• • •

Alexander departed with Lilah, who was still quite sleepy and leaning against her son as they descended the stairs. I washed up and changed clothes, carefully emptying my pocket of the evidence I had accumulated the night before. I was anxious to analyze the hairs and cigar ash I had found in the Renault. I suspected I already knew what the results would be, but I hadn't the time now. I put it on my worktable for later inspection.

I unlocked my motorbike, which I kept in the hall in front of my parents' door, and rode off toward the assessor's office on Lambeth Road, where a college friend of mine worked. I turned down Park Lane with the midday sun in my face. Weaving in and out of traffic, I tried to interpret the strands of Mrs. Smithwick's web. She had directed Watson and me to the building where her young Latin "companion" tried to murder us. She said she owned the building. I assumed that was true. She had been complicitous in the murder attempt or had been directed by someone to send us to the location. It is possible she did not know there was to be an attempt on our lives, but judging from her reaction when Watson and I showed up at her door, I believe she was aware what her mission had been. Daisy had confirmed that she had a prior relationship with the young Latin man, Sergio, and it was a good bet that the hairs I found in the Renault would match the one I found in Watson's apartment after the burglary. Unfortunately, without Sergio's body I would be unable to make a verified match. Christ, why hadn't I swept the area of the building for hair samples when I returned last night? Holmes would have thought to do it. I stopped at a traffic signal on Piccadilly. "It's the details," Holmes used to say. That's where the truth lies. The truth does not contradict itself. It leads to one indisputable conclusion. But in the category of contradictions, the hair from the Renault might have belonged to Sergio, but he surely wasn't driving the automobile last night as dead men make very poor drivers.

The light changed and I zagged into Green Park, a favorite route of mine because of the vast lawns, abundant trees and lack of traffic. I had spotted the Renault while at Wiggins's brothel, an unlikely coincidence. But still I couldn't imagine what motive Wiggins would have for killing Holmes. And why now?

I shot out of the park along Birdcage Walk, crossed Westminster Bridge and parked in front of the assessor's office on Lambeth Road.

My friend Colin was from a Scottish farming family. He had a broad, freckled face that years in the field had made almost brick red. He hoped to go into politics and had taken a job at the assessor's office as a first step. He had told me the job was viciously dull, and spent most of his time trading crop futures, which had financed his way through Oxford. Colin was as good as anyone I've ever known at keeping countless calculations in his head. All of us would check with him after exams as he could repeat back every question and equation. When he saw me, Colin broke into that big, friendly Scottish grin of his. "Wha' are you doin' 'ere. Ya coom ta take me ta lunch, aye?"

"Fish and chips on me if you do me a favor."

"It is legal?" he joked.

"Not strictly."

I had Colin look at the tax rolls for Beatrice Smithwick and found that she owned an astonishing twenty-two properties, including the three I had already visited. Many were due to be reassessed as they were undergoing improvements. There were building permits pending on many of them, and most interesting was the fact that attached to the files were directives to the building department to have the projects expedited per request of the office of Lord Andrew Fitzroy. In all, this elderly lady had purchased and commenced renovation on eighteen properties in the last year.

I took Colin to the corner stand and had one of the greasier pieces of cod to be found on this side of the Thames. I did not discuss with him the reason for my inquiries or my suspicions of malfeasance in the matter. My obvious conclusion was that someone else was using the old lady to buy these properties, and Fitzroy was exerting influence to push them through for renovations, but Colin didn't need to know these things, and he happily munched on a second helping of fish and chips as I bid him farewell with a list of properties in my pocket that I felt required investigation.

The first property was on Freemasons Road, not far from Wiggins's headquarters. It was a nicely renovated three-story brick building very much in the character of Wiggins's own. However, unlike Wiggins's "gentlemen's club," the front door was wide open and children were running in and out, laughing and playing on the stoop and the stairs.

I climbed the steps and entered the lobby. The mailbox showed sixteen different names on the various slots. There was a sense of gaiety inside the building. Sunlight poured in through the front windows. I could hear women's cheerful voices socializing with each other in the hallways of the apartments above. Three little girls were on the floor of the spotless lobby playing jacks. All seemed idyllic in this small oasis on the gritty East End street. The only thing shadowy here was the identity of the owner.

I proceeded to a second address on Waterloo Road. The building was an austere, gray granite with a Roman-pillar façade of the kind used in banks and government buildings, which I speculated the structure had been at one time. It was a rather imposing edifice and took up half the block. The street was not well traveled and a group of boys were playing marbles in the road. The goal of their game was to flip the marble into the grooves of a manhole cover that was in the center of the street. They were playing for pennies, as opposed to when I was a child and we would play for each other's marbles, the winner getting the pick of the loser's collection. I was a tolerably good player, but my neighbor Charles Dawkins could flip a cat's eye into a thimble at ten paces. His collection was quite impressive as he accumulated the top-grade marbles from all the neighborhood boys.

As I walked along the front of the building, I noticed that all the windows were draped from the inside, without a ray of light getting in or out. The front entrance had a gate of steel bars with a wide glass door behind it. Nothing could be seen through the glass. There was a buzzer beside the gate and I pushed on it. After a few more attempts and several minutes of waiting, it was apparent that no one was going to respond. The boys playing marbles had begun to eye me as if I was some kind of fool.

I ambled over to them in my most unthreatening way. "Hello, lads. Could one of you tell me what goes on in that building?"

One youngster with the largest pile of pennies and best collection of marbles sneered up at me. "If you don't know, then maybe you shouldn't know." The boy, who was about eleven years old, had a manner reminiscent of Wiggins in his youth. He took the stub of a cigarette from behind his ear and put it in the corner of his mouth as if making a show of ignoring me and resumed the game of marbles.

"Half a crown to the one who tells me what goes on in that building," I declared, regaining their attention.

One boy with a wool cap and smudged face squinted up at me. "Bet he's a copper."

"I'm not a cop," I assured them.

"Doesn't matter. Creed pays off the cops anyway," blurted a chubby one proudly.

"Shut up, Snail!" snapped the leader. He motioned to the others and the five boys left off their game and huddled by a post box. When they returned, their leader spoke for the group. "We'll tell you, but we need a pound."

I produced a pound note from my wallet and held it up for all to see. "Give it here," said the leader assertively. I scowled down at him. There was only so much of his impudence that I was willing to take. Reading my expression, he surrendered the information. "It's for tarts and bets," he said.

"You mean they use it for a gambling house and brothel?" I asked.

"Brawful?!" exclaimed Snail, apparently unfamiliar with the term "brothel."

They all peered up at me like I was an idiot. "Do ya know wha' a whorehouse is, mister?" said the leader, as if speaking to a simpleton.

"Yes, I do."

"So when the lucky ones is done winning downstairs, they go upstairs to the girls."

"I see." I handed the leader the one-pound note. "Another pound to the one who can tell me of a different 'whorehouse' within a mile of here."

"You don't need another whorehouse," said Snail. "This is the best one around."

The boy in the woolen cap chimed in, "Snail should know. His mum works there."

"Does not!" protested Snail and pushed the other boy as they all had a good laugh at his expense.

"Does anyone have an answer? I must be going."

"Coin Street. Long white building with the doors all in rows," volunteered the leader.

"How many blocks from the river?" I asked.

"Four," he answered with authority.

I handed him the pound note. Snail immediately piped up, "Hey, we get part of that, too, Wyatt!"

"Shut your mouth," responded the leader, and they quickly gathered up their marbles and headed off down the street squabbling about their proper share of the earnings.

One of the addresses on my list that I had yet to visit was indeed 400 Coin Street. I climbed on my motorbike to take a pass by. It turned out to be a long, white-plaster set of typical row houses, with two rooms downstairs and two rooms up. I stopped and straddled my motorbike as an older man in a top hat and long coat exited one of the front doors. He kept his eyes averted as he hurried off down the street.

I decided I had done enough investigation of Mrs. Smithwick's properties. Whoever was her heir would inherit interest in several very upscale whorehouses, at least two gambling parlors and some nicely renovated residential buildings. How she had the time and why she had the inclination to accumulate all this property in the prior year, and also be complicitous in the attempted murder of Watson and myself, was still a mystery. Lord Fitzroy was helping her procure permits and Fitzroy was advocating for Moriarty. This Sergio character was involved with Mrs. Smithwick and now both were dead. All of them were acquainted with Wiggins and the mention of Creed's name by the boy called Snail confirmed the fact that Wiggins was either managing the operations at these properties or was the party for whom Smithwick was fronting. Some or none of this might have anything to do with Holmes's death. There were many strands to follow. I determined to follow the one that led me to the home of Lord Andrew Fitzroy.

• • •

Fitzroy lived in one of those gaudy, dynastic mansions along the Thames. I was halted at the gate by his oversized chauffeur, who had a pronounced Irish accent and a thick, waxed moustache. I announced myself, and he told me to wait at the closed gate while he passed the word on to Fitzroy's aged butler. The chauffeur returned and smugly told me that Lord Fitzroy could not see me presently. I said, "Please tell him that I'm here by request of our mutual friend on Butchers Road." The chauffeur eyed me impatiently and then went back to the house to relay my message. I suspected that conjuring Wiggins's influence might get me over this barrier, and I was correct as the chauffeur returned and grudgingly opened the gate. I courteously thanked him for his assistance and proceeded to the house where the aged butler, whose name I learned was Phelps, led me into an extremely formal living room with the traditional portraits of aristocratic ancestors covering every inch of the walls. Such paintings in such houses made me bristle, as I had become increasingly uncomfortable with the notion of aristocracy. As a youth, I was taught to accept the fact that there was a privileged class descended from wealthy landowners and friends of the king upon whom privilege and benefits were heaped by virtue of class distinction. Upon growing up, I had become more and more resentful that these elitists had long since abandoned any sense of noblesse oblige and took their entitlement as divinely ordained and absent of any obligation or responsibility. Mostly, it seemed to me they used their positions to further aggrandize themselves and attempt to drive progress off the road and into a ditch to forestall the inevitable day when they would be seen as what they are—relics of a medieval past, a vain and heartless hierarchy created to manage an ignorant population of people who were pronounced unable to reason for themselves or provide for their own welfare. I have to admit that the communist ideology had some limited appeal for me, but primarily I was devoted to progress, both social and scientific, and in my mind this ancient notion of a ruling class was diametrically opposed to both.

I waited in this chamber of pomposity with growing resentment as the centuries of Fitzroys stared down at me with their regal poses. Finally, after twenty minutes, Lord Fitzroy deigned to enter.

"Mr. Hudson," he said extending a hand. "How can I help you?"

"Lord Fitzroy, so glad to meet you," I said, shaking his hand. "Thank you for giving me your time."

"Yes, well, what is it that you need?" he asked, already beginning to get impatient.

"Do you know Beatrice Smithwick?"

"No. I do not."

"At her home I saw a picture of you and her at a groundbreaking."

"I go to many ceremonies and meet many people. To be quite candid with you it's hard to remember everyone I meet at those events. Many are quite pro forma," he said, making his best efforts to remain affable.

"I see. But your relationship with Mrs. Smithwick is such that your office has expedited over a dozen projects for her in the last year." I decided to press a little harder and see what his reaction might be.

"Well it's possible she knows someone in my office and that person is trying to help with some worthy projects that this Mrs. Smithwick is pursuing," he answered, tossing off the implications of my question.

"Some of these worthy projects are whorehouses." I intended there to be no mistaking the implications of that statement. After the last couple of days, I was feeling irritable and was in no mood to fence about with this fat aristocrat.

"What are you implying Mr. Hudson?" he asked with a dangerous glare.

"Do you know a man named Sergio, a 'gentleman friend' of Mrs. Smithwick?"

"As I told you, I don't know either of these people, and I'm growing impatient with this conversation."

"They are both dead, Lord Fitzroy." I could see from his eyes that this was new information to him, but he immediately hid his surprise.

"Are you threatening me, Mr. Hudson?"

"Not at all. I'm merely informing you that as of yesterday those two people are dead, and I am not displeased about that as they attempted to murder Doctor Watson and me."

Lord Fitzroy stared past me for a moment as he absorbed this information then regained his regal composure. "Would you excuse me for a moment?" he asked and didn't wait for an answer.

"I would rather not," I said tightly as he quickly left the room.

I strolled over to his liquor collection and toyed with the idea of pouring myself one of his eighteen-year-old whiskies when I heard a woman's voice from behind. "I like the way you stand up to him."

It was the diminutive Lady Fitzroy entering through the French doors that led to the garden. She was wearing narrow tweed slacks and a matching blazer. Her dark hair was short and parted at the side. "Pour me some of whatever you decide on," she said as she approached. I poured a glass of whisky and handed it to her as she stood suggestively close to me and took a sip.

"This may seem like an impertinent question," I said, "but how well do you know your husband?"

"Too well." She slithered around behind me and slipped her hand into the pocket of my trousers. "Lord Fitzroy and I have an understanding. I'm a modern woman. You seem like a modern man," she said, fishing around with her hand.

"Are you searching for a handkerchief? I keep it in my breast pocket." I produced my white handkerchief and waved it at her.

She put her chin against my back and whispered, "I have a friend. She could join us."

I pulled her hand out of my pocket and turned around to face her. "That's a generous offer, but…"

"I hope you don't think I'm too old," she said, acting wounded. "I'm only thirty-two. That's not much of an age difference."

"I will take all factors into consideration," I said, trying to sound open-minded.

She smiled and swallowed the rest of her Scotch. "Lord Fitzroy wouldn't murder anyone."

"Did someone suggest he was a murderer?" I probed.

"I know who you are, and I know you're investigating the murder of Sherlock Holmes."

Now I was interested. "So why are you sure he wouldn't murder anyone?"

"Because he's a coward," Lady Fitzroy said with perfect confidence. With that, she turned and wandered back into the garden.

I sat down on the couch with my Scotch and waited for Fitzroy to return. After another five minutes he did so, accompanied by his bulky Irish chauffeur.

"I'm 'air ta esskoort ya out," he said, with his heavy Irish accent.

"I'll leave after a few more questions," I said calmly.

"Do you know who you are talking to, boy?" fumed Fitzroy, finally showing his temper. "I had lunch with the king last week."

"Does the king know you bugger twelve-year-old boys?" I didn't appreciate his attitude, and I was determined to indicate that to him.

Livid, Fitzroy motioned to his chauffeur to take care of me.

"If you move toward me, you will regret it," I cautioned the brawny chauffeur. But the Irishman took no heed and stepped forward with fists raised. This is a common mistake nowadays. The ill-informed belief that fights are won from the waist up remains prevalent among a class of boxing ring and barroom brawlers. The notion that I would engage this oaf in some sort of bare-knuckle battle was absurd. He swung and I ducked, and, as I spun away, I stomped down hard on the inside of his bent left knee. There was an audible snap, and he dropped to the floor in excruciating pain.

"That will require hospitalization," I informed him as I looked down. "I have just damaged your medial collateral ligament, however, luckily for you, a friend of mine is a surgical resident at Westminster Hospital doing research on just such injuries." He continued to writhe on the floor.

"What is it you came here for, Mr. Hudson?" demanded Fitzroy imperiously.

"I want to know why you advocate for Moriarty. Is he blackmailing you as well?"

"I am not advocating for him. I am advocating for justice," he proclaimed.

"Please, Lord Fitzroy, can we get past this horseshit? I am sick of listening to your protestation." I stepped right up to his face with an expression that communicated how deeply serious my intentions were. "The man I most admired was murdered and then somebody tried to murder me, and I will spare nothing to get to the bottom of it. If you have something to do with it, I will see you hanged."

This finally seemed to penetrate his lordly pretensions. "I knew and respected Sherlock Holmes and can assure you and Doctor Watson that I had nothing to do with his death." He was quite convincing. "And if you continue to make slanderous and reckless statements about me I shall be forced to sue you."

He turned and stormed out of the room, and I determined that the best course was to leave it at that for the moment. Phelps, the butler, entered accompanied by the cook and the gardener for support and held out a hand tentatively. "May I see you out," he said with a quiver in his voice.

I glanced down at the chauffeur who was still on the floor clutching his knee and gritting his teeth. "My friend's name is Doctor Linus Newell," I told him and then found my own way out.

• • •

As the gardener opened the front gate for me, I gave a little wave to Lady Fitzroy, who was sitting in the garden smoking a cigarette. She merely stared and continued to smoke.

I was just about to unlock my motorbike when a Rolls-Royce Silver Ghost limousine with closed curtains rumbled up to the curb. Wiggins's lieutenant, Creed, emerged from the back and motioned for me to get in. Sir Patrick was sitting stoically behind the wheel looking straight ahead as the car idled ominously. Clearly I was displaying some reluctance regarding getting into that foreboding backseat when Wiggins poked his head out the door.

"Get in, Christopher. We'll take care of your motorbike." His head disappeared back inside the car as Creed, without waiting for a response, hoisted my bike onto the roof rack of the limo and motioned once again for me to get in. This time I complied.

The spacious automobile was upholstered with thick gray velvet and smelled of leather and tobacco. I sat down on the rolled velvet couch facing Wiggins with my back to Sir Patrick. On one side of Wiggins sat his impassive "nurse." On the other, Creed seated himself and closed the door. Wiggins was wearing a purple velvet jacket with fur collar and a black derby hat. He had his Jesse James revolver tucked in his belt. The car instantly rumbled off, and Wiggins leaned forward with that inscrutable grin of his. "Now, Christopher," he said soothingly. "I know you are keen to find Mr. 'olmes's murderer. Clearly, you are becoming quite an excellent detective, and, if you should choose, perhaps an heir to Mr. 'olmes 'imself. But you are barking up the wrong tree 'ere, gent."

"Is that what Fitzroy left the room to do? Call you?" I asked, trying to sound as nonconfrontational as possible. I was not interested in drawing Wiggins's ire.

Unfortunately, my strategy didn't seem to work as Wiggins gave me a cross look and called to Sir Patrick. "Patrick, takes us to Narrow Street, eh."

"Narrow Street?" I thought to myself. That's by the river in Bethnal Green, the area where I suspected Holmes was murdered.

Wiggins settled back in his seat and folded his hands across his lap as if commencing a lesson. "Lemme explain some things to you, Christopher...I'm a person 'oo 'as to straddle two worlds, and I've always done so. That has been my fate. It was determined the day me mum's boyfriend beat me so bloody that I left home and took to the streets, and mind you, my story is no 'arsher than many what runs with me. But mine 'as a happier ending than most." He held up his index finger for emphasis. "I made myself a success, and, on the way, I've learned that there are things tha' 'appen in life that are unavoidable and unforeseeable. Even I cannot conduct all the strings, try as I might. Sometimes there's no satisfaction. You must get used to this, Christopher. You will find that life is a series of complications."

"Fitzroy, Smithwick, this Sergio fellow, who tried to murder Watson and me. All these things are interconnected, and I would like to know in what way."

He leaned forward again. "'Ave I not been kind to you? 'Ave I not been extra gentle? You're very brave. I get that. I'm brave myself. But you can be too brave." Wiggins glanced at his nurse, and she immediately withdrew the velvet pouch from her satchel lying on the floor of the limousine. She prepared the injection as Wiggins continued. "You must understand that if I get arrested...get pinched for something serious, they'll make a right sanctimonious hue and cry for justice. There's plenty that would just as soon see me disappear. But I ain't goin' nowhere, right, Creed?" He gave Creed a jocular elbow. Creed smiled joylessly. He was a individual absolutely incapable of mirth. "Now suppose you was to run 'round askin' questions about Spanish gentlemen who may or may not be in my acquaintance," continued Wiggins. "In that case someone who gave you that information might get into trouble."

Wiggins saw the concern register on my face. That "someone" he was referring to was Daisy.

"You see, one thing that I demand of my people is loyalty. They must be trustworthy o' else trouble follows. I'm very 'ard on those that I believe cannot be trusted." He stared at me silently. I felt myself turning pale imagining what might have become of the woman who had entrusted me to protect her as my source of information.

Wiggins noted my distress. "Don't you worry young Master 'udson, I would not 'urt Daisy any more than I would 'urt one of me own children. Ordinarily, she would never break such a strict rule, but she has a soft spot in 'er heart for you. I wager, 'owever, that she will not make the same mistake again."

The nurse pinned Wiggins's forearm to her lap, found a useable vein and injected him. He took a deep, relaxed breath and rolled down his sleeve. "Now, I believe it is adequate to accept that this unfortunate Spanish chap is dead, so let that be an end to it."

"I can't, Wiggins. I have to know the answers." I knew this wasn't the response that Wiggins wanted, but it was the only one I was willing to give him.

He looked up at the roof of the limousine and closed his eyes in exasperation. "Might we talk about somethin' else? You're a sports fan, are you not? Who do you think will be the champs this year? Bolton or Newcastle?"

"I think it will be Blackburn," I answered.

"Crompton is good, I grant you that, but my money's on Newcastle." The limousine rolled to a stop. "Get out, Christopher," he commanded.

I twisted around and looked through the windshield to see where we were. Dusk was settling and we were parked in a poor and desolate part of Narrow Street no more than a fifty-yard dash from the Thames. Wiggins stared at me with his arms crossed. "What d'ya think? I'm goin' ta tie rocks to your ankles and throw you in the river? Get the fuck out. I want to show you something."

Sir Patrick had already exited the car and opened the back door for me. I climbed out to find we had stopped in front of a newly constructed four-story brick building with granite-framed windows each with its own flower box. There was a fenced park next to the handsome structure that took up half the block, and children cavorted on the swings and in the sandboxes, their chatter drifting toward us like happy music.

"Welcome to Narrow Gardens, Christopher," gloated Wiggins as he climbed out of the limousine with Creed at his side. At the sight of Wiggins, children started rushing forward from the building, from the park, from the hopscotch games on the sidewalk. All flooded toward him declaring, "He's here!" "It's Wiggins!" "Hello, Mr. Wiggins." They tugged at his pant legs and the hem of his coat, yammering and clambering.

"All right, children…All right." He beamed down at them, reaching into his coat pockets and pulling out fistfuls of paper-wrapped taffies and showering them down on the youngsters, who dove and squealed, gathering up all the candy.

"You see, Christopher," he said turning to me. "I'm a bit of a Robin Hood." We walked up the steps into a pristine, marble-lined lobby with an elevator and mail compartments for twenty-four families. We took the stairs with Creed and Sir Patrick trailing close behind us. Wiggins's silent nurse stayed behind in the limousine.

On the second floor a group of women had clearly heard of Wiggins's arrival and they were waiting in the hall like a welcoming committee. Some were holding babies, others had toddlers hanging from their aprons. "Hello, Mr. Wiggins," they greeted him like an adoring chorus.

"'Ello, ladies," answered Wiggins with a tip of his hat.

One woman ran into her apartment and returned with a mincemeat pie and humbly offered it up to him. "I made this for you special, Mr. Wiggins."

"That's my favorite, Mrs. Douglas. You will make me fat with that," he joked, shaking a finger at her and handing the pie to Sir Patrick.

We walked to the next set of stairs. "You see these people," said Wiggins as we ascended to the next floor. "'Omeless they were. Sacked by the factories, beat by their fathers and husbands, abandoned by this proper English society."

"I gather you own this building," I said as we reached the third level.

"Not officially, as you might 'ave learned from your research at the assessor's office." Wiggins was remarkable. He seemed to have eyes everywhere. "I 'ave people like Mrs. Smithwick assume title of the property for me. Makes it easier to get permits and such."

"Especially for the gambling parlors and brothels," I observed.

"There's plenty of business outside the East End. A businessman always has to look to expansion," he shrugged as if that statement was self-evident and the morality of the enterprise of no significance. "Sometimes the neighbors get a little touchy with the likes of me opening up one of my establishments in their area."

"And I assume that's where Lord Fitzroy comes in."

"It's useful to 'ave friends in 'igh places. It's funny, you know. It's the women who give us resistance with construction. They've been gettin' very active with their suffrage and all that. To my way o' thinkin', the prime minister should put a woman in his cabinet, so someone could reason with those suffragettes." He sighed. "All things in good time, I suppose." We reached the third floor and the residents were lined up outside their doors to enthusiastically greet him.

"Welcome, Mr. Wiggins. So good to see you," smiled a woman holding an infant in her arms.

"Always a pleasure to see you, Mrs. Greeley." He kissed the baby's forehead and gave Mrs. Greeley's bottom a squeeze as we moved on. "Very sweet lady," he said glancing over at me.

We climbed to the top floor. It reminded me very much of the floor that Mrs. Smithwick directed us to when Sergio attempted to murder us. It had the same deep-red carpeting and elegant sconces on the wall. It also appeared to be deserted. This penthouse was clearly off-limits for the other residents of the building. Sir Patrick bounded past us and unlocked a door marked only with a "W."

The inside of the flat struck me more as the headquarters of a company than a residence. Two banks of windows looked south across the Thames to Surrey Quays and West as far as Buckingham Palace. The floor was richly carpeted and the walls paneled. There was a mahogany conference table, a dozen leather chairs and an easel with a large map of the city and pins indicating the location of various properties.

Wiggins walked me to the window. The light was fading over the city. "This town is changin', Christopher," he said as he motioned to the view. "It used to be all about what last name you was born with. Very soon it'll be all about success. That'll be the standard. What you've accomplished not what some ancient ancestor accomplished." Wiggins guided me over to the west-facing window with a brass telescope on a stand. The sightline extended beyond Tower Bridge, the dome of St. Paul's Cathedral, all the way to the Palace. "From 'ere I can see twenty-seven of my properties. Over 'alf are outside the East End." He nodded contentedly, pulled out a cigar and lit it. Creed and Sir Patrick watched silently from the other side of the room. "Some of my buildings," said Wiggins with a sweep of his arm, "are like this one. Others are places of business. One feeds the other. That's 'ow business works." He put his arm around my shoulder. "Yes, I had Mrs. Smithwick purchase property in 'er name for my benefit. And yes I 'ave Lord Fitzroy and others use their influence on my be'alf occasionally…Again, that's business. Now I tell you these things because I want you to understand the interconnections. I am trying to be as open as I can. But I caution you, young Mr. 'udson…stay out o' my business. Mr. 'olmes was not killed because of any real estate deal. I can guarantee you that."

"And what about Freddy Carson? Why was he killed?" I asked.

"What is the life of one fat prison guard?" replied Wiggins. The dusk light was rapidly fading and Wiggins's face was half shadowed. A cloud of smoke drifted from his mouth toward the ceiling. "You 'ave a bright future, and you will learn that over the course of time that you will 'ave to overlook some questionable and perhaps even distasteful situations. This is the great irony of life. The Jekyll and 'yde of it all. A man can't be judged by a few acts of kindness nor can he be judged by his mistakes. The measure of a man is the sum of his deeds."

"That's an admirable philosophy, Wiggins. But I need to deal in facts. What do you know of the black Renault that I chased from outside your Butchers Road building last night?" I asked, emboldened for reasons I couldn't even explain.

Wiggins glanced at his two men across the room. I could see from the slight glimmer on Creed's face that they knew what I was talking about. Wiggins looked back at me without a trace of the jovial tolerance he had displayed up until now. "I will tell you somethin', Christopher. Professor Moriarty 'as placed 'is hand of protection upon you as 'ave I, and none who fear us will harm you. I will say no more on this matter. You must let this go." He turned and strode out the apartment. Creed quickly joined him and Sir Patrick stared at me, waiting for me to follow.

"After you, sir," he said with his perfect diction.

I took a last gaze at the darkened view of the venerable city of five million souls and then let him escort me out.

● ● ●

On the way to Baker Street, Wiggins received another injection from his nurse and dozed off. Both she and Creed sat silently, staring straight ahead. I wondered if the nurse was able to speak. I never heard her utter a word. I knew Creed preferred not to speak aloud. It struck me that they were quite good companions for Wiggins, who liked to speak excessively.

The limousine pulled smoothly up in front of 221 Baker Street. Wiggins was slouched over, snoring. Creed got out and retrieved my motorbike from the roof rack. I thanked him and watched the taillights of the Silver Ghost recede into the darkness. Due to the unexpected intervention of Wiggins, I had missed my appointment at Scotland Yard with Watson, Lestrade and Gregson. I trusted that Watson would fill me in later. I rolled the bike into the hallway, parked in front of my parents' flat and went upstairs to analyze the evidence I had collected over the past few days.

When I got to my apartment, I saw that my mother had tidied up and changed the linens. I sat down in Holmes's trusty armchair and contemplated my list of things to do. Mother, clearly having heard me come in, brought me up a rather early dinner of leg of lamb and roasted potatoes. I was glad to have it since I ate very little of the greasy fish and chips that my friend Colin had feasted upon at lunch.

I finished my meal in minutes and retrieved the cigar that Wiggins had given me several nights before and lit it in order to compare the ash to that which I had found in the backseat of the Renault. The cigar was the same rare type that I observed Moriarty smoking in his cell, and I was fairly confident of what the results of the comparison would be.

32

WATSON

Christopher seemed to have taken the information in stride, but I was still occupied with thoughts of Lilah as I unlocked my refurbished front door. I suppose that was one of the advantages of youth and a more progressive way of viewing these things. I decided to sit at my desk and take notes on everything that had transpired since the moment I had heard of Holmes's death. Essentially this would be an expanded version of Christopher's timeline but using my own personal point of view. This was the process I employed when writing about the cases that Holmes and I had pursued. I would record copious notes and later piece together my accounts with the benefit of those notes and the informed perspective of hindsight. I found the note-taking to be most beneficial in focusing my mind in the midst of a case and was hoping I would find it additionally therapeutic in this particular situation.

Holmes always accused me of romanticizing our experiences in my accounts. I disagreed with him vehemently. He regarded the world in black and white, pertinent or not pertinent, accurate or inaccurate, and I, on the other hand, through the process of my writing, revealed to myself a world full of nuance. I suppose this is where Holmes and I most differed in our view of the world, and why he claimed I romanticized it through my retellings. I have always firmly believed that the facts don't tell the whole story, only the solution. Sherlock Holmes, for his part, sought only the solution.

I wrote from late morning to early afternoon with nary an upward glance. I recorded every event, every word I could recall. I could have kept on into the late hours of the night if it wasn't for an appointment I had set up with Holmes's solicitor to go over some paperwork for the estate.

I was due at Pearson's at three o'clock and arrived a half hour late. Such was the trance of writing I found myself in for those several hours. The solicitor was waiting for me, and I was escorted into his office by the tortoise-like secretary, Dora. There were documents to sign and papers to go over.

"By the way, I have located Lilah Church," I informed the solicitor.

"Yes, I know. She was here not more than a few hours ago," he responded as he passed me another document for signature.

"Was she!" I said in astonishment.

"Her son came in at first and wanted to see the will. I told him that, as he was not named in it, I would not read it to him, but, if his mother were present and consented, I would have no problem. He returned with his mother in less than an hour." Pearson told me all this matter-of-factly which assured me that they hadn't revealed the true nature of the relationship. "Is there a problem?" he asked seeing my perplexed expression. "The will shall become a matter of public record in a few weeks anyway."

"No, you're absolutely right. Not a problem," I said distractedly. I found it disconcerting that Alexander should not take my word for his absence from Holmes's will, but then again, he was in all likelihood Holmes's actual son, and therefore things could get complicated if he chose to assert a claim. This was not something I intended to disclose to Pearson at that time, but I was anxious to make sure we were getting all our parties straight. "What did Lilah Church look like?" I asked Pearson.

He looked up from a document, as the tone of my question appeared to raise his level of concern. "She was quite pretty, actually. Dark ringlets of hair. A touch heavy with the makeup for my tastes. She seemed a bit tired. They gave me an address on Averill Street."

"Yes, that all sounds correct," I reassured him. I supposed that Christopher must have taken Lilah home sometime during the day and, in all probability, had a conversation with Alexander. I was anxious to hear what the content of that discussion had been.

"Good," said Pearson, as if putting the Lilah Church matter to rest.

"I should like to make the distribution to Miss Church immediately," I declared.

Pearson looked up again as if mystified by my doggedness on affairs regarding Delilah Church. "That can be arranged," he said warily. My purpose was to keep Alexander and Lilah satisfied until I determined how to deal with them. My sense at the time was that both understood the obvious desire for discretion, and I was sure Christopher communicated that to them.

After Pearson directed me to sign a few more documents, I still had time to walk the mile plus to Victoria Embankment to have our scheduled meeting at Scotland Yard. As I approached the building it occurred to me that Holmes and I had visited it innumerable times, but I couldn't remember a single occasion of going there on my own.

When I was led into the commander's office, Lestrade and Gregson were waiting for me. Lestrade had a very unpretentious manner of occupying the most important room in the building. I believe this endeared him to his underlings. Gregson was the only one that seemed frequently annoyed by Lestrade's often plodding and warm manner.

We chatted for fifteen minutes while waiting for Christopher to arrive, with Gregson hardly participating. Small talk was never Gregson's strong suit. I'm not sure I ever heard him express any interest outside the job. He mentioned a motion picture now and then, but hadn't gone to the theater since Gilbert and Sullivan retired. As Lestrade and I were discussing the imminent opening of the London Museum, which would be devoted to the history of the city, Gregson interrupted, "Shall we get started? Mr. Hudson can catch up if he manages to arrive."

"Yes, certainly," I said. "I'm not sure what has detained him, but I'm confident he will arrive soon."

"I hope he hasn't had any trouble," said Lestrade with a hint of concern.

"I've found that the lad can take care of himself," I assured him.

Gregson opened up the file that had been waiting on his lap. "We have analyzed the fingerprints from the Renault," he began. "They are from three different parties. One belongs to the owner, whose prints we took when he came down to claim the vehicle. The second belonged to a Sergio de la Iglesia. He's a Spanish citizen who has a record of car theft and petty crimes."

"That is the man who tried to murder us," I informed them.

"That was a big step up for a fellow like that," said Lestrade and knitted his brow.

"He had few known associates, but one told us that he boasted that he was working for Wiggins." Gregson looked up for a reaction. Both Lestrade and I remained silent. "The third print we could not identify, however it matched the print taken from your flat after the burglary, Doctor."

"Not this de la Iglesia fellow?" I was extremely surprised. Both Christopher and I had concluded that the Spaniard had been the burglar. "Then you say it was a conspiracy."

Gregson passed no judgment on that opinion, but continued evenly, "An examination of the Renault suggests that Hudson's theory might be plausible that Holmes was run over. We have definitively matched the car to the tracks left at the granary where Holmes was found. Time of death was put at somewhere between two and three in the morning. We've found no eyewitness to either the murder or the disposal of the body. We questioned people we know are likely to have been on the streets of the East End at that time of the night since Mr. Hudson suggested that is where the murder took place. No one saw or heard anything." Gregson closed the file. "All in all we are not much closer to solving this. It's possible that it was an accident, someone panicked and disposed of the body out there in Kent."

"You don't believe that, do you?" I asked pointedly.

"Not really, but I have absolutely no motive. This Spaniard tried to kill you and that is evidence enough that there was foul play, and he might well be the culprit and you two were threatening to discover it, but now there's no body and frankly all we have to go on is your word, trustworthy as it is."

"Yes. *Corpus delicti*," Lestrade chimed in. "In this case we know a crime was committed, but we have no evidence of the perpetrator."

"And the unknown fingerprint? I'm sure you have Wiggins's prints," I asked.

"It doesn't belong to Wiggins," Gregson said with certainty.

I was unsure whether to impart our newly discovered information about Lilah with Lestrade and Gregson. I had not yet resolved whether

I intended to keep it secret or not. There were others who shared the secret of Holmes's relationship with her, so it may not have been solely mine to keep, but it didn't seem that it was relevant information to be shared at the moment. "And what of the driver of the Renault last night?"

"Yes, I thought about that," Gregson said. "Suppose it was this de la Iglesia character who killed Holmes for whatever reason. You and Hudson are a threat to him and he tries to kill you. Now, after he's dead, his conspirator or conspirators attempt to get rid of the car, but by chance Christopher sees them and the chase is on."

"And who killed de la Iglesia?" I asked.

"I haven't a clue," said Gregson grimly. The three of us stared in frustration.

We concluded the meeting by resolving to meet again in two days' time. That would give Scotland Yard a chance do an investigation of a flat they had located in Whitechapel that they believed to belong to this Sergio de la Iglesia character and to question and round up any known associates.

• • •

I caught a taxi in order to be on time for the confidential dinner that Mrs. Hudson had requested of me. I had the cab drop me off a block away so that Christopher would not be alerted to my arrival. I felt a little uncomfortable about this clandestine affair, but, after all, we were talking about Christopher's mother, so I knew she had her reasons.

As I stealthily approached, Mrs. Hudson opened the front door of Baker Street and ushered me into her flat. I was heartened to see Christopher's motorbike parked in the downstairs hallway for it had crept into my thinking that he might have met with some more foul play, since I was sure he would have made every effort to keep his appointment with Lestrade and Gregson.

The aroma inside the Hudsons' flat was sumptuous. She had prepared my favorite, leg of lamb, and the table was set and waiting. "Thank you for coming, Doctor Watson," she said in a hushed tone though I could tell her from experience that there was no way for voices to be heard from inside her flat all the way up to Baker Street B. "Would you like a glass of wine? Dinner is ready to be served."

"If we're ready to eat, I would welcome a glass of wine with dinner." I walked into the dining room just as Captain Hudson entered from the kitchen with a bottle of Burgundy and a corkscrew. Captain Daniel Hudson was a tall, blond, Nordic man. He was tailor-made to be in command of a ship. His bearing inspired confidence. There was no arrogance. He merely exuded a sense of the utmost competence. The Captain spoke little of his work and even less of his early life. I know he had been in the navy and, like many of us from that era, preferred not to recount his history of service. He was stingy with his words but not his smile. He was a good listener and often would sit enrapt by Holmes and me over a brandy as we told him the tale of one our latest cases.

"Good evening, Doctor," said Captain Hudson as he pulled the cork and poured wine into all three crystal goblets on the dining room table.

"Good evening, Captain. Always a pleasure to see you," I answered sincerely.

"Please sit. I'll get the lamb," said Mrs. Hudson and hurried into the kitchen.

Captain Hudson and I sat down at the table. "How are you enjoying retirement, Captain?"

"It suits me, Doctor. How about yourself?"

"I was quite enjoying it until the recent events hit."

"Yes, I'm sorry." He clearly felt bad for reminding me of the sore subject.

"No, no. There's no need for such sensitivities between two old friends," I said trying to put his conscience at ease. I raised my glass and toasted, "To retirement."

Mrs. Hudson entered with a platter of leg of lamb surrounded by roasted potatoes. "I hope the lamb isn't overdone for you." She put the platter down in the middle of the table and we all served ourselves.

The lamb was delicious, coated with coarse salt and smeared with mint jelly. After a few bites I looked up and said, "Well, Mrs. Hudson, the lamb is perfect, but I'm afraid I might get dyspepsia from the mystery regarding the confidentiality of this meal."

"Yes, you are quite right. I am going to get directly to the point," she said, putting down her fork and knife and delicately wiping her mouth with a blue-and-white checked linen napkin. "Christopher has a very promising future in medicine. I think you can appreciate that as well any of us."

"And you don't want to see him follow in the footsteps of Sherlock Holmes," I said finishing the thought for her.

"Exactly," she said, quite pleased and relieved.

"I can fully appreciate how you might prefer your son to go into the field of medicine instead of crime-solving," I said agreeably.

"Wouldn't any mother?" she said with deep conviction. "Would you please convince him to go to back to medical school? As you know, no one admired Mr. Holmes more than I. But he had a special gift. He had a calling."

"Your son seems to have a bit of that gift." I didn't mean to be contrary, and given a second chance, I probably would have retracted that statement in that it seemed to distress Mrs. Hudson unnecessarily.

"His gift is for medicine. You should see his grade, Doctor Watson. We talked to his dean at Oxford, and he was more than clear that our boy should be a doctor like yourself."

Captain Hudson, always the dutiful husband, sat quietly as if a spectator. It was unclear what his opinion was on the matter. He had always been a bit of a hard read. It wasn't a matter of him trying to be deceptive but rather that subdued Scandinavian manner. I wanted to alleviate Mrs. Hudson's anxiety and so I quickly acquiesced. "I will try and convince him to go back to medical school."

"Oh thank you, Doctor Watson," she said, brimming with optimism. She picked her knife and fork up. "Now, let's all enjoy the rest of our dinner."

I didn't have the heart to tell her I felt I had very little influence over Christopher in this matter, so instead I gave her a bit of false hope, finished my wine and lamb, thanked her for dinner and went upstairs to Baker Street B.

• • •

I knocked on the door and heard Christopher's distracted voice approving entry. The door was unlocked and I found him sitting in Holmes's armchair and staring at his timeline, which now dominated the wall like a papier-mâché map of the continents. "What did my mother want of you at her secret dinner? To convince me to become a doctor and not a detective?" he said without looking up.

"Yes. How did you know?" I was relieved that he had figured out the situation. I knew from the first there would have been no way to approach the subject without Christopher seeing though the charade.

Christopher rose from the chair and stretched. "Where do I begin? First off, I heard the door open to let someone into my parents' apartment, but the bell was not rung which means it was someone my mother knew and was expecting, even watching out the window for. She brought up my dinner early and still has not come to retrieve my dishes, another sign that she had guests. She made your favorite meal, leg of lamb, and lastly, since I deduced you were the guest and I was not invited, it is clear that she wanted to discuss me with you."

"Your observations are spot-on," I told him. "Where is your mind on that matter?"

"My mind, good doctor, is on other matters at hand. Please tell me what you learned at Scotland Yard. I apologize for not attending, and I hope you weren't worried about me. I had an encounter with Wiggins which I shall recount, but, please, you first."

I told Christopher what Scotland Yard had to contribute. He was most interested to hear that the fingerprint at my flat was not from this Sergio de la Iglesia character.

"Yes," he uttered as if this fact had answered a riddle, and he moved energetically across the room to Holmes's old microscope, which he had set up on the cluttered, six-foot-long research table. "That squares with what I found. I recovered two black hairs from the Renault. I assumed they would match the one I recovered from your flat, but only one did. Take a look." He beckoned me to the microscope. I accommodated him and looked into the eyepiece. "You see the middle one is the same as the hair found at your flat, but the other is thicker and hasn't that little wave in it." Honestly, I couldn't see the difference. "So there were three different parties in that car."

"Three?" I said falling a little behind the logic. "We know Sergio was in the car from his fingerprint and we know that some unidentified person broke into my flat and that same person was also in the car given the match of hair samples—"

"And we know Wiggins was also in the car, because of this cigar ash." He held up one of his collection tubes with a piece of intact cigar ash in it. "I finally had time to do a comparison when I returned home this evening. This ash is from a cigar imported from the Caribbean and sold at the St. James Street Tobacconist. It is the exact same cigar that Moriarty was smoking, which leads me to believe that it is Wiggins who supplies Moriarty with his cigars and his information."

"So Moriarty is in on this, too," I said.

"Wiggins picked me up outside Fitzroy's estate this afternoon and we had a very interesting conversation. Among many things, he told me I was under the protection of him and Moriarty and no harm would come to me."

"I certainly don't think Sergio was aware of that," I said wryly.

"Agreed. And now he is dead, which means Wiggins believes there is someone I still need protection from."

"Yes, I follow that logic." I considered the likelihood that there was someone out there still anxious to kill us. It did make one a bit uneasy.

"I believe Wiggins knows why Holmes was killed, and I believe he knows who killed him and that is the person he is protecting us from."

"Then why doesn't Wiggins tell us who it is?" I said, posing the obvious question.

"Because I believe it might implicate him."

"Now wait," I cautioned. "It's not often that I stick up for Wiggins, but I don't believe he would either murder Holmes or allow him to be murdered. He might have been in that automobile at some point, but it doesn't mean he was there during the time of the murder."

"Fair point," he conceded. "But whoever lured Holmes to the East End that night either killed him by accident or did it impulsively. No one premeditates a murder using a car. You bring a weapon, a knife or a gun."

"So what are you saying?"

"I'm saying what I've said from the beginning. Holmes went there to meet someone he was familiar with, perhaps even trusted. It's possible that Wiggins arranged for him to go to the location but didn't expect for him to be murdered. Given all the evidence, there's just no way around it. I believe Wiggins had a hand in this somehow."

My emotions were torn by Christopher's conclusion. I had known Wiggins since his teens. He was Holmes's faithful servant. Never resentful. Never a disrespectful word. Could he have killed Holmes in some insane rage? In some psychotic state? I could not believe it. Could he have set him up to be killed by another? Not intentionally. For me, the pieces still were not fitting together. "What of the prison guard? How does he fit in?" I asked.

"I believe Freddy was a go-between for Moriarty and Wiggins. Moriarty said as much," replied Christopher.

"But what could he have done that would induce the Professor to murder him in public?"

"I haven't a clue," said Christopher. "What could possibly threaten Moriarty? What would he be afraid of?" he said as if thinking out loud.

"Perhaps he did it for sport," I suggested, but I could tell that Christopher hadn't heard my last supposition. He was ruminating about the questions he had just posed and then something seemed to occur to him.

"I must go see Moriarty," he suddenly announced. "I think I can get the truth out of him. I know what he's afraid of."

"And what is that?" I asked, completely intrigued.

"Being alone," he answered. He hurriedly started pulling on his boots. "I think you should go have a talk with Wiggins. He trusts and admires you. To him you are the closest thing to Holmes. Tell him we have evidence against him, which we do with the cigar ash, and tell him you are giving him this opportunity to talk before you set Lestrade and Gregson on him."

"All right," I said. "I shall go see Wiggins. If he had a hand in this, perhaps I can get him to confess."

"I believe tonight one or both of them will tell us the circumstances of Holmes's murder." Christopher put on his leather jacket and rushed out of the flat.

33

CHRISTOPHER

My mind was filled with strategies to approach Moriarty as I rode through the night toward Bedlam. The motorbike felt as if it were driving itself, and the ride passed in a blink. I galloped up the stairs of the hospital and burst into the reception area. I had been given clearance to visit Moriarty at any time and one of his Scotland Yard guards came up to escort me down to his cell.

I found Moriarty lying on his bed, his hand still manacled. He was reading a book entitled *The History of Western Philosophy*. Without looking up he said, "So you have come to speak to the Oracle again, eh, Master Hudson." He tossed the book aside and rose from the bed. "You wouldn't happen to have a cigar, would you?" he asked jokingly.

"I need you to tell me what you know, Professor," I said sternly.

"Well, that would take a lifetime," he answered offhandedly as he went to his desk, opened a drawer and searched around in it until he withdrew the stub of a cigarette. "Where is Watson? Can't face me anymore?" he said derisively as he lit the stub with a wooden match.

"Watson is twice the man you'll ever be," I sneered. "Just because he can't tolerate your evil…" I stopped myself. I was being drawn into Moriarty's game. I had to regain my composure and prepare to spring my trap when the moment was right.

Moriarty's lips curled in a smug smile when he saw my discomfort. He motioned toward the philosophy book on the bed. "The hospital has a rather weak library. No Nietzsche at all." He took a deep pull on the cigarette butt. "Tell me, Christopher, who do you favor, Rousseau, who thought man was basically good and moral, or Hobbes, who believed man was basically evil and immoral?"

"I'm not here to discuss philosophy, Professor."

He sat down behind his desk. "Did you know that Rousseau had a child by a woman whom he took in as his servant and his lover? He abandoned that son, giving him up to a foundling hospital."

"I'm tired of your riddles. I know about Lilah, if that's what you're alluding to," I said icily.

Moriarty seemed quite pleased to hear that piece of gossip had been revealed to me. "Yes, the whole thing is a bit of Greek tragedy, isn't it? You must have felt like a son to him," he said. "How ironic that she should be in the building right above me for all that time, and me, her alibi, locked down here in this dungeon. There must be some symbolism there, no?"

"I need answers, Moriarty," I said with deadly seriousness.

"Oh my! Now we're getting formal. Please continue to call me Professor." He crushed out his cigarette stub and glared back at me with equal seriousness. "I will answer one question other than who killed Sherlock Holmes since I have already given you the answer to that."

"Why did you kill Freddy?" I demanded.

"Because he got greedy," he fired back.

"What does that mean?"

"I answered the question," he responded. "I've told you everything you need to know. You hear, but you do not listen. How can you step into the shoes of Sherlock Holmes if you can't figure these things out for yourself?"

"You'd like to go on with these games forever wouldn't you?" I said, having run out of patience.

"I consider this more than a game," he said gravely.

"You'll answer me, or I'll give you what you really fear, Professor," I declared, ready to spring my trap.

"And what is that?" he said mockingly.

"A confinement where you'll see no one, speak to no one, not a soul to play your games with, alone in a silent cell with only your own thoughts to amuse you. I can arrange for that at the new Rampton Secure Hospital."

Suddenly I saw something I had not seen before in the eyes of Professor James Moriarty: fear…or as close to fear as the professor could convey. The game had changed and he knew he was no longer in charge.

"You need me more than you know, boy," he scolded and shot to his feet.

"I'll manage," I responded defiantly.

"Who do you think protected you?" he shouted bitterly. "Who do you think saved your life? Who do you think had 'Sergeant Archie' watching you?"

I was genuinely astonished by this revelation and it put me slightly off-balance. Moriarty saw this.

"Yes, lad. He's one of mine," Moriarty said curtly.

"From whom were you protecting us?"

"That Spanish ponce," he scoffed, as if the obvious answer was the whole answer.

"Did Wiggins put him up to it?"

Moriarty took a deep breath as if deciding whether to respond to that question. "No," he said convincingly. "Fortunately for you, Wiggins is a sentimentalist. He's a bright boy and tougher than a coffin nail, but he has too big a heart. Someday that will lead to his undoing."

"And what led to yours?" I asked pointedly.

"Sherlock Holmes," he answered without hesitation. A silence descended over the cell. He removed his stare, lay back down on the bed and picked up the book.

"Do what you'll do, boy. Whether it be here or at Rampton, you'll be back." He returned to his reading and I turned to leave, but he had one last swipe before I departed. "On second thought, young Hudson, you best become a doctor."

• • •

On my chilly ride back I pondered all Moriarty had just said, but one particular statement was echoing in my mind. How could I presume to fill the shoes of the great Sherlock Holmes? Even when I thought I had the upper hand, it seemed as if Moriarty was just toying with me.

Inwardly, I felt lacking. But that was his game, to plant doubt, to seize the situation and direct it for his own purposes. The nature of crime-detection dictates that one is always chasing. Those on the other side have the advantage of knowing while we are always uncovering the truth. I had to decipher the puzzle of information that Moriarty gave me. I had to put extraneous feelings out of my mind. His insults were designed to test my mettle.

I returned home and trudged up the stairs playing our conversation back in my head. Moriarty always came at things in a roundabout way. The first thing he said to me on this visit was, "So you've come to talk to the Oracle again." And he called the situation a "Greek tragedy" when I told him I knew about Lilah. I unlocked my door and entered the flat. It was a strange reference and seemed out of character. Moriarty was certainly not a classicist. He prided himself on being modern and progressive. I gazed at my timeline and reviewed both the conversations I had with him. I carefully scanned all the information from Holmes's disappearance in 1891 to the present moment, and suddenly it struck me. "Oracle" and "Greek tragedy" were references to Oedipus. I had suspected it, but somehow didn't think it could be true. I had kept it buried in the back of my mind, but it was the only logical solution. It fully explained the circumstances of Holmes's murder.

I rushed to my microscope. The phone rang. I didn't want to answer it. I wanted to carefully examine the evidence. I had to make sure what I now believed was the case was actually true, but the phone kept ringing insistently and I grabbed it. "Hello," I said. "Christopher Hudson speaking." It was Lilah. Her voice was desperate and heartbroken.

"He killed him, Christopher." Her voice trembled with sobs. "He killed Mr. Holmes. What will become of us?"

"Lilah, where are you?" I asked urgently. I was now quite concerned for her safety as well as her sanity.

"The angels will take us, Christopher," she said in utter despair. "Won't they?"

"Are you at home, Lilah?" I asked, hoping that she could make sense of my words.

"Yes. I must go home," she said with a sudden dreaminess in her voice. "I'm going home."

"No, Lilah! Where are you? You must stay there. I will come get you." But she had already hung up. I rushed down the stairs and jumped back on my motorbike.

• • •

I sped through the streets, leaning forward over the handlebars. Thankfully the pavement was dry and, ignoring the traffic signals, I was able to pull up in front of the grim Gothic building on Averill in less than fifteen minutes. I ran inside and bounded up the stairs to the third floor. The door to Lilah's apartment was wide open and I rushed in. The room looked as if there had been some kind of altercation. Some of the botanical pictures were smashed on the floor, the contents of Lilah's embroidery basket had been strewn all over. "Lilah! Alexander!" I called out. There was no answer.

I went into Lilah's bedroom and it was also in a shambles, drawers pulled open and bedclothes ripped onto the floor. It appeared as if a child had indulged in a tantrum. I heard footsteps enter the apartment and reached into my pocket for my switchblade. A voice shouted, "Who's there!" It was the old crone of a landlady. She was carrying her butcher's knife. I stepped into the drawing room, and when she saw me, she turned and shot out of the door in a panic. I caught up to her in the hall and grabbed her by the back of her collar.

"Don't hurt me, sir," she squealed.

I released her and she turned around. "Where are they?" I demanded.

"They're both gone."

"What happened in there?"

"They 'ad a big, screamin' argument." The old woman was now willing to volunteer the information, as if she finally sensed I was an ally. "He locked 'er in the bedroom, but I came and let 'er out."

"What were they arguing about?"

"I don't know."

"Where did she go?"

"I didn't see 'er leave. She musta snuck out. That poor woman. That poor woman," she grieved. "He's a drunk and a no-good. In and out with that Spanish friend of 'is."

"You're talking about Alexander?"

"Who else?" she said with disgust.

"Wiggins owns this building, doesn't he?"

"Yes," she admitted. "'E tells me to watch out for 'er. 'Elp 'er, sir. 'Elp 'er. She's a good soul."

"I will," I assured her. The old lady had a genuine affection for Lilah. It made me look at her with new eyes. "Thank you for telling me." She retreated down the stairs, and I went back to the apartment.

Looking around the disheveled room, I realized that when Lilah spoke to me on the phone of "going home," she didn't mean to this place. This wasn't her home. I understood what home meant to her. It was the place that for one year of her life she had been the happiest. It would take me at least two hours to ride down to the cottage in Sussex and hopefully, in that time, no harm would befall her. I picked up the phone and called the East Sussex Constabulary and got a Sergeant Barnett on the line. "Hello, this is Christopher Hudson. I'm involved in the investigation of the murder of Sherlock Holmes. I spoke to Chief Constable Gentle about it."

"Yes, Mr. Hudson, we were all made aware of the investigation by your Superintendent Gregson."

"I would like you to send an officer out to Mr. Holmes's cottage at the end of Shoreham Road," I continued as calmly and concisely as possible. "There's a woman who might be having emotional problems and needs assistance. Her name is Lilah Church. I fear for her safety, so please exercise caution."

"I understand, sir," Barnett answered briskly. "I will send a constable out there immediately."

I was a bit reassured when I hung up the phone. I immediately rang Wiggins's headquarters. Fortunately, I had committed that phone number to memory, as I'm sure it wasn't listed in any of the directories. The phone rang at least ten times and finally Sir Patrick picked up on the other end. "Good evening," he said with his usual sonorous composure.

"Sir Patrick, it's Christopher Hudson."

"Yes, Mr. Hudson. How good to hear from you."

"I must speak to Doctor Watson. He is there, is he not?"

"He is in conference with Wiggins," said Sir Patrick calmly.

"Please deliver a message as soon as possible. Tell him Lilah has run off. Tell him I'm on my way to find her in Sussex." There was a brief hesitation from the other end.

"Yes, I thoroughly understand," Sir Patrick answered finally, and he hung up.

I dashed out of the building and jumped on my motorbike for the ride south.

34

WATSON

I had told Christopher that if Wiggins had a hand in Holmes's murder, I would get him to confess. As my taxi pulled up in front of Wiggins's foreboding headquarters, my confidence in that statement began to wane. If I went into that building and accused Wiggins of being involved in this heinous crime, there was a real possibility that I could disappear forever. I wanted to believe that Wiggins and I had a deep and unbreakable bond, but it occurred to me that I might be dwelling in a romanticized past. It is said that history is written by the victors. I suppose, in the same sense, nostalgia is felt by those who survived well. It was unclear to me what camp Wiggins felt he fell into.

I sat for a moment in the taxi and considered going straight back to Scotland Yard and having them haul Wiggins in for questioning, but that urge quickly passed. I owed him more than that. I had to go in and give Wiggins his options.

I climbed out of the taxi, mounted the stairs and pressed the buzzer. Presently, the door swung open and I was confronted with Wiggins's sullen lieutenant, Creed. He stared at me a moment and then stepped aside, allowing me to enter.

Inside there was hammering and sawing. The first floor was newly furnished since my last visit and smelled of fresh leather. The men who had formerly been playing cards at the far end of the room were busily constructing and mounting shelves and mirrors behind a massive, ornate bar. A large, imposing chandelier had been installed and glowed with a rather elegant grace. I followed Creed up the stairs to the second floor.

We found Daisy and a coworker sitting at the "reception desk." The right side of Daisy's mouth was quite swollen and there was a significant bruise on her cheek. "What happened to you, Daisy?" I asked solicitously. She gave me a lopsided smile but said nothing. Creed kept me moving up the next set of stairs and Daisy's eyes followed us until we were no longer in her sight.

On the third floor we found Wiggins lying on a bed that had been added to the sparse furnishings of this dwelling. He was perusing an auction catalogue by the light of a standing lamp. The only other illumination was the halo surrounding the raised platform with Wiggins's empty satin, throne-like armchair. He propped himself up on one elbow to greet me. "I just spent the afternoon with Christopher. I'm sure 'e tol' ya all about it. I guess you two just can't leave me alone."

"Is something the matter with Daisy?" I asked, trying to put no particular emphasis on the query.

"She'll be fine. She's just learnin' ta keep 'er mouf shut," he said, as if that were an adequate answer. "So wha' 'ave you come for now, Doctor?"

I suddenly felt quite defenseless and fainthearted under his gaze. I again began thinking it might be advisable to abandon this confrontation. Creed stood by the door impassively. Wiggins studied me suspiciously, waiting for a response, and there was an uncomfortable silence in the room. I could have offered up some weak excuse. Inform him of some insignificant piece of evidence and take my leave. Wiggins slowly rose from the bed as if sensing what my intentions were. "Wha' is on your mind, Doctor Watson?" He drew a few paces closer to me.

I saw beneath his smoking jacket that he had his Jesse James revolver holstered on his side.

"Wiggins, I'm going to tell you the truth because you are far too clever for me to try and lie to you," I heard myself saying. "We have evidence that ties you to the car that killed Holmes. We have information that ties you to the Spaniard who made the attempt on Christopher's and my life. Before I give this evidence to Lestrade and Gregson, I wanted to come to you and give you an opportunity to make a clean breast of it. Christopher has determined, and I agree, that somehow you are involved in Holmes's death."

"Leave us. Leave us. LEAVE US!" thundered Wiggins, and Creed immediately withdrew. Wiggins took another stride toward me and squinted. "You know I could 'ave you killed right 'ere, Doctor Watson, and no one would ever speak of it." He glared at me and then shouted, "Nurse!" The unseen door opened and the silent nurse came clicking toward us from the darkness with her velvet pouch.

"No. He doesn't need any more," I called to her, but she didn't even break stride. It was as if I were a ghost that she could neither hear nor see.

For some reason Wiggins changed his mind. He waved her off with a flick of his wrist, and she instantly turned and disappeared back into the shadows. He sat down on the step of his platform and hung his head in his hands. "I should have prevented all this, Doctor."

"I will do all I can to protect you, as long as justice is done," I told him.

"Justice!" He sprang to his feet and shouted in my face. "You sent a sixteen-year-old boy and 'is band of beggars around the city to do your bidding and your good friend ends up fuckin' one of those beggars! I have no use for your justice, Doctor Watson." He turned his back and moved away from me, fuming. "Do you know what it feels like...lookin' in those windows when you're 'ungry...cold...no one to protect you?"

His words filled me with shame. "You're right, Wiggins," I said. "There's no excuse. I wish I...had done more...seen more clearly."

We were both silent for several moments. He kept his back to me. When he finally spoke I could hear the tears in his voice. "I sat in the street and put 'is 'ead in my lap. 'E knew 'e was dyin', and you know what 'e said to me?" Wiggins turned back around. The tears were running down his face. "'E said 'e was sorry. 'E said that 'e was wrong to have used us so. And 'e asked that we all forgive him." He fell silent again.

"Tell me how it happened," I asked softly.

Wiggins wiped his face with his sleeve. "It was a foolish plan. Alexander and Sergio dreamed it up. They would pretend that Alexander 'ad been kidnapped and get Mr. 'olmes to pay a ransom. Alexander thought 'is father owed him that. 'E's a bitter lad."

"But Holmes always saw to their well-being, him and Lilah," I said, offering up a feeble defense.

"Well, sometimes you want more than well-bein'," said Wiggins. "The boy wanted to be important to 'im. Like Christopher was important to 'im. 'E used to follow Christopher secretly sometimes. Watch Holmes and 'im go into that fancy club on 'is birthday. I tried to give the lad this and that to do, you know, because 'e's Lilah's kid, and that makes 'im one of us. But 'e's undisciplined. The both of 'em—'im and Sergio—totally undisciplined. I swear I'd 'ave killed 'im if 'e wasn't Lilah's child."

"Tell me about that night," I said, trying to coax the whole story from him.

He shook his head remorsefully. "They asked me to be the go-between. Said they'd give me ten thousand. Somewhere in me mind I figured maybe 'e's entitled, you know. This little cast-off. I know what that's like. 'E is 'is rightful son after all. So I told 'olmes that the kidnappers 'ad contacted me and 'e was to bring the money to Narrow Street, over by Rope Fields…A 'undred thousand pounds. Then the 'kidnappers' would let his son go." Wiggins scoffed. "Mr. 'olmes saw through it from the first. 'E showed up without the money and they was, what, a hundred feet away in that black car that Sergio stole. The two of 'em—Alexander and Sergio. And I'm out there in the street with 'olmes, pretendin' to be the middle-man, ya understand. And 'e gets right to it. 'E says 'e knows what's goin' on. It's nonsense. 'E's not payin' any ransom. 'E just wants to speak to Alexander. So now I'm feelin' like the fuckin' fool that I am, and I go back to the car and tell 'em the jig is up. And 'olmes comes walkin' toward us to talk to Alexander…and…" Wiggins's voice starts to tremble, "…the boy runs 'im down…runs right over 'im just like that. Like he 'ad a little fuckin' fit o' temper. Or maybe 'e meant to from the beginnin'. And 'e gets out cryin' and cursin' and askin', 'where's the money?' And I'm in shock. I genuinely don't know what to do. And the little piece of shit says, 'Pu' 'im in the car. I'll take 'im home and make it look like an accident.'" Wiggins placed his hands over his face.

"Why didn't you turn him in?" I asked, deeply disturbed by what I had just heard.

Wiggins looked over me as if I was as naïve as a newborn. "There was no way to get on the right side of this one, Doctor. Not for a man like me. I only work from the background in your world. Your court would 'ave me 'angin' by my neck in less than a week. You know that. Wouldn't no one be comin' to the defense of the infamous Wiggins."

"Tell me why Freddy was killed," I asked.

"That was my fault," he said flatly. "But 'e brought it on 'imself as well. I used Freddy to slips things to Moriarty. Cigars and such… So that night, when I get back, I'm out of my 'ead yellin' at Sergio, 'oo 'ad always been a useless, li'l whore. 'E's the one brought me the Smithwick woman after 'e 'ad bled 'er dry by gamblin' away the money what 'er ol' man left 'er. And Freddy over'ears what I'm yellin' about as 'e's comin' up the back stairs to pick up Moriarty's stuff. The next day Freddy asks Sergio for a loan. It wasn't proper blackmail but that's 'ow it starts, believe me, I'm an expert on the subject. I couldn't let 'im go 'round talkin'. Moriarty offered to accommodate us. 'E 'ad nothing to lose long as Fitzroy keeps 'im from the 'angman. We slipped him the weapon and 'e took care of the rest…gladly."

"So I gather you and Moriarty are quite close," I said, still trying to remain even-keeled and not let on how troubling I found Wiggins's account to be.

"Moriarty is not a man you want as an enemy. Only Mr. 'olmes could 'andle that. Moriarty let me take over certain interests o' 'is like the brothels when 'e went into prison. In exchange I supply influence with certain parties and various luxuries."

"And what do you know about Sergio's attempt to kill us?" I asked.

"I 'ad nothin' to do with that," he said emphatically, raising a finger. "If that li'l bastard wasn't dead already, I'd put 'im in the Thames personally. I underestimated 'ow colossally stupid 'e was. Fortunately, Moriarty was 'avin' you followed to make sure you was safe. I believe 'e's quite fond of Christopher in 'is own way."

The thought of Moriarty being our savior disgusted me. "Do you know the man who saved us?" I asked.

"I've met 'im, but I don't know 'oo 'e is. 'E's always disguised. Never comes 'ere. Make me meet 'im in different places. Sometimes 'e's a priest. Sometimes 'e's a barrister. If it's important to Moriarty, that's the man what shows up."

"And where is Alexander now?"

"Last night, while Christopher was 'ere, Alexander came to this room to make peace and try to convince me that 'e 'ad nothin' to do with the break-in at your flat or the attempt to kill you." Wiggins's expression turned steely. "I tol' 'im the only reason 'e wasn't dead was because of Lilah. Lilah will always be one of us. I tol' 'im his only choice was to leave town. I tol' him go somewhere where we'd never 'ear of 'im again. We'll take care of his mum. 'E left 'ere and that's when Christopher saw 'im driving off and chased 'im all the way to the river."

Wiggins rubbed his hands down his face and took a deep breath, as if relieved by the recounting of all the events. It was as though hearing himself confess made him feel less culpable. Just then, Sir Patrick entered the room, calmly moved to Wiggins's side and whispered something in his ear. As he listened, Wiggins's eyes moved to me.

35

CHRISTOPHER

The engine of my Harley-Davidson strained at top speed and the wind off the channel froze my face. At last, I sped onto the road that led to Holmes's cottage. Happily, the tunnel of trees sheltered me from the stinging wind. It also blocked out the shining half-moon, leaving only my headlight to pierce the darkness for a distance of no more than a hundred yards. I lowered my speed, fearing I might crash into something by overrunning the range of that lonely beam. Soon, the road opened up onto Holmes's gravel driveway. I could smell the smoke even before I saw the gray column rising from behind the darkened cottage. An orange glow flickered from above the steeply peaked roofline of the home. Two automobiles were parked in front. One was an East Sussex police car.

I skidded to a stop and noticed something slumped on the ground not far from the front door. I laid down my bike and cautiously approached. It was a young constable lying in a heap on the gravel. I carefully turned him over and found that he had been shot in the stomach. He was dead.

I instinctively got into a crouch beside him, fearing I might be the next target. There was little doubt in my mind who had done this. The question was, should I leave to seek help? I quickly decided that I couldn't do that. I had to see to Lilah's safety. Scanning the area, I saw no one, then I heard a crash of wood and glass from behind the cottage.

I stole to the side of the cottage and peeked around the corner. The glow of a growing fire threw shadows that waved to and fro across the back lawn. I could see neither the flames nor the source of a second loud crash.

Carefully I stalked down the side of the house and got a full view of the back lawn. Flames were jumping through the upstairs windows of the cottage, igniting the shingle roof. Swarms of Holmes's bees were circling ferociously overhead, swerving back and forth toward the blaze, hundreds falling to the ground with scorched wings. Alexander was in the process of destroying the last of Holmes's dozen hives with a garden hoe. He pounded the wooden hive with a deranged viciousness, tossed aside the hoe and, seemingly satisfied, wiped away a bee that was attached to his cheek by the stinger.

Another upstairs window exploded and flames leaped out. I looked for any sign of Lilah and saw none. A hundred feet from the back door the lawn was swallowed by the darkness. I knew another hundred yards beyond that were the cliffs. Alexander swiveled his head back and forth as if looking for something else to destroy. I carefully stepped out from beside the house. "Alexander, where is your mother?" I called to him and tried to ignore the bees circling wildly above me.

Alexander looked around the yard until his eyes found me. He reached down to pick up something off the ground and I stiffened. It turned out to be a bottle of whisky. It was half empty and from the sound of his voice I deduced it had been full when he found it. "Ahhh, Mr. Hudson. How nice. Come a little closer so we can talk." He took a gulp from the bottle.

"Where is your mother, Alexander?" I demanded loudly.

He motioned at the night. "She's hiding...Come closer." He waved me over drunkenly.

The answer that she was hiding alarmed me to no end. I looked to the cottage. Thick smoke was pouring out of the open French doors. The downstairs was completely obscured.

"Is she in the house?" I asked desperately.

He cocked his head and said as if annoyed, "I told you, she's hiding." The flames suddenly burst through the shingle roof. I considered running in through the back door to see if I could find Lilah, but it would have been a hopeless gesture. The cottage was now engulfed and nothing inside would survive.

"She loves this place," said Alexander as he motioned toward the raging flames with his bottle. "Doesn't want to leave," then added mockingly, "She'll have to leave now." He took another slug from the bottle and whispered loudly, "She's crazy, you know. But still...she's my mum."

I didn't know how to humor him, how to reason with him. He seemed completely unreachable. My only concern was Lilah's safety, and I feared it might be too late for that. I took several steps toward him with my hand held out docilely. "Alexander, let's go find your mother together."

He suddenly produced Watson's Webley from his waistband and pointed it directly at me, stopping me in my tracks. "I was his son!" he yelled angrily. "His rightful son! But he cared nothing for me. He left me nothing. He left you all his things. Look at your things now." He held his hand up to display the burning cottage.

I reached in my pocket and felt for my switchblade. I was too far from him to throw it with enough force. I had to get a bit closer. "He loved you," I said soothingly and slowly took a few more steps toward him. He fired a shot. I heard it whistle over my shoulder in the darkness.

"Stand where you are or I'll shoot you dead." He held his arm stiff as board with the gun pointed straight at me. "Fuck him!" he said venomously. "He left us here! That's what drove her mad."

Out of the corner of my eye, I saw something at the edge of the small forest of chestnut trees that bordered the yard. It was Lilah, glassy-eyed and hugging the trunk of a tree as if it were the mast of ship in a storm-tossed sea.

Alexander noticed her as well and took his eyes off me for a second. In one smooth movement I pulled out my switchblade, clicked it open and whipped it underhand through the darkness. Alexander gasped as it lodged squarely in his rib cage. He gazed down at the handle of the knife as if trying to recognize what could possibly be protruding from his side. He took an unsteady step sideways but did not go down. He looked at me hatefully with the gun pointed directly at my chest. I heard the crack of the gunshot. My body jerked. An electric jolt surged though my legs. I couldn't tell where I had been shot. I felt no pain. I looked across at Alexander and he was lying on the ground clutching his chest.

I turned around and behind me, holding his Jesse James revolver, was Wiggins. He was flanked by Watson, Creed and Sir Patrick. "Look a' that," remarked Wiggins. "It still shoots straight."

Watson rushed to my side. "Are you all right?"

"Yes, Doctor," I assured him. "I'm all right."

We both moved quickly to see Alexander's condition. He was lying on his back, staring lifelessly at the sky. Doctor Watson reached down and closed Alexander's eyes.

Sir Patrick strode over to Lilah, who had fainted onto the grass by the woods. He picked her up in his huge arms and gently carried her back toward the front of the house as Wiggins came up behind us. "She belongs with us," he said, looking down at me and Watson. "You will take care of this, will you not, Doctor?"

I rose to my feet and answered for the both of us. "We will take care of this."

Wiggins handed me the gun and without another word walked off with Creed at his side. There was a loud groan of timbers and I looked up to see the cottage collapse in on itself.

36

Lestrade was perfectly willing to accept our version of the story. Gregson was a bit dubious. He wondered how Watson had managed to gain possession of Wiggins's prized Jesse James revolver, and how it was that he had been dropped off at the cottage by a "helpful stranger." In fact, the story we told Scotland Yard was essentially accurate, excluding Wiggins's involvement and Alexander's relationship to Holmes. It was adequate to claim that Holmes had always taken an interest in the boy's well-being and had been drawn up to London through threat of the kidnapping. Gregson stared knowingly at me for a full minute and, despite his misgivings, declared himself satisfied that the case was closed. We left on a cordial note, and I felt I had genuinely made some headway in the respect department with Superintendent Gregson.

My next stop was at my parents' home in Hampstead Heath. I informed my tearful mother that at present I was not going to proceed to medical school. I told her that, though I saw medicine as a noble profession, I was not an individual who tolerated tedium easily. This was not to offend those who do pursue this venerable occupation, but I felt a career in crime detection would suit me better at this point in my life.

After inquiring whether I might reconsider going to medical school at some future date and getting the response she was hoping for, Mother kissed me on the forehead and gave me her blessing. "Oh, if only Mr. Holmes could see you. He'd be so proud." I considered my mother an authority on that topic and therefore was content to believe her statement to be true.

Next, I took the underground to the Green Park station to pay a visit to Dr. Watson. The Harley had sprung an oil leak on the way back from Sussex and would take at least two weeks to repair while we waited for a part from the States.

When I arrived at his flat on Stafford Street, Watson was already at his desk documenting the final events we had confronted only the day before. I did not question whether he intended to publish all the sensitive facts of the case. That was totally up to his discretion, and I would not presume to try and influence him one way or the other. What Holmes and Watson had can never be questioned or duplicated, and it certainly was not my place to even imply that I should have any opinion or input on the matter.

After Watson greeted me, he resumed his position at his desk. "I should like your point of view on the case when I get finished doing my notes and recollections," he said as he scribbled a last thought.

"You are more than welcome to it," I answered. "It should be interesting to compare experiences of the events."

"How did your mother react to your news about medical school?" Watson asked, putting down his pen.

"I believe she took it as well as can be expected," I answered.

He nodded and smiled as if visualizing my mother's face. "You may never be able to fill his shoes, you know," he said with as impartial a tone as possible.

"That is why I came here. To ask you to join me," I answered. I could see from his expression that this was not an unexpected request and I could also see it was not an easy one for him to answer.

"It is so hard to let the past go," he said with a wistful look in his eyes. "That is both the push and the pull of what you are requesting."

"I know it will never be the same, Doctor Watson. But Holmes chose me. And how often was he wrong?" I couldn't help grinning as I offered up the strongest part of my case.

A smile grew across Doctor Watson's face as well. "You make a powerful argument, young Master Hudson." He gave me a pat on the shoulder. "Let me think on it."

• • •

I left Watson's flat and proceeded to the underground to take the train to Oxford and withdraw from medical school. No on could ever take the place of Sherlock Holmes, but I would try to follow in his footsteps. That was the path that he had laid out for me those many years ago without me even realizing it.

I was about to step onto the train when someone tapped me on the back. I turned and saw a tall, young, blond-haired man who I took to be Australian, based on his accent. "Is this the train to Piccadilly?" he asked.

"No," I told him. "Try the orange line. You can pick it up on Bond Street."

"Thank you, mate," he responded with a broad smile.

I stepped onto the train, and just before the door closed, he reached out and put something in my hand. "A souvenir from the Professor," he said, without the least trace of an accent.

The doors sealed closed and the train moved forward. I opened my hand. In my palm was the slug that I had searched for back at the building where the attempt had been made on the lives of Watson and myself. When I looked back the man had disappeared into the throng.

37

WATSON

I let Christopher do most of the talking at Scotland Yard. We had pieced together that after Lilah called Christopher she got on a night train to East Sussex and returned to the cottage. Alexander, knowing that his childhood home was her likely destination, stole a car and drove down after her. The hundred and ten thousand pounds that was taken from my flat was recovered in the car. Obviously, Alexander intended to use the money to go off to wherever it was he was trying to convince his mother to go off to. As we mutually determined beforehand, Christopher omitted the more sensitive facts of the interrelationships.

Lestrade was more than satisfied. This Alexander Hollocks was certainly the culprit and just as well dead. Gregson was clearly not as sanguine. He knew Christopher was not telling the whole story but did not press the issue.

After leaving Scotland Yard, I returned home and sat down at my writing desk trying to decide whether to divulge all the facts of Holmes's murder. It made me remember that in his final letter Holmes asked me to deliver his eulogy, saying there is no one who can speak the truth about his life better than I. Holmes always sought the truth, and that is why I have decided to write the truth without reservation. I am convinced that Sherlock Holmes paid in full measure for his mistakes. In a moment of weakness, a man with sublime talent betrayed himself and quietly paid for it the rest of his life. And he did not pay in legal tender, for that was the decision he made on that last, fateful night. He knew the price of his error might well be greater than gold. It might well be his most valuable possession—his name. Instead, it merely turned out only to be his life. His name remains intact. His humanity is secured in the acts of bravery and justice that are his alone. I, Doctor John H. Watson, have written of them. I have written the truth about the finest man I have ever known, the perfectly imperfect Sherlock Holmes.

ACKNOWLEDGEMENTS

I would like to thank my friends and family who were gracious enough to read my manuscript and give me their thoughts, support and encouragement, particularly my brother Dennis for his always indispensable counsel. Thank you to Califia Suntree for her immaculate editing of the manuscript. Thank you to Margot Frankel for her excellent artwork. And thank you to Bob Wallace for his invaluable advice.

ABOUT THE AUTHOR

David Fable is the pseudonym for an award-winning screenwriter, playwright and network television producer.

Fable is currently the artist in residence at a major university where he lectures on writing for the stage and screen.

CPSIA information can be obtained
at www.ICGtesting.com
Printed in the USA
LVHW080212151021
700530LV00012B/242